Filthy Phil

Filthy Phil

K.L. Corum

The Book Factory

Filthy Phil
by
K.L. Corum

The Book Factory
an imprint of New Tradition Books
ISBN 1932420371

For information contact:
The Book Factory
newtraditionbooks@yahoo.com

To those who believe in love at first sight.

Also for my first love.

I want you to want me.

I hated his guts. Filthy Phil, I mean.

Did she love me? Does a woman ever really love a man? Sure, she loved me. About as much as any woman could. "Of course, I love you, Ray."

Ray. That's my name, Ray. It says so on my paycheck.

Filthy Phil—I even hated saying his name—was the kind of guy that Jim Croce wrote songs about. He was the kind of guy you just don't fuck with. He was a huge motherfucker, way over six-foot, way over two-hundred pounds of pure unadulterated meanness. He came from England or Scotland or Ireland or some place where even their own kind don't understand a damn word they're saying.

He was almost a foot taller than her. She told me once, "Baby, we're all the same size in bed."

She tormented me. That's what she did. It didn't stop me, though. It should have, but it didn't. But women who look as good as she did could torment men. It's their life's work.

I could go on and on about her looks, but what good would that do? She looked good. Well, better than good. She was movie star gorgeous with deep blue eyes and a perfectly sculpted face which had more than a few freckles scattered across it, which made her beauty less intimidating. It wasn't so much her looks, though, it was how she carried herself. She was overly confident, if there is such a thing and in her case, there was.

I was tending bar then. I didn't have much to do during the day, but at night I was *the man* in some pathetic kind of way. Drunks gave me power. I had them in the palm of my hand. But what good is a drunk to anybody? Mostly, I just wished they'd get their drinks, move away from the bar and leave me the fuck alone.

A lot of pretty girls came into the bar. That helped matters considerably. I mean, somewhat. Most of 'em would rather die than give a guy like me the time of day. You know the kind of girls I'm talking about, the kind who think of bartenders as a piece of furniture or second class citizen.

She wasn't like that. I guess that's what drew me to her. She didn't see me as some loser. She liked me. She said I made her laugh. Chicks always say that, though, don't they? Make 'em laugh and the rest is easy.

If only.

The bar doesn't warrant much description. It was a bar, what else do you need to know? It was an older, Irish-type establishment, just like the one in your city. You know where it is. The bathrooms stunk, the beer was sometimes warm and if you wanted some kind of mixed drink, you were shit out of luck. I didn't know how to make many.

There's not much to my past that really needs mentioning. I never married. I was only in one long-term relationship, which I broke off, for some reason. The girl…well, she wanted more than I could give. Isn't that the way it always works? I think it had to do with the "freedom" issue. Freedom to do what? Grow old and die alone?

The city doesn't matter either. We could call it New York or Chicago. We could call it New Orleans or Nashville, maybe even Vegas. It could happen anywhere, really. Let's call it New York, for obvious reasons. Most stories seem to take place in New York.

Me? I was just your average guy. I guess I looked pretty good, though I'm not the type of person to brag on myself.

2

I've got dark hair and blue eyes and a good, solid build. The chicks seemed to like me. It was either me or the prospect of free drinks. Either way, it didn't matter as long as they did. Like me, that is.

Needless to say, I wasn't an unhappy person. In fact, I was pretty content. I had dreams of owning my own bar someday but that was about it. I didn't fantasize about winning the lottery or about being discovered by a talent scout; those dreams are for fools anyway. About the most exciting thing that had ever happened to me was that once someone lost a bag of money at the bar but I handed it over to management. Sometimes I wished I'd kept it. But it's gone now.

I was just meandering through life, living, eating, and breathing like we all do. I was in my element then. I was in my element because I was comfortable. So we seek, so shall we find...

Then I saw her. I should have looked away.

Do I believe in love at first sight? No. And I still don't. I do, however, believe in lust at first sight. The love comes later, when you see if you're compatible, if you jive in bed together. And if you're not compatible in bed, then why bother?

It was a Wednesday night and uncommonly crowded in the bar. Some sort of celebration was going on outside. Some sort of parade. It could have been St. Patrick's Day, I don't really remember. All I know is I had been there since six and it was going on two in the morning.

The crowd was unruly, rambunctious. They were dancing on the tables. On the bar. Destroying property. Doing things people will only do if they're drunk. Someone had put on *Crimson and Clover* on the jukebox. The Joan Jett version. I'd always loved that song, always loved Joan but it was getting late and I wanted everyone out so I could go home and crash. *They*, however, had no intention of

3

leaving the party too soon. *They* were having the time of their lives.

It was getting on my last fucking nerve.

Over the tops of many heads doing an assortment of things, I saw her. I can still see her standing there like it was yesterday, like it just happened. She was standing still, trapped in time. She was looking to the side, a sly smile about to play on her sensual red lips.

My heart skipped a beat as I stared at her gorgeous face. Her long, dark hair was pulled back into a perky ponytail. The way she looked, she could be going anywhere—to the track to make a bet or to the airport to catch a plane to some exotic location, maybe Madagascar. She could be coming in to shoot the place up. She could be coming in for a drink.

What took her so long to get here?

She looked around like she owned the place but was just visiting and was glad to see everyone was having a good time. She didn't smile, but the look on her face was far from disagreeable. Just then, she turned and her eyes fell on the bar. She began to walk towards it, towards me. I looked away.

To the beat of *Crimson and Clover*, I saw us doing it—fucking, making love, having sex. Screwing. I saw me holding onto her, so tight. I saw us in the shower, on the bed. I saw her bouncing on top of me. I saw me giving it to her doggie style. I saw me fucking her like we lived in a trailer park.

I saw us holding hands. I saw us taking long walks at night through our neighborhood. I saw me playing guitar and singing *Candida* to her in the park. I saw us laughing together at the movies. I saw us sharing an ice cream cone. I saw us—

"Hello?"

I looked up. She was standing right in front of me, impatiently tapping her fingers on the bar. I couldn't think of anything to say. What do you say to a girl like her? Ask her what her sign was? Ask her what she was doing in a place like this? Nothing would do and it wouldn't do because it would come out all wrong. Then I remembered why she was there. She wanted a drink. Oh.

"Yes?" I croaked, like some fucking old man. I cleared my throat and lowered my voice, "What can I get you?"

Good God, I sounded just like Barry White. *Ba-by...*

She eyed me. "Do I know you?"

I shook my head and straightened up. If she knew me, then I would know her and I can assure you, I had never laid eyes on her until that very moment. I would have remembered it. Believe me, *I would have remembered it.* She was the kind of girl you'd screw your best friend over for.

"No," I said quickly. "I don't think so."

She pointed over her shoulder with her thumb. "You were staring at me like we know each other."

Oh, God, she was already onto me. Was I that obvious? Yes, yes I was. I stared at her in a panic but she just smiled. She was being really nice, flirty even. That surprised me because girls who look as good as her usually aren't very friendly.

"I don't think so," I stammered.

"Ah, well. Get me a...." She considered the liquor bottles behind the bar, clucking her tongue as she peered over my shoulder. "I guess a mai-tai."

A mai tai?! She had to be kidding. I stared at her anxiously. She stared back, almost daring me to reply in the negative. I looked behind me at the liquor bottles. I didn't even know what was back there. It was rare that anyone who came into this bar wanted something as exotic as a mai tai.

"Coming right up," I muttered and got to work.

What the hell was in a mai-tai? I picked up a few

5

bottles and studied the labels like I knew what I was doing. I heard her groan and then she came around the bar and bumped me out of the way with her hip.

As she picked up the various effects, "Mai-tai. Glass. Crushed ice. Light rum. Dark rum. Lime. I need a lime. Get it for me."

She shooed me away. Miraculously, I found a lime. It was warty as hell. I held it out to her.

"Juice and peel it," she ordered. "Okay, now we need some...what's it called?" She snapped her fingers as she looked through the old bottles then pulled out some crème de almond. It was dusty as hell. "Cool," she breathed and began to prepare the drink.

She had a Southern accent which meant she wasn't from around here. I wondered if she lived in town or was just visiting. I could tell she had some money, she had that look. The clothes fit exactly right; they looked casual, but I could tell they cost a fortune. The boots were the good kind of leather, the watch was... I looked closer. It was a Mickey Mouse watch. *Who was this chick?*

I watched in amazement as she mixed the drink and poured it in a glass. After she squeezed the lime, she bent down and rummaged under the bar. Out of nowhere, she pulled out a little blue umbrella and topped the drink.

My eyes nearly popped out of my head. Where the hell did that thing come from?

"Ta da!" she exclaimed and handed me the drink. "Try a sip."

A guy came to the bar and called, "Lite on tap."

She winked at him, then at me and fished a can of Lite out of the cooler.

"I said tap," he said.

"I said three bucks," she replied curtly and held out her hand.

He handed her a five, told her to keep the change and

another guy came up and asked for a shot of Jack, which, by the way, was never in short supply. She poured the shot and set it down in front of him. He stared at her for a moment, nearly smiling. She smiled back, took the shot and downed it and told him it was "three bucks".

He chuckled, handed her a ten. "Now can I have one?"

"Only if you let me join you," she said and poured them both another shot as I stood there holding a pink drink topped with a little blue umbrella. They took their shots and the guy walked off. She turned and grinned at me. "I've always wanted to be a bartender."

I just stared at her.

"How's the drink?" she asked and reached for it and took a tiny sip. "Damn, that's good. You try it?"

I nodded, though I hadn't.

"Cool," she said and went to the tap, where she poured a Guinness. "Sweetie, you got any matches back here?"

"Uh…yeah," I said.

She said, "Put me a pack in my pocket, would you?"

I fished the matches from under the bar and slipped them in her jacket pocket. I realized I had touched her, her jacket. *Her.* I stepped back nervously and wondered what she would do next.

"I'll run a tab," she said and skipped away, carrying her drink and a bowl of peanuts tucked under her arm.

"Okay," I called weakly and watched her make her way to the other side of the room.

I knew right then and there that this was the woman I'd been waiting for. The woman I'd given up ever meeting. The one who'd make everything right, the one who didn't exist before she stepped into the bar. There she was. I smiled broadly. She glanced over her shoulder and winked at me. I gave a little wave and she nodded, carefully placing the drinks and the peanuts on a table that was filled with men in business suits. I didn't recognize any of them. Besides, all I saw was her and that cute ass of hers.

She turned, stepped backwards and fell into the lap of none other than Filthy Phil. She might as well have been on the moon.

Filthy Phil had been a ruffian, a hooligan, a thug—whatever you want to call it. I liked to think of him as a swindler. *I'd* even go as far to call him a nincompoop.

He'd worked his way through the "ranks" and was now the successful proprietor of various gambling establishments. On top of that, he did a lot of other underhanded stuff. He had his paws in everything, which made him very rich and very powerful. It also made him very callous. Many men had met their demise with Filthy Phil and his gang of lackeys. If you didn't pay with cash, you'd pay with a finger or a toe—you know how it is. The price went up according to how much you owed him.

Filthy Phil didn't eat young children, but he looked like he might. He was that kind of guy. She was a different kind of girl.

She had come to New York on a dare. For a bit of fun. Someone from her little town, located somewhere in the South, had dared her to come here alone. She'd stepped off the bus and into the city with no illusions. She wasn't looking for anything other than a good time. She was just taking on a challenge. She'd do anything to spite you.

She hadn't intended on staying for very long, just until her money ran out. And once it did, she took a trip to the track, hoping to win enough to extend her stay. Filthy Phil just happened to be there. She placed her last ten bucks on a horse called Sunshine and won enough to stay another week.

The fact that Sunshine hadn't actually *won* the race didn't matter to her. The fact that she'd caught Filthy Phil's eye didn't concern her. To her, he was just some lug with a weird accent. He was just another guy that was being nice to her. Lots of guys were.

"I mean, he didn't pull me out of the gutter, Ray."

She became the twinkle in Filthy Phil's eye. Their courtship was brief. Soon she was staying at his luxurious penthouse, but she didn't like it.

"It's too stuffy," she told him and found a loft somewhere in Greenwich, saying, "I like it better over there. It's more like I imaged New York being."

She told him he could stay with her if he liked—he was paying for the place, after all—but she'd prefer he didn't. She liked her space. She didn't mind being alone. She didn't like picking up after "some man". He could visit anytime he wanted. He could take her out to dinner. He could buy her flowers. Occasionally, he could spend the night. But he had to leave in the morning.

Contrary to what she said, he moved in almost immediately, giving up the lease on the penthouse to stay in a loft with bare wood floors, a bathtub in the middle of the kitchen and a leaky faucet. All of which were fixed soon enough after a short visit with the landlord who was told to do so and to do so promptly. After the necessary threats on his life, he was more than happy to oblige. He even threw in a Jacuzzi just to make his new tenants happy

All this information, whether or not it's pertinent, was gleaned from many conversations, in and out of bed.

She became my lover soon enough. She didn't love me; she needed me to do something for her. Apparently, she thought I was the only man in New York capable of such things. She knew I loved her and used that to her advantage. Yet, what she wanted really couldn't be accomplished without immediate threat. To me, I mean.

"I want you to kill him."

Yeah, that's right. You heard it here first. She wanted me of all people—ME!—to kill Filthy Fucking Phil, one of the most feared men in New York City! A man who was known to take pleasure in tormenting his deadbeats or so the fable goes. A man who was bigger, meaner and certainly craftier than yours truly. A man who was…well, you get the picture. It wasn't like she was asking me to take out the garbage or paint her toenails.

I dropped the glass I was drying and stumbled back. She watched it hit the floor, sighed, bent and began to pick up the pieces.

"What the hell's wrong with you?" she asked, peering up at me.

"I don't even know you," I said as this was, in fact, our first meeting of the minds. It had been past closing time when she came in and I was just closing up. Again, the heart palpitations. She was wearing another outfit that fit just right and her hair was down in her face, as if she'd just made love and ran her fingers through it. It was so sexy. She always walked around with that fresh-faced-just-fucked look. Regrettably, I later found out why.

She told me to watch my foot. I stepped aside, then bent to help her.

"And you know who I'm talking about," she said.

"I do not."

She clucked her tongue. "Ray—that's your name, right? His name is Phil, they call him Filthy Phil. He owns this bar and a lot of other stuff. He thinks he owns me."

I stumbled back. "He owns this bar?"

She groaned under her breath and said, "Yes."

"Well…"

She sat back. "Look, I need some help and you seem to be just the person who can help me."

"What makes you think that?"

She sighed and pulled a pack of cigarettes from her pocket. She offered me one—I declined—then lit one, inhaled, exhaled and said, "You look like you ran away from the circus."

"Huh?" I said and shrugged, feigning indifference, but I was hanging on her every word.

She went on, "You have this look of loss about you, a look of frustration, though you don't know why you're frustrated or what you've lost. You've never been close to anyone or anything. You don't have a wife or kids or a girl. You were probably in some long-term relationship, which you screwed up and walked away from because you were afraid of commitment, or some other such excuse that means you just weren't interested. Coulda been because you didn't think you had enough to offer. Coulda been you were scared shitless."

What *was* she getting at?

She ashed on the floor and continued her pop psychological account of my entire life, "You think about love and the future but you never get close to it cause you're content. You're satisfied. You probably pick up the occasional skank in here, take her back to your rathole and fuck her. The next morning she disappears and you're glad, right?"

I only stared at her.

"You're one of those guys who doesn't know or care about anyone else. You probably read Tolstoy though you certainly didn't understand a damn word of it, but thought it might make you look smart to carry around a shabby copy of *War and Peace*."

I looked away. It wasn't Tolstoy. It was Dostovesky. And I did understand it, thank you very much.

"I prefer Cèline." She took a hit off the cigarette. "I mean, if you're trying to make an impression always go with the more obscure reference."

11

Whatever.

"There's nothing mentally, emotionally or physically wrong with you," she continued. "You're stable. You're capable of great things if you would just get up off your ass and do something. But you won't. Cause you're satisfied. You prefer to carry on with life, flying along like a fucking Peter Pan, not worrying about tomorrow, today or yesterday."

It was true. But it still pissed me off. I asked, "What's so wrong with that?"

"Nothing, if you're an earthworm."

I frowned. Was that what I was to her? An earthworm?

She scooted in closer to me. "But in the back of your head there's this little thing, isn't there? It could be a voice, it could be a hunch, it could be a gut instinct. But you know there's more out there. You just don't know if you can lay your hands on it."

I swallowed hard.

She took my hand. "I'm here to tell you that I know where you can get it." She placed my hand on her breast. "And it all starts here."

Years later, I might reflect back and know that I should have never fucked her that first night. That I should have told her to leave and to never come back. That I should have gotten up and ran away from her and from what she was offering, from what she wanted. But what she was propositioning was something I wanted and I wanted it bad. Maybe I needed her to give me that initial kick in the ass to get me going, even though I knew I might have to pay for it with my life.

Somehow, it didn't seem to matter at that moment. Maybe it didn't matter cause it really didn't make much sense. It was all lies, I knew that and I also knew she was humoring me, hooking me, pulling me into something—what, I don't know. Again, it didn't make much sense but it really didn't have to.

She leaned in and brushed her lips against mine, just like that. That's all she had to do. Shivers went down my spine. Her lips were nice, soft, wet. I pulled her close and pushed my tongue into her mouth. She moaned softly and her hands came up to play in my hair.

I should have stopped there. But what good is a "should have"? I wanted to love her to the point she could no longer take it. I pushed her back against the floor. It all moved very quickly then. My hand went up her shirt; her hand went down my pants. Soon, we were naked from the waist down and fucking on that cold, dirty tile floor. We were making a lot of noise, but then again, there was no one around but us.

She was squirming beneath me, opening her legs and pushing me inside. I couldn't get enough of her, of the moment. I began to pound against her. She pounded back and soon we were fucking like crazy. It was the best feeling, ever. One I would always remember and, later, try to recapture.

When it was over, we held onto each other and she whispered in my ear, "I think I love you."

That was all I needed to hear. Even if it was bullshit.

Pussy-whipped.

"He hangs around my neck like a fucking noose," she said, opened her front door and motioned me in. "He's not here. He's in Miami. Won't be back until tomorrow."

I followed her through the spacious loft. It was nice. Decorated perfectly, tastefully, yet there was a little kitsch to be found here and there. Like the pod chair in the living room, which sat opposite the big, brown, leather sofa, which had a patchwork quilt thrown over it, as if someone had taken a nap and another person had covered them with it. Funky, psychedelic artwork on the walls, with a few black and white pictures here and there. Solid walnut bookshelves lined an entire wall and were stuffed with family pictures, books, knickknacks and a very expensive stereo, which was a little dusty. An entire section of the shelf was stuffed with CDs. They were also strewn all over the place. Mostly hard rock, which she soon told me, was her favorite kind of music.

I stepped in and stared at a few of the pictures. A little girl with pigtails grinning happily up at the camera, that had to be her. I smiled. A shot of Filthy Phil glaring at the camera. I stepped away quickly.

"I did it all myself," she said and smiled widely. "Like it?"

"Yeah, it's very nice."

She nodded and turned on her heel. "Want a coke or something?"

"Sure," I said and watched her head off into the kitchen.

"Hi, Truman," she said.

I looked around. Who the hell was she talking to?

"Say hi to the cat, Ray. His name's Truman."

I looked down to see a big white ball of fuzz with a face. He didn't look too friendly.

"Say hi, Ray. He's a weird cat. You have to be nice to him, to let him know you're on his side. If not, he ends up shitting on the windowsill."

"Oh. Hi, Truman."

She didn't crack up like I expected her to. Wasn't that a joke?

"Come in here," she called.

I went into the kitchen. A big steel refrigerator, custom Swedish cabinets with silver handles. The counter was a thick slate. Nice. Filthy Phil lived very nicely.

She handed me a glass with coke and ice and sipped one she'd poured for herself. She was watching me, gauging my reaction. She was going to test me, I knew that. And she was going to get a big kick out of it, too.

"Thanks," I said and cleared my throat.

"Welcome."

I took a sip. "So, he's not here?"

She jerked her head to the side. "Come on."

I watched her walk away. She had the cutest twist to her walk. It wasn't affected, either.

I followed her to the bedroom. All it contained was a big bed and a white shag rug. It wasn't so much a room for sleeping as for fucking. I stared at her, then to the left at the closet door, then back again. She smiled at me and patted the bed.

"Custom made," she said and leaned back on the bed invitingly. "Come here."

I cleared my throat.

"You're a good lay, Ray. Oh, look, I made a rhyme! Ray's a good lay, so he doesn't have to pay!" She giggled and motioned me over with her finger.

"I don't feel comfortable being here," I said, but leaned down for a kiss anyway.

"He's not here, Ray. Don't worry. Besides, I fuck around on him all the time. He knows."

My mouth fell open. "You do?"

She shrugged, "Well, no, but I tell him that anyway. I say, 'Hey, dickhead, I fucked the plumber, the delivery man, the janitor.' Whoever's available."

"What does he do?"

"He stares at me with this stupid, dumb look." She mimicked a stupid, dumb look. "He doesn't care. He doesn't care because he knows it's not true."

I didn't know what to think then. I didn't know what to say.

She perked up, "Do you know when a man leaves town that he actually starts manufacturing more sperm?"

Where *the hell* did that come from? I asked stupidly, "Huh?"

"So when he comes back and fucks his girl, his sperm will kill any other sperm that might be inside her. In case she cheated on him."

I could only stare at her.

She pulled me down on the bed. "It's true. Sperm competes with each other. That way, it's kind of insured that his sperm will be the one to father the child. I saw it on TV."

"Oh," was all I could think of to say.

She climbed on top of me and smiled.

"Why are you doing this?" I asked.

"Doing what?"

"Fucking with my life."

"I'm not fucking with your life, Ray," she said and bent down to stare into my eyes. "When we met, didn't you feel a spark between us?"

"Yes, I did. Did you?"

"I brought it up first, didn't I?" she said sweetly. "I was so attracted to you that I was afraid to speak."

I had a feeling she was lying. That was okay.

"I was afraid you'd see right through me," she said, taking my hand.

I pulled my hand back and asked, "What do you want from me?"

"Right now, I want to fuck you," she said and moved in my lap.

"And after that?" I said and moved against her, grinding my dick against her.

"I want to fuck you again," she said and bent to nibble on my ear.

"You haven't told me your name," I said and moved to

16

brush my lips against hers.

She pulled back and smiled. "My name isn't important, is it?"

The truth was I knew her name. After that first night, I asked around about her. That's how I'd found out all the things I knew about her past, how she'd met Filthy Phil, about how he'd never let her go. The only thing I didn't know was her birthday, her social security number and her favorite color.

"Just call me Kat," she said. "That's what my friends call me, Kat, with a 'K'."

"Alright, Kat, what happens next?"

"The direction you want to take is up to you. You can be wishy-washy about it or you can help me. If you help me, there's a lot of money we can split. I won't fuck you out of it, either. I don't care about it that much. All I want is for Phil to be out of my life."

She only called him Phil. She never called him by his rightful name, Filthy.

"And why do you want him dead?" I asked.

She stared at me and said, "I told you. He thinks he owns me. He won't let me go. I've tried to leave him but he always comes after me. This is the only way for me to be free."

"And what does this have to do with me?"

"Everything," she said. "After we met, I knew I had found an ally in you. We're very much alike, Ray. We're perfect for each other. Can't you see that?"

I could see that she was perfect for me, for any man. But was I perfect for her? I didn't know, but I did know I wanted to be.

"He's cruel to me," she said dramatically. "He keeps me locked up, he beats me. He won't let me have any friends. He won't let me go anywhere. He gets angry. He gets mean."

In my gut, I knew she was lying. There were no marks

on her body, only a few faint scars we all have from rambunctious childhoods. She didn't look at all like an abused woman. She didn't have that vacant, faraway look in her eye. She smiled too much, she was too quick to laugh, to make a joke, to tease. People who are in that kind of hell don't usually do those kinds of things.

"And is this why you hate him?" I asked.

"Well, yeah," she said and touched my face with the tip of her finger. "Besides, he said I was short once."

"You are short."

"Yeah, and I'm still pissed off about it, too," she said and glared at me.

I almost smiled. I couldn't. It was a bit unnerving to be sitting in Filthy Phil's apartment, on Filthy Phil's bed and with the love of Filthy Phil's life.

"He makes me miserable, Ray," she said. "He's not a nice person, he's a criminal. A guy like him doesn't deserve to live and he certainly doesn't deserve a girl like me."

I couldn't have agreed more.

I'm with stupid.

After that first night, I began to see her on a regular basis. She'd come in, sit at the bar and make small talk. As the bar began to empty each night, she'd start asking when I was going to "do it". But the more she talked, the less convinced I was of doing it. And she never gave me a good reason either. Her main excuse was that she hated him and something about an insurance policy, which she'd let me have most of.

One night, around midnight, she said, "Ray, we have to talk."

By this time, I'd totally talked myself out of it, so I said,

18

"I don't want to talk about it."

"Ray, I could have gotten any guy to do this, but I picked you. You know why?"

She had picked me. Why had she picked me? My money? My charm? My ass? No. She had picked me because she thought I'd get the job done. It was that simple.

"Why?" I croaked then cleared my throat. "Why?"

She studied me and sighed. "Because I want to be with you."

I rolled my eyes and checked her out, looking for signs of deceit. She stared back at me, looking like such a little cutie, almost like a little girl. I wanted to buy her a lollipop and kiss her cheek. But I really didn't want to murder her boyfriend.

"I don't know how to do it," I said.

"I know. It's not an easy thing to do."

I sighed loudly, poured another beer, took another bill.

"But it has to be done, Ray," she said. "Soon. I can't wait much longer."

"What does that mean?" I asked.

"It means, if you won't do it, I'll find someone who will."

I turned to her. "So do it."

"Maybe I will," she hissed.

"Maybe you should."

She glared at me and grabbed her jacket.

"Hey, come on! I was only joking!"

But she was out the door in a flash. I didn't see her again for nearly two weeks. It almost killed me. All I thought about was her. Her penchant for lying, for story telling. The way she wrapped her legs around my waist and held me tight while we fucked.

But I was weak. I was no more a killer than she was a saint, and God knows she was no saint. But then again, who is?

19

As fate would have it, I saw her boyfriend before I saw her again. I was behind the bar with my back turned, counting out the register. I heard a very masculine voice with that indeterminable accent say, "Pardon?"

"Be right with you."

"Alright," Filthy Phil said.

I froze. I'd never heard his voice before, but I knew it was him. Who else could it have been? Of course, the bar was completely empty. Except for him. And for me. That figured.

I turned and the look on my face must have made him crack up. He laughed, "You're white as a sheet, mate."

I didn't reply.

"Listen, get me a pint, would you?"

I nodded and walked stiffly over to the tap. He watched me. As I've said, he was a big motherfucker. He had a very imposing physicality, all of it muscle, none of it fat. And his face was sculpted looking—sharp cheekbones, big red lips and piercing blue eyes beneath thick black eyebrows. Was he handsome? No. He wasn't handsome cause he looked mean. He looked as though he'd just soon kill you as to look at you.

I placed the pint in front of him.

"Thanks," he said very politely. He took a long gulp, sucking about half of it down. He set the glass on the bar and motioned with his hand, "Got any matches?"

I retrieved a pack and flipped them over to him.

He lit a cigarette, inhaled deeply and said, "I haven't had a fag in two years."

I nodded. I hoped to God he was talking about cigarettes.

"Bloody fucking women," he said and took another drag.

"Excuse me?"

"Bloody fucking women, that's what I said," he replied

rather dryly.

"Oh," I said but didn't venture a comment. I valued my life. I know when to keep my big mouth shut.

"You know her," he said and eyed me.

I know I must have looked really stupid then. I must have looked like some cartoon character. My eyes nearly popped out of my head. In the back of my mind, I heard a foghorn blow. I was shaking a little in my boots, too. Impending fear of death will do that to you.

I stammered, "Wha…aahhh?"

"You know her, don't you?" he asked, smoking.

"I know a lot of girls."

"Yeah, that's what she is, too, a fucking little girl," he said almost cheerfully. "That's the truth, init?"

"I'm not sure…"

"Her name's Katherine, Kathy Cumberland. She goes by Kat, that's what we call her. Kat. I gave her that nickname. Kat, with a 'K'."

I stared dumbly at him. I knew all of this already.

"She drops by here a lot, doesn't she?"

I shrugged.

"Yeah, she does. She came home late one night and I asked where she'd been and after she chewed me arse because I dared ask such a personal question, she told me she'd been hanging out. Here." He knocked on the bar, then gulped the rest of his beer down and motioned for another.

I played dumb, "Huh," and switched the glasses.

"Thanks," he said. "So, have you seen her?"

I shook my head.

"Oh, come on. You're Ray, right? She told me all about you."

All about me… Oh, Jesus! I tried to appear cool, "She did? Why?"

"Listen," he said and leaned across the bar. "Just between you and me, she's a nutter. I love her more than anything, but she's a bit of a nutter. You know what a nutter is, right?"

I stared at him and nodded stupidly.

He nodded back. "She picks up these people, brings them home, gives them food, clothes, money. I come home one day to find me closet has been emptied. She's dressed half the bums in New York in me bloody Armani suits. Not that they fit 'em, either."

He shook his head at her foolish behavior. I leaned back and stared at him. If I didn't hate him so much, I'd probably start to like this guy. He was quite affable. But I couldn't like him. I hated his fucking guts. He was what was standing in the way of my happiness. Him and the rest of the world.

"And you know why she does this shit?" he asked, lighting another cigarette. "She does it to take the piss. She doesn't care about being Mother Teresa. She only does it to get under me skin. And when I don't get pissed, she gets pissed. At me, I mean. Makes me life a living hell, that one."

I knew what he meant.

He sighed heavily, the weight of the world on his shoulders. The weight of loving a woman he didn't understand made him sad, disillusioned. He went on, "But then, y'know what she does? She'll always flying about like a little bird, always looking for something she's misplaced or what-have-you. She'll stump her little toe and cry like a bloody baby, crumbling to the floor. And I'll scoop her up, put her to bed. And then she'll say, 'I love you, Phil, you know that, right?' And everything's good again."

I was about to throw up. I wished he'd just shut the fuck up and get out of my sight. I didn't need this shit.

He, however, was on the verge of breaking down. "She didn't come home last night."

I stood to attention. "Where is she?"

"I don't fucking know. Why do you think I'm here? She's always threatening to leave. I never believe her, I mean, why should I?" He took the glass between his massive hands and squeezed it. "If something happened to her...if someone hurt her...I'll..."

The thick glass splintered and shattered, driving his point home quite effectively. He wiped his hands clean on his pants. He didn't have one nick on his hands. He was one tough son of a bitch.

"I'll get that," I said and grabbed a small broom and dustpan and cleaned up the mess.

"Sorry about that," he said sheepishly. "It's just she—"

Before he could finished, the door opened, slammed. We both looked over and simultaneously let out a sigh of relief. There she was, breezing into the bar, walking into our lives to add some sunshine and a lot of fucking misery.

She stopped short when she saw Filthy Phil, whose look of anguish was now replaced with elation. His eyes just lit up when he saw her. It was almost unnerving.

"What *the fuck* are you doing here?" she snapped.

He dropped his head.

She glowered at him as she approached the bar. She turned her gaze on me.

"Mai tai?" I asked cautiously.

"Baby?" he asked timidly.

"Go fuck yourself, Phil," she snapped and sat a few stools down from him. "Just give me a beer, Ray."

He motioned for another one, too. I wanted to say something to her, but he was there. I wanted to say how happy I was to see her. But, that wouldn't have been a good idea, would it? I got the beers and set them down in front of them. She ignored hers. He took a long gulp and tried not to look at her.

Filthy Phil said quietly, "Where you been?"

She held her hands up and stared at me in amazement. "Get a load of this guy."

"Kat—"

"Shut it, Phil."

I was momentarily stunned, even more so when he did, in fact, shut it.

"How you been, Ray?" she asked.

"I can't complain," I said.

She nodded. "No, but you still do sometimes, don'cha?"

I couldn't help but smile. She almost smiled back, but then she caught Filthy Phil smiling and shot him a look of pure disdain as if that comment wasn't intended to amuse him.

He cleared his throat and looked up at the ceiling. The anguish was back. I almost smiled. Then everything got really quiet and the room shook with silence. I started to leave. I had to get away and let them do whatever they were going to do. I went to the other side of the bar and pretended to busy myself.

Phil cleared his throat. "Where you been?"

"None—of—your—fuck-ing—business."

"Fine," he muttered.

"Besides, I beeped you earlier and you didn't call me back."

A glimmer of hope crossed his pathetically sad face. "I didn't get it."

"I figured as much," she growled at him, then to me, "He was probably off fucking that little cunt."

Again, the grimace.

She faced him, "Ain't that right?"

"I am not fucking anyone."

"And certainly not me."

He groaned in misery. "I told you, I am completely devoted to you."

"You liar!" She picked up his glass and threw the remainder of his beer in his face. He didn't even blink. I knew I should leave and let them have at it but I couldn't stop myself from watching. It was like a train wreck. You

24

want to look away, but you just can't.

He motioned for a towel. I quickly handed him the one I'd been using all night. He took it, sniffed, threw it down and motioned for another. I got him a clean one. He wiped his face.

"You could at least be honest with me," she muttered. "I mean, I like a little variety, too."

She stared at me knowingly. *Why was she doing this?!*

"I'm warning you, Katherine," he muttered with no visible malice in his voice.

She chuckled. "Warning me? Oh, right, big man. Just like you to pick on a little girl."

He looked away, then at me, shaking his head. "You can't win, mate, you can't fucking win with women! You do everything they want, let them shit on you and they still end up walking all over you."

He had that down.

She stared at him. "At least I didn't fuck someone else."

She's a damn good liar. Here I was her lover—hopefully not former—standing in front of her and her "man" and she was lying right to his face. Oh, she was really good at being a woman and that meant she was really good at her job of driving men crazy. If I hadn't been terrified, I'd been amused. But I should have been terrified.

"For the last time, I did not fuck her," he said and put his head on the bar and groaned. His head shot back up and he snapped, "I want me wallet back!"

She eyed him slyly, rolled her eyes and pulled a wallet out of the pocket of her jacket. She chucked it at him. He caught it and opened it. It was empty.

"Should I even ask?" he asked.

"No, you shouldn't," she replied smartly.

I almost laughed. Good enough for him.

He shook his head and slipped the wallet into his suit jacket, placed his head in his hands and fell back on the bar.

He'd had it.

"What are you doing here, anyway?" she snapped.

"I was looking for you."

"Oh. Get up, man, you're making me sick."

He sat up, rubbing his eyes. "Have you eaten yet?"

She shook her head.

"Are you hungry?"

She nodded.

"Would you like something to eat?"

She shrugged.

He stood and held out his hand. She hopped up, jerked away from him and proceeded out the door, calling over her shoulder, "You coming, Ray?"

Filthy Phil and I glanced at each other.

"It's alright," he said. "You can close up early."

He did, after all, own the bar. I didn't mention the fact that it was past closing time anyway. I locked the door on my way out.

Taking liberties.

We walked down the street and into a packed all-night diner. I found a booth near the kitchen and sat down. Kat waltzed in, plopped down in the other seat, leaned back and stuck out her legs, taking up the whole seat. Filthy Phil stopped short when he saw her sprawled out. He motioned me over with one finger. I scooted over and tried not to breathe as his massive frame took up the majority of the seat.

It took forever to get waited on. We sat there for about twenty minutes, yet we didn't attempt to make small talk. Filthy Phil stared up at the ceiling, past me out the window, and at his gigantic paws. I took a good look at his watch. It was some fancy Swiss kind. I could tell it cost a fortune. He caught me staring.

"Oh, nice watch," I said quickly.

"Kat got it for me birthday," he said and took it off. "Here, try it on."

"Oh, no, that's okay."

He ignored me and placed it in my hands. It weighed a ton. I slipped it on. I tried to smile and said, "Nice," like I cared.

Kat was eying us. "You gonna try on each other's dresses, too?"

We stared at her.

She rolled her eyes. "Where the fuck is that mother—"

"Now, Kat," Phil said gently.

"'Now Kat'," she mimicked him and faced us. "He better not count on a tip from me."

I took the watch off and handed it back to him.

Just then, a waiter whizzed by. She grabbed his shirttail and pulled him back. He nearly dropped a tray of dirty dishes.

"We're ready to order if you have the time," she said.

"I gotta take these to the kitchen."

"No, you gotta take our order."

He stared at her, rolled his eyes, put the plates down and took out a notepad. "What can I get you?"

Filthy Phil said, "I'd like some bacon and eggs and—"

"No, you would not," she told him. "You know what your doctor said. More fruits and more vegetables."

"But I want—"

She turned to the waiter, "He will have the grilled chicken salad with vinaigrette dressing on the side. No bread, no croutons, no crackers. And I know I'm being a bitch right now so if you spit in it, I'll come after you."

Filthy Phil chuckled a little at her.

"However, I will have the cheeseburger platter. No

mayo, with bacon and a coke." She closed her menu and handed it to him.

The waiter sighed and said to me, "For you, sir?"

"I'll just have some coffee," I said quickly.

She said, "He'll have the same as me."

He hurried off. I saw him stop at the counter and talk to some guy, who must have been the manager. He jerked his head over towards us. The manager glanced over and his eyes nearly popped out of his head. He grabbed the guy's shoulders and shook him. He must have recognized Filthy Phil. People always seemed to have that reaction to him.

Our drinks and food arrived in record time and was delivered by the manager, who asked if we needed anything else.

"No, we're fine," Kat said and smiled at him.

"Let me know if you need anything," he said nervously and took off.

She nodded and began to arrange her burger. She wiped most of the ketchup and mustard off, arranged the lettuce, bacon and tomato on it *just so,* then she put a just a dab of ketchup and mustard back on it, then and cut it in half. She handed part of it to Filthy Phil and said, "Just so you'll know I'm not mad at you anymore."

He smiled at her. She smiled back. Then it dawned on me. It was obvious, wasn't it? It was a love triangle, simple as that. I loved her. He loved her. She loved herself.

"How's your food, Ray?" she asked.

"It's okay."

"Good," she said merrily and took a small bite off her burger. She ate about two French fries, took one more bite, then pushed the plate away. "Done," she said wiping her hands with a paper napkin.

"You didn't eat anything," Filthy Phil said.

"Well, it wasn't very good."

"Eats like a bird," he muttered.

"At least I'm not hung like one," she said and they both laughed. "Sorry, Ray. Private joke."

I stared at him, getting a little satisfaction. And his feet were so big too. Shame, really.

"I was thinking, Ray," Filthy Phil said. "That you could come work for me."

No. No. No. And no.

He stared at me and his face took on this menacing look. It was almost as if he was daring me to turn him down.

"I can't, really," I said.

"I was thinking, Ray," he repeated. "That you could come work for me."

"He can't," Kat said quickly. "He works for me."

Filthy Phil turned to her.

She shook her head. "So?"

He narrowed his eyes. Here it comes. He's gonna figure it out now. I'd be dead soon. Oh, Father, who art in Heaven…what was the other part?!

"So, that means," he said and smiled. "That he's been working for me all along."

I was fucked beyond redemption.

"I think it's a great idea," Kat told me a few days later.

I stared at her. We were driving in her car, a sleek silver Mercedes Benz. As I looked around the expensive interior, I asked, "I'm still a little fuzzy about a few things, Kat."

"Oh?" she asked. "Like what?"

"Like why do you want him dead," I said.

"Why wouldn't I?"

"Well, for one thing, he bought you this car."

"*He* didn't buy me this car," she said and shook her head. "*I* bought me this car."

"Oh," I said. "Still, I can't work for him, Kat."

She rolled her eyes. "Look at it this way. You'll get to know him better, learn all of his habits and it'll make it easier for you when you get ready to knock him off."

"What I mean is, I don't know if I want to kill him or not."

She stared over at me. "You don't know him like I do, Ray. Once you do, you'll *want* to kill him."

I wasn't so sure. The only thing I really detested about him was the fact that he had her and I didn't. But that really did piss me off.

"Listen," she said. "It's not that hard. You get a gun, you shoot him, it's over."

"Why don't you kill him?"

She shrugged. "I tried to once. I broke a lamp over his big fucking head. The bastard didn't even flinch."

Then how did she expect me to get to him? Even so, I said, "So, let me get this straight. You want him dead because...?"

"I told you," she said. "I hate his guts and he won't leave. Besides that, there's this big insurance policy we're going to split, okay? Do you always want to be a bartender, Ray?"

I thought about that. No, I really didn't. I also didn't want to spend the rest of my life alone. I thought about Filthy Phil. He didn't deserve her. Maybe I didn't either but he sure as hell didn't. In truth, I'd love to take her away from him. In reality I didn't want to have to kill the guy to do it.

"Maybe I should just go back to the bar," I said. "It's not that bad."

She sighed. "You can't. We already replaced you."

Then it was settled, wasn't it?

"If you loved me, Ray, you'd just do it," she said. "And stop asking so many stupid questions."

30

"Kat," I told her. "I just don't know about this."

"It'll be a cakewalk, I tell you," she said and stopped at a red-light then turned to me. "It's simple. He always counts down the receipts at night. Around midnight, he'll leave the shop and go out the front door. He'll continue to his car where Tiny will be waiting on him."

Tiny? Did she just say Tiny?

"I'll tell him I'll pick him up so he can give Tiny the night off," she said. "He likes to give his driver the night off occasionally. And then, slam, bam, thank you ma'am."

Good God. This was the craziest thing I'd ever been caught up in. I chewed on the inside of my jaw and stared out the window.

The light turned green and she put pedal to metal and the car lurched forward. She was a terrible driver and would be a perfect cabbie. I held onto to the door handle and said a little prayer.

"Light me a cig, Ray," she said as she steered the car around a delivery truck.

I lit her one.

She smoked a little and continued, "And, of course, I'll be late getting to the scene of the crime. You'll enter through the back alley; his back will be to you. You'll fire and he'll go down. I'll drive up, scream, call 9-1-1 and then it'll all be over."

She grinned from ear to ear. She was so damn proud of herself. She had to be crazy. There *had* to be something wrong with her. I watched as she drove, smoked and pulled something out from under the seat—all at the same time.

"Here," she said and pushed a brown paper bag at me.

"What is it?"

"Open it!" she said excitedly.

I opened it and pulled out a gun. An old gun. It was way older than me. Hell, it was probably older than my great-grandmother, God rest her soul. But to be so old, and

31

so big, it was in good shape.

"Isn't it cool?" she asked.

I just stared at her.

"I mean, I know it's a gun. It was Old Hank's gun. He used it in the war. He gave it to me."

I didn't care to know who Old Hank was or which war she was referring.

"Does it even work?" I asked.

She stared at me, as if she'd never considered such a thing. "Of course, it works!"

"What if he kills me, Kat?" I said, suddenly realizing this could, in fact, be a possibility. Dear God, how had I let her talk me into this? Why was I even riding in her car with her? I needed to get out, run away. But then again, I thought about Filthy Phil having her and I knew I'd never have her as long as he was in the way. Besides that, he was a menace to society.

"You're going to jump him!" she said. "He won't know what hit him."

I wasn't so sure.

She leaned across the seat and kissed me. "Then it'll just be us, okay, Ray? Just us."

I melted. The things a woman can do to a man with one little kiss and the bat of an eye. The things... She made a sharp left turn. I was slung up against the door and back into reality. I looked straight ahead. I couldn't do this. I just couldn't. I'd just have to tell her no, sorry. And then what? She'd find someone else, that's what.

We drove for a little while in silence. She rolled the window down and threw her cigarette out. "So, anyway, I was thinking about going to Jamaica. I hear it's real nice. I read that Ian Fleming had a place down there, so it must be pretty cool. You ever been?"

It was amazing how quickly she could jump from subject to subject. I realized God put people like her on earth to baffle the rest of us. It was kind of annoying, too.

"Uh, no," I said and heard a siren. I turned to see a motorcycle policeman behind us.

"Shit!" she squealed and stared at me anxiously. "What do we do?"

"You better pull the fuck over!" I said and looked down. *Fuck!* The gun! I pushed it back into the bag and under the seat. She stopped the car and I pretended to whistle. The cop tapped on the window. She rolled it all the way down.

"Is there a problem, Officer?" she said and flashed him a big smile.

That wasn't going to work with this guy, I could just tell.

"You threw a cigarette out the window," he told her. "Littering."

"I did?" she asked.

"Yes, you did," he said and began to write a ticket.

"Really?" she said. "I did?"

"Yes, really, you did."

"Huh." She turned to me. "Did I do that, Ray?"

"I wouldn't argue about it," I told her.

"Okay, I won't," she said sweetly and leaned out of the car and smiled up at him. "Do I know you?"

I sat up. She'd tried this line with me, too.

"I don't think so," he said but paused.

"Yeah, I do," she said. "You once came by my apartment. You know my boyfriend, Filthy Phil."

He stood a little taller. She grinned at him. He cracked a smile and began to shred the ticket.

"That's what I thought," she said with a wink. "Oh, hold on a minute."

She leaned across me and dug into the glove compartment. Everything in the world was in there—candy, cigarettes, papers, a rubber ducky—everything. She finally found a big, bound stack of tickets. They were tied with a pretty pink ribbon, as if she were preserving them.

"See if you can take care of these, too, why don't you," she said with a smile.

He took them without resistance. "I'll see what I can do."

She winked, "I'll tell Phil you said hello, Officer…"

"Officer Farmer," he said and held out his nametag.

"You have a great day, Officer."

"You too, Miss…"

"Miss Cumberland," she said with a smile.

As she pulled away from the curb, I was amazed. How did she just do that? I wasn't sure but I did know she was playing games with me. I wanted to tell her that, tell her I knew she really didn't love me. That she never would. But I didn't want to say it cause I didn't want to believe it.

I stared at her, sitting there driving in New York traffic like an old pro, which meant pedestrians beware. My heart twisted in pain then. She had been right. I wanted something more; I was just too scared to admit it. My life had been boring until I met her. I never thought I'd be mixed up with bookies or thugs or people called Filthy Phil. I never thought I'd be involved with a girl who looked as good as she did. Everything comes with a price, though, doesn't it?

"We'll work out all the details later, Ray," she said and smiled at me. "Until then, just relax."

I didn't respond and she pulled off into a garage a few minutes later and we got out of the car. She threw the keys at a small, skinny parking attendant.

"Hey, Butch," she said. "Be careful with it."

"Who's this?" he asked and pointed at me.

"He's with me," she said. "Come on, Ray."

"He's working for Mr. Phil now?"

"No, he isn't. He's working for me. Now shut your trap and park my fucking car."

He didn't even flinch like most guys would have. He was probably used to her.

We walked around the corner and into what appeared to be a jewelry shop. She waved sweetly at everyone in there, they waved back, obviously happy to see her. We walked straight through to a back office, which was piled high with mean looking guys and in the back of it all sat Filthy Phil, who grinned like a fool when he spotted her.

"Hey, baby," he called.

She went over, plopped down in his lap and gave him a big kiss, which was reciprocated. With vigor. Which pissed me off.

All the thugs in there tried not to stare at them, tried not to gawk as he patted her ass, as he ran his hand up her back. They probably wanted her like I wanted her. We should have known we'd never have her. She belonged only to herself.

She finally pulled back and stared me dead in the eye, a satisfied look on her face. She had me then. And she knew it. I wanted her like he had her. And I knew what I had to do to get her.

Besides, he was a badass motherfucker. He was mean and he was cruel and he was all the things society despised. I was actually going to do the world a favor.

At least, that's what I told myself in order to do it.

It went down a little something like this:

I got there a little late. I got lost, okay? I'd only been there once before. And the son of a bitch was already waiting on the curb! I had come around back, so he didn't see me, but there the fucker was, larger than life. He was whistling, leaning back on his heels.

Damn him!

He seemed to remember something. He stepped away from the curb and went back towards the store. I jumped away into the shadows. He didn't notice me. I wondered if he could hear my heart, which was beating anxiously inside my chest and threatening to come out. I almost wished it would. Then I wouldn't have to go through with this. But it didn't. So I had to.

He was unlocking the door. This was it. I had to do it now. *Get up there and do it! Step to it!*

Maybe I should just flee the scene of the crime before it happened. I hesitated, turning my head left and right, left and right, looking for an out. There was no out. Damn it. It was now or never. So it was now.

I stepped up and caught my breath. Then I almost doubled over with nausea. I felt sick, terrible. Oh, God, I was going to do this! I'd never done anything like this before, never even dreamed about it. So why was I doing it now? I closed my eyes and thought about Kat. Oh, that's why. *Fuck!* Love was a lot of damn trouble when you got right down to it.

I'd just do it. I'd just do it. I'd just point the gun and fire. Maybe it'd miss him and I could run and tell her I tried. I was a pretty lousy shot anyway so it would make sense. That's what I'd do. I was going to do it. I was going to do it now. Now. *Now!* My hand shook as I pointed the gun at him and fired. And missed. Would that be good enough? He turned, seemed momentarily stunned and stared at me in disbelief. No, I better fire again, so I did. This time the bullet hit him right in the belly. He stumbled back at little, staring down at the bullet hole. Should I fire again? The bullets didn't seem to be affecting him. I fired again, hitting right above the previous spot. He stared at me, but he wasn't

36

going down. *Why wasn't he going down?* He couldn't be that fucking hard.

I should just run.

But I didn't have time. All of a sudden, I heard more shots and they weren't coming from my gun. They were coming from his gun! And they were hitting me, left and right. I fell to the ground and blacked out momentarily.

The last thing I felt was him pulling the ski mask off my head and the last thing I heard was, "Ray?"

That's the last time he addressed me by that name. More on that later.

It's a shame about Ray.

I was in and out of consciousness for the next few hours, well the next few days. Or weeks. I don't really remember.

Kat had arrived right after he gunned me down. She had pulled him off me and shouted, "Why did you kill him?!"

"He was shooting at me!"

"I can't believe you, you dumb son of a bitch!"

She didn't say the last part. I added it in.

They carried me to her car, put me in the backseat. They conversed but I couldn't make out the words. It was almost as if they were speaking gibberish. Well, I know he was, but I couldn't make out what she was saying at all.

"Here," she said and handed him a cell phone. "Call Dr. Harold."

"Hallo, this Dr. Harold?" he said. "Phil here. Meet us at our place." He hung up and handed her the phone.

"I need both hands to drive, dumbass!" she snapped and turned around to look at me.

"You need both eyes too!" he yelled and grabbed the wheel.

"Damn, it, I had it under control," she muttered and turned back to me. "Shit, he don't look good at all."

He turned around and stared, too. "It's just a stomach wound. He'll be fine as soon as we get the bullets out."

She hit him on the arm, hard. "Just a stomach wound? Oh, is that all? Jesus, Phil!"

"Sorry!"

"I can't believe you did that!" she yelled. "If he dies, I'll kill you!"

"I'm sorry," he said. "It was accidental."

"You're such an idiot!"

"WATCH OUT!" he hollered.

The car swerved. I thought I was going to throw up. A horn honked. She honked her horn and hollered, "If you can't handle driving in New York, get the fuck out!"

Phil sighed.

I mumbled, "Am I going to die?"

They stared at each other.

"What'd he say?" he asked.

"I dunno," she replied, then asked softly, "What is it, Ray?"

I tried again, but I blacked out. I don't remember anything after that.

? ? ? ?

I didn't die. I got hit in the stomach, in the arm and in the thigh. I'd probably walk with a limp the rest of my life.

Now I was living with them. I was an invalid ensconced in their loft, in their world. I had my own room and everything. I wondered why once, but then, it didn't seem to matter. I wondered why he helped her save me when I was trying to kill him. He had to know that. It was too obvious. Why wasn't he asking questions? But I let it go. I mean, why mention it if you don't have to?

I wondered why they hadn't taken me to a hospital. But I didn't ask. I knew why.

Kat, with the help of a good-looking hired nurse—we'll call her Delores and she wasn't a "real" nurse, just one of Kat's friends—mended my wounds and helped me back to health. They both dressed in these little white nurse's uniforms, showing cleavage like there was no tomorrow. God, they looked so damn good. They even put on the little white hats. They gave me wonderful, glorious sponge baths, just like in some porno. They gave me pecks on the cheek, spooned soup into my mouth, and pumped wonderful painkillers into me so often that I was living in this beautiful, tranquil dream world.

They'd tease each other, thusly, teasing me. They'd brush up against each other "accidentally" and say things like, "Oh, you have a little baby powder on your nose," and wipe it off with lingering touches. It was the best fucking medicine. If hospitals would start serving this kind of thing up, there wouldn't be so many sick people in the world. But, then again, no one would ever leave either.

Kat would crank the music and they'd dance, sometimes grabbing things like the remote control and singing into it like a microphone. They'd crack me up. Kat once got so into that Journey song *Loving, Touching, Squeezin'* that she nearly passed out. She wailed, hitting all the high notes like a professional. She was really good.

Occasionally, Filthy Phil would watch us but he never said anything. He knew I was in too much pain to fuck (but, God, how I wanted to) or even move, so why should he worry?

One day, Kat said, "As soon as you're better, we'll try again."

"I'm not trying again!" I shouted. "I nearly got killed!"

She rolled her eyes. "That damn bulletproof vest! How could I have not remembered?"

I glared at her. "How indeed."

"I can't believe he shot you," she said and held my hand. "The son of a bitch."

I nodded in agreement and studied her. "Why did he save me when I was shooting at him?"

She eyed me back. "Ray, I already told you this once."

"No, you didn't."

She sighed and withdrew her hand. "I told him you thought he was trying to rob the store."

"Oh. And he bought it? Even with me wearing a ski mask?"

"Well, it was cold that night wasn't it? There's no crime in wearing a ski mask if you're cold."

"This doesn't make sense to me," I said. "He can't be that stupid."

She yawned. "Well, he is Phil."

"Well, there you go," I replied dryly. "But I just don't understand it."

"It's because you're on drugs, baby," she said and gave me a little pout. "Have you been able to get an erection?"

"Where the hell did that come from?!"

"Well, have you?"

I looked away and crossed my arms in a huff. "No!"

"See? It's the drugs."

"Please stop saying that."

"You'll get your little fella back soon, Ray. Don't worry."

My little fella? *Little?* She just said that, didn't she? Little. Like she was insinuating I was not very...well endowed. How could she have said that? Sure, I wasn't a large man, but I had some length. Some.

Then it occurred to me. That night, at the diner, she

40

had said, "hung like a bird". Had she been talking about me and not Phil? And why had he laughed? I knew right then and there I'd have to find out how big his dick was just to make sure that comment wasn't addressed at me. (Please remember that I was on drugs, so I wasn't thinking straight.) (And that I'm not gay.)

"I want out of this!" I shouted at the top of my lungs.

She leaned back and glared at me. "You've come this far, Ray. There's no going back now."

"I just want my old life back. I want a little security."

"Why? No one is ever secure, we pretend we are, but we aren't. I mean… Well, look at you."

"Yes! Look at me!"

"You'll be fine," she said and smiled gently. "Right now, I have to go work."

"What?"

She sighed and said, "I volunteer at the shelter a few days a week. You know that. Now close your eyes and go to sleep and I'll be home in two shakes of a lamb's tail."

"But, but—"

But she was gone. She shut the front door quietly on her way out.

Damn her. Well, see you later, too. GOOD-FUCKING-BYE! Little fella indeed. I'd get to the bottom of this if it killed me! I huffed and puffed and shook my fist in the air for a few minutes, then closed my eyes and drifted off to sleep. I awoke with a start after the front door slammed shut.

"Baby!"

Filthy Phil was home. He always called out to her like that. The son of a bitch.

"Baby!"

Why didn't he just shut up?

I heard him mumble something and stomp into the kitchen. I drifted off. Next thing I knew, he was in my room

41

next to my bed. I nearly jumped out of my skin when I saw him standing there. He was peering at me like a gorilla in a zoo peers at the people. His head was cocked to the side and he studied me, then he jerked it to the other side.

It was unnerving as hell.

"How you doin', Boy?" he finally asked.

It should be noted that Filthy Phil had taken to calling me "Boy" with a capital "B". I don't know why. I didn't argue. You usually don't try to pick a fight with a guy that could break you in half on whim. I don't think he meant anything by it. He didn't say it with malice. He just thought it was a clever little nickname, and, he explained, everyone should have a nickname. Yes, everyone, even if it was, perhaps, not a very imaginative one.

I shrugged, "As well as I can be."

He grinned. "Want some pizza? I want some pizza. I'll get us one."

He took off out of the room. I heard him pick up the phone, dial and order a pizza with everything, including anchovies. He came back in.

"Want to watch telly with me?" he asked.

"What?"

"Telly. Come on, I'll help you."

He leaned over and in one fell swoop, I'm ashamed to admit, had me up in his arms and was carrying me into the living room, where he deposited me gently on the couch. I got an idea then.

"You got any porno?" I asked.

He grinned. "Of course. You wanna watch one?"

I nodded eagerly.

He shrugged and went to the bookshelf and rummaged around for a minute or so then pulled out a DVD. He popped it in, went for some beers, came back and we watched the porn. I kept glancing over at his crotch, hoping he'd get an erection, which is a strange thing for me, or any other heterosexual male, to want. But I had to see, didn't I? I had to know if she was talking about me. That little comment, "hung like a bird" was driving me crazy.

He didn't get an erection. Neither did I.

The bell rang. Soon, we had pizza and a short, skinny delivery boy wearing a dirty baseball hat watching the porno with us. I don't know why, he just came in, exchanged pleasantries with Filthy Phil and then Filthy Phil said, "I'm watching a porn with Boy. Come join us."

They seemed to know each other. But maybe the delivery boy was some spy or…undercover agent or… Fuck, who cares? I really didn't have the energy to speculate. It just made me wonder. But this was a strange household, where eccentric people resided. I even thought I saw Elvis a few times, which was pretty fucking weird. But I had been on some heavy pain medication. (I know I've already mentioned that.)

The delivery boy said, "You got any more beer?"

"In the fridge," Filthy Phil said and jerked his head towards the kitchen.

"Anyone else?" he asked.

I nodded, as did Filthy Phil who was gobbling up the pizza in record time.

"You gonna eat any?" he asked.

"Oh, sure," I said.

He gave me a piece on a paper napkin. The delivery boy came back with the beers. And we watched the porno.

I turned to Filthy Phil, who was guzzling a beer whilst watching the TV out of the corner of his eye. I still couldn't get over how big he was. In comparison to Kat, or me even. He would have made two of the skinny delivery boy. He was just so fucking large. He caught me staring at him.

"You got a problem?" he asked.

I looked away quickly. "No problem at all."

He shrugged and let out a gigantic burp that brought

the house down. I was nearly lifted off the couch. I hoped to God he didn't have to fart. I would have surely shot through the ceiling.

"Pardon," he said.

He and the delivery boy cracked up. The delivery boy gave it a shot. His burp was a little less hardcore. Pardon the pun.

"Give it a go, Boy," he told me.

"I don't have to burp right now," I said and turned my attention back to the TV.

"Oh, come on, give it a try," he said, then slapped me on the back hard, which made me...well, burp—loudly.

Filthy Phil and the delivery boy roared with laughter. They were nearly rolling in the floor. Finally, I cracked a smile. It was kinda funny, I mean, if you had the mentality of a twelve-year-old boy or of a Filthy Phil.

The delivery boy, still laughing, asked, "Where's Miss Kat?"

"She's working," Filthy Phil and I both said at the same time.

We gave each other a quick glance. Here it comes, he's gonna beat the shit out of me right here, right now. Yet, he merely grinned.

"She'll be home later," he said.

"Filthy Phil," the delivery boy said. "How old is Miss Kat?"

"Wha'?" he asked.

"Miss Kat. How old is she?"

"Maybe you should ask *her*."

"I did, but she wouldn't tell me. She said, 'Old enough to know not to answer that question'."

Filthy Phil cracked a smile and considered, "Let's see...she had her birthday in December and she said this year she was twenty-seven."

"She's twenty-seven, then?" he asked.

"Well, she told me she was twenty-seven when I met her."

"When did you meet her?"

"It's been about four years we've been together."

I stared at him. She'd lied to me. She told me she'd only known Filthy Phil for about a year. "The most miserable year of my entire life," she had said.

"So really, she's about—what—thirty-two?" the delivery boy asked.

Thirty-one, Einstein.

"Yeah, but don't tell her that," he warned. "Don't ask, don't tell, that's me motto."

"Yeah, right," the delivery boy said and smiled. "She only looks like she's about nineteen."

"And she acts like she's thirteen," Filthy Phil said, then added with a wink, "But don't tell her I said that."

"Oh, come on, she's the coolest chick I know."

He nodded in agreement, "Yeah, she is pretty cool."

Truman entered, hopped over to Filthy Phil and placed a paw on his leg, like he was a dog instead of a cat. Filthy Phil leaned down, scratched the cat under the chin and fed him an anchovy.

"How's me little mate?" he asked the cat, which sat back on its heel, fish in mouth and stared up at him. Filthy Phil gave him another scratch then the cat hopped up on the couch, sat right next to him and began gnawing at the anchovy.

He must have known the secret language of animals. But then again, why wouldn't he? He was one of them.

"How do you know Kat?" I asked the delivery boy.

"Oh," he said and turned his attention to me. "I was a runaway. She rescued me."

I was flabbergasted. "Really?"

"Yeah," he said. "She works at the shelter sometimes. She's a volunteer."

Yeah, I knew that. Then I thought, if she was doing all of this shit, how did she have the time to arrange the termination of one Filthy Phil and plan a future with me? On top of saving runaways, she nursed me, cleaned the entire loft and did a lot of other stuff. Where the hell did she get the time?

The delivery boy leaned over and picked up another slice of pizza, took a bite and said with full mouth, "I ran away when I was about fifteen. I lived on the streets for about a year. She walked by my box one day."

"Your box?" I asked.

He swallowed. "I was living in a cardboard box, Boy."

What was this shit? Now this kid was calling me Boy, too?!

Filthy Phil said to me, "That's no way to live, either."

"No, it isn't," he agreed. "Anyway, I was really hungry and I saw this pair of legs stopped in front of the box. I had a hole cut where I could see out."

"Okay," I said, wondering where this was going.

"She was wearing cut-offs, you know Levi's, shorts. And, just let me say, she has the nicest legs. Right, Phil?"

"Fuck yeah."

"So, she was stopped and I was so hungry that I just reached out and grabbed her."

"Why?" I asked seriously. "Were you gonna eat her?"

They cracked up again, laughing so hard they spit out food and beer all over the place. They laughed for at least five full minutes. I smiled, pleased with myself. After they were done, Filthy Phil surveyed the mess.

"I better clean that up," he said and exited into the kitchen.

The delivery boy was still laughing, "No, Boy, I wasn't going to eat her." He leaned in and whispered, "But if I ever get the opportunity, I wouldn't mind a taste, if you know what I mean."

Oh, yeah, I knew what he meant. Too bad he wasn't her type.

"Anyway, I was going to snatch her purse. Problem is she doesn't carry a purse."

I'd noticed that, too.

"So, I grab her leg and she screams like, 'Ahhh!' and kicks me. I was really weak cause I'm so hungry and I just gave up. But she doesn't move; she just bends down and knocks on my box."

I nodded.

He smiled widely, shaking his head. "To make a long story short, she saved my life. She got me out of that box and into a shelter. I was sick, too, with pneumonia, and she paid for my doctor bills. She got me an apartment and a job. I go to college part-time right now. I want to be a DJ."

"Wow," was all I could think of to say. "You have to go to school to be a DJ? I just thought you had to sell drugs and go to clubs."

"Not that kind of DJ," he said. "The radio kind."

"Oh," I said. "I didn't know that."

"Yeah," he said, then concluded, "Kat's a fucking saint."

Filthy Phil came back into the room with a towel and some spray cleaner, "But don't tell her that."

They laughed again, this time more quietly.

I watched as he cleaned the table. It was a ridiculous thing to witness. Here was this big lug cleaning up his little mess so his woman wouldn't tear him a new one. He missed a spot.

"Hey, Phil," the delivery boy said. "You forgot your apron."

"Oh, yeah, fuck you," he said and pretended to squirt the boy in the eye. They laughed and Phil went to put the cleaner up and came back with three more beers.

"This is my last one," the delivery boy said. "Then I got to get back to work."

Filthy Phil nodded and gulped his beer. He was in good spirits and I was curious, so I asked, "How did you two meet?"

"What's that, Boy?" he asked, glancing at me, then back to the TV.

"You and Kat. How did you two meet?"

"Oh, we met at a horserace. I told her not to bet on a horse, she told me to fuck off and the rest is history."

"What?"

He turned to me. "She wanted to bet on this loser horse, Sunshine...I think its name was Sunshine. I knew the old mare wasn't gonna get it, if you know what I mean."

I knew exactly what he meant.

"She insisted on betting on her with her last ten bucks and she lost. We were sitting together and she threw a bag of popcorn at me and told me I had steered her wrong and demanded I get her money back."

"What did you do?"

"I gave her the money back out of me pocket, then gave her some extra."

I was surprised he gave it to her.

He continued, "But it's never easy with her. She wouldn't take it until I explained the gambling system."

"How'd you do that?"

"She's a woman. Women usually don't know how to bet, no offense to any of them, but they usually pick a horse cause it's pretty or they like its name. So, I just explained it, in a roundabout way until I had her good and confused and gave her a little money. You know, to get her through the next week or two."

"Oh."

He chuckled at the memory. "I didn't see her for about a week or so then I saw her in a bar. By this time all I can think about is her, right?"

I nodded.

"So, when I see her, I'm just...just happy, mate. I'm over the moon for this girl. And she looked bloody damn good, which makes it harder, y'know what I'm saying? She ignored me, which meant she at least knew I was in the room."

I sighed heavily. Maybe I didn't want to hear this.

"So, I offer to buy her a drink. She doesn't want one. It's a bloody fucking bar and she doesn't want a drink. Then some guy tries to pick her up. She could see this would get me, so she starts to flirt with him."

"And?"

"And I tapped him on the shoulder," he said, demonstrating by tapping me on the shoulder. "And told him to fuck off. Which he does, for obvious reasons, which pisses her off. She flies out of there and onto the street. I go running after her, feeling like a prat, wishing I had never laid eyes on her."

I definitely knew what he meant.

"So, she slows a bit and I catch up and we get to conversing and I'm falling harder and harder, making a bloody fool out of myself, wanting to snog her so bad I could hardly stand it."

"What's that?" I asked.

"Huh?"

"You said 'snog'. What's that?"

"Oh, it means to kiss," he said and looked at me like I was a complete idiot. I felt like one. That was not the visual I was looking for! I thought he meant he wanted to hit her or something.

He went on, "I really wanted to impress her, y'know? I wanted to show her...I dunno...I wanted to show off, plain and simple. Strut round like a rooster, y'know?"

He pushed his chest out like a rooster. He looked like such a dumbass. The delivery boy and I cracked up.

"Back then I was riding round on me Harley and asked

if she needed a ride. I wanted to get to know her, y'know what I mean?"

How many times could he say "y'know?" I rolled my eyes and nodded. The delivery boy, who was obviously tired of this story, had his attention back on the TV. Two nude women were making out. Damn, what was she doing with that cucumber? I forced my attention back on Filthy Phil.

He continued, "She said sure, why not? She got on and we rode round for a while, over the George Washington Bridge and what-have-you and then we come back into Manhattan and I stop at a red-light, turn round and she's fucking gone."

"No way!"

"Yeah! She's gone! I started to panic, thinking she could have fallen off the bike or God knows what! I didn't know what to do or what had happened. I almost went to the police, but, for some reason, I didn't."

I knew why he didn't. That was probably the first time he'd ever considered such a thing, too.

"So I just went about me business, hoping she was fine," he said with a sigh. "A few days later I see her walking in Central Park without a care in the world. I rush over and ask her what the bloody hell happened. She said, 'I got bored and decided to get off.'"

Yup, that sounded like Kat.

Filthy Phil threw his head back and roared with laughter. The delivery boy laughed, too. I cracked a smile. Ahh...umm...

Filthy Phil laid a hand on my shoulder and said, "And the rest, as they say, is history."

Filthy Phil was the luckiest man in the whole fucking world. God, I hated him so much.

"I gotta take a piss," he said.

He got up and stomped towards the bathroom. I glanced at the TV. The two women had been joined by a man, who was a plumber. I still wanted to know. Did I dare?

"Excuse me," I said to the delivery boy. "Be right back."

"Okay, Boy."

Boy! I tried not to growl at him as I got up. But immediately my attention was focused on my leg as a sharp pain shot through it like a bolt of lightening. I nearly howled but only allowed a tiny whimper to escape my lips. I hobbled to the bathroom. The door was open a crack so I couldn't see a damn thing.

I stood there for a moment considering my options. The most feasible one was for me to go back into the living room. Another would be to throw the door open. I considered that one. Yeah, I could just throw open the door and pretend I didn't know he was in there—"Oops, *sorry*." Another alternative would be for me to recall my senses from where-ever-the-fuck they had gone and get a fucking life.

I was about to do just that but all of a sudden my leg began to attack me. It started twitching on its own. And it hurt like hell. This happened from time to time. Kat sweetly called these little hells "healing pains". I grimaced and tried to hold the damn thing still but it was like someone had inserted a gerbil in there and let it loose to do whatever the fuck *it wanted to do*. It felt like the damn thing wanted to escape.

As fate would have it, I didn't have to make the decision on my own. It was made for me. I didn't have to open the door cause the fucking cat did it for me. He slithered right past me and into the bathroom, leaving me standing there like a damn pervert.

My leg was still shaking. I looked so bad then and I knew it. I knew it looked like I was...let's just say, by this time, my entire body was jerking and it just didn't look good.

Filthy Phil was finishing up. I stared at him, mouth agape, suddenly recalling my mission there in the first place.

The bitch hadn't been talking about him. The whole "hung like a bird" thing was about me. She was talking about me! Not him! I had proof right there, didn't I? He was not hung like a bird. He was hung like a fucking horse. Everything about him was big. Why wouldn't his dick be big, too? What had I been thinking?

I hated him even more, if that were possible.

"Excuse me?" he suddenly asked.

The cat meowed.

I stared up at him. My head joined the rest of my body began to shake on its own. I stammered, "Oh…no…I thought… It's just, I…uh…you were…finished…"

"Is there something you want?" he asked and nonchalantly zipped his pants, then leaned over and flushed the toilet.

My head was still shaking. I couldn't make it stop.

"You need help taking a piss?" he asked.

"Oh, no, no I don't. I just… I just thought I left something here…" I stepped to the sink as if I were on official business, rummaged around, and found a razor. I held it up and said, "Oh, there it is."

Filthy Phil stared at the razor. I looked, too. It was pink. As was my face.

"Come on, nothing to be ashamed of," he said and pulled me to the toilet.

"No, Filthy Phil, I'm okay," I said but he was bigger than me and a lot stronger. He pulled me over the toilet, yanked my sweatpants down and made me attempt to take a leak while he held me steady.

It was the most awkward position I'd ever been in in my entire life.

He glanced over my shoulder. I couldn't believe he did that! How could he have done that! When you're at a urinal, do you look over at the other guy?! No, you do not!

Needless to say, I couldn't piss.

"Go on," he said.

"I'm fine now. You can leave."

He was now shaking slightly as he tried to contain his laughter. The motherfucker.

"You can leave now," I hissed.

"You're not finished."

"I am almost finished and—"

I heard a gasp. I looked to my right. Kat was standing there, mouth agape. Oh, God. When did *she* get here?

"Hiya, baby," Phil said and smiled his goofy smile at her.

It took her a minute to respond. She just stared at us, apparently more than a little confused and replied weakly, "Hey, you two."

"Hey," I called feebly.

She shook herself, regained her composure and blurted, "What the fuck are you doing?!"

"He needed help taking a piss is all," Filthy Phil replied.

"Huh?" It seemed to take her a minute then she exclaimed, "Ooooohhhh! Oh. I thought for a minute... Oh, nevermind!"

He glanced over at her and smiled.

She smiled, came over and kissed his cheek. "You're sweet for helping him like that, baby. Even if it does look a little weird."

Baby! Fucking baby! He was her fucking baby?! What about me? What did that make me? What the hell did this mean?!

She gave me a peck, too. "Glad to see things are...alright down there, Ray."

I melted. The bitch.

She hopped up on the vanity, settled in and began swinging her legs. Was she planning on staying? She winked and smiled at me. I guess so. Okay, now I really couldn't piss.

"Boy, I'm waiting," he said.

"I don't really have to go right now," I said.

"Oh, for God's sake, piss, Ray, no one cares in this house," Kat said. "Phil sees me pee all the time."

Filthy Phil cleared his throat.

"Any pizza left for me?" she asked sweetly.

"I think so," he said, smiling at her.

I tried again. A little squirt came out. Phew, thank God. I could now get out of this embarrassing situation and kick myself in the ass.

"I'm done now," I muttered.

"So, you *did* order pizza?" she asked.

He groaned. She got him! I chuckled. Good girl. Rip him a new one. And make him leave me alone.

"Phil," she began, shaking her head. "We had pizza two nights ago. Now, it's not me with the heart problems in my family, it's *you*."

He grunted and shook his head desperately. "Listen, I wanted to see Zack."

She said crisply, "They have salads where Zack works."

"I'm finished!" I yelled and tried to step away. Trouble was his big paws were still on my shoulders holding me tight.

"Come on, love," he muttered. "Let's not fight."

"Okay, fine," she said and hopped down. "You know, I get sick of having to be the bitch when all I'm trying to do is look out for you."

What the hell did that mean? If she was trying to look out for him, then why the hell did she want him dead?

"I know," he said. "I'm sorry. I just had it today. I'll do better tomorrow."

"Really?" she said and crossed her arms. "If that's so, then what did you have for lunch?"

He paused.

"Ah ha!" she exclaimed and pointed at him.

"No, let me think! Give me a fucking minute... I had...grilled chicken and..."

"Don't lie to me. I went over to the shop today and asked Valerie. She said you ordered in gyros."

He cursed under his breath, "Blimey!"

"I can forgive the pizza or the gyros, but I can't forgive both on the same day, Phil!"

"I'm done," I muttered.

They ignored me, of course. He stared over at her. She stared back, shaking her head.

"And you didn't have to order anchovies," she said and went to the door. "I fucking hate anchovies!"

And with that, she was gone.

"You done yet?" he asked.

"Yes, I'm done. You can let me go now."

He released me. I almost fell into the commode. I steadied myself just in time and pulled my sweatpants up. *Phew*. Kat would have to stop giving me so many drugs. I wasn't going to take any more. Ever again. Well, I'd have to keep using them until I healed but after that I was going cold turkey.

I turned to leave but he was still standing there in the same position. He crossed his arms as if he were about to give me a lecture or something. God, he got on my nerves so bad.

"What?" I asked and leaned over and flushed the commode.

"Did you get a good enough look?" he asked.

He did not just say that. Did he?

"You hear me?" he asked.

I turned my attention to the commode and wished I was in there being flushed down with the water. The sewers of New York would be better than this. They *had* to be.

"Boy?"

Oh, good God in Heaven. Why me? What did I do to

deserve this? I gathered what I had left of my dignity and put on my cool face. I turned to face him. "Excuse me?"

"Did you get a good enough look?"

"What do you mean?" I asked.

"You wanted to see me tool, right?"

"What?"

"Me fella…me…dick."

I nearly choked on my words, "No! I didn't want to see your dick!"

He sighed heavily as if he were humoring me. As if he were doing me a favor and I should just be good and damn grateful that he was willing to take the time. He leaned in and said, "It's like this. I'm a big guy. Look at me! I'm big! I like being big. That's why I'm so good with the ladies."

I looked away quickly.

"People are curious. I can't tell you how many times people have asked me to pull it out," he said proudly.

"Well, I've never had that problem," I snapped.

"And urinals? Forget it. All eyes are on me."

I do not look at urinals. I do not look at urinals. I do not—

"So, did you get a good enough look?"

Through gritted teeth, I said, "I don't know what you mean."

He grinned, then leaned in and whispered, "Right at nine, with great width, which is what the birds dig the most. It gives them something to grab onto. Length, who gives a shit? If you ain't got width, you ain't got shit."

Then apparently, I didn't have shit. I glared at him. He had it all. It wasn't fair! I would kill him one day. I would do it just to even the score a little.

"Well, that's nice," I replied dryly.

"And, Boy, size does matter. It makes all the difference."

How would he know?

"I'm used to it. Everyone wants to see. First day I met Kat, she made me show it to her."

I groaned. I did not need to hear this.

"And the rest, shall we say, is history."

That's exactly what it is. History. I hoped to God no one ever found out about it.

Jealous again.

The next day, I sat in the living room and watched Kat work out. She was doing everything, too—push-ups, sit-ups, free weights. She was wearing this little sports bra which showed off her tits in the most fantastic way and pair of black shorts that didn't quite cover her ripe ass. The cheeks of her ass peeked out just a little as if they were trying to say hello, but were too shy.

Not that I gave one shit. I was mad as hell at her and I had a big fucking ax to grind. I didn't care how good she looked. And she looked pretty damn good.

I began, "That comment you said—"

"Huh?" she asked and sat up from stretching. "What did you say?"

I growled, "That comment you said about someone being hung like a bird was about me, wasn't it?"

She stared at me, obviously baffled. "Ray, I say a lot of shit. I can't remember everything that comes out of my mouth."

"At the diner that night I met Filthy Phil, you said—"

"Oh, I remember now."

I glared at her. "Was it about me!?"

She jerked back. "About you?"

"Look, just tell me. Am I the one who's hung like a bird?"

"Ray, you've got a good size dick, okay? No need to be insecure about it."

I snapped, "I wasn't insecure about it until I saw Filthy Phil's dick!"

She burst out laughing, covering her mouth with both hands. "When did you...why did you—"

"He is not hung like a bird, but someone else is. That's me, right?"

"No, it's this guy that works for him, his driver."

I glared at her.

She groaned. "His name is Tiny, though he's a big fatass, get it?"

Oh, I get it. Very clever. Wonder who came up with that one?

"One day we had a party and Tiny came to it," she said and drew a breath. "He was really drunk and stumbling around and then I noticed that he was pissing into a potted plant I had. Which made me mad but once I got a look at him... Well, he was hung like a bird."

I put my head in my hands and groaned. Oh, shit, oh shit, oh SHIT! I groaned, "I can't believe this! I actually saw Filthy Phil's dick!" I didn't add, *And I wanted to see it.*

"Everybody in New York has seen Phil's dick," she said offhandedly. "Big deal. I mean, the more opportunity for him to show it off, the better. Is that why you wanted to see it? Cause of the comment?"

I nodded and muttered, "I feel like such an idiot."

"Oh, don't," she said and scooted over to me. "You men are so weird about shit like that."

I rubbed my eyes.

"You shouldn't have let him order pizza, though."

I glared at her, willing myself to hold it back. But I couldn't. I ripped into her, "What the hell does that mean?!"

"What?" She jerked a little.

"You know damn well what I'm talking about!"

58

She stared at me for a moment then let out that sigh she had that said she was through with the conversation. Well, I wasn't.

"I thought we were going to kill him," I hissed. "I thought that was the plan and then you're all concerned about his weight and what he eats."

"Well, I don't want to live with a fatass. No, hear me out! Until you get back on your feet, I've got to act like I care and stuff! Geez, Ray, get a clue."

"I don't think you want him dead!" I yelled.

"Like hell I don't!"

"Kat, where is this going?"

"Anywhere you want it to, Ray, that's where's it's going."

"But you…you…act like you love him."

"It's animal attraction, that's all. I'll get over it."

I shook my head. "You never answer my questions."

"That wasn't a question. It was an accusation."

"Well, so?"

She shook her head, sat back, opened her legs and leaned forward into a stretch.

I decided to test her, "I love you, Kat."

"I love you, too, Ray," she muttered.

I looked to see if her fingers were crossed. I couldn't tell.

"Well, did you at least enjoy the porno?" she asked, changing the subject.

"It was okay."

"We've got better ones than that. I don't know why he always wants to watch that one. Might be because one of the chicks in it reminds him of a girl he used to date."

Like I cared. She waited. I shook my head and snapped, "Oh, really?"

She sat up and stretched her arms over her head. "Really. He left her back in England."

"So, he's from England?"

"Yes, *Northern* England."

"Oh," I said. But then my curiosity got the better of me. "Why did he leave her if he loved her?"

"Well, he had to leave. He was about to get busted."

"For what?"

"For some shit that all boys do. You know, he came over here when he was only like eighteen."

No, I didn't know that. How could I?

"He said it was the first time he'd ever been scared in his life, coming to America. You kinda feel sorry for him." She stared away, brought her hands down and rested them in her lap like Buddha. "Poor thing."

"Yeah," I said sarcastically. "Poor thing."

She nodded, not catching my sarcasm. "And you know he had to make a living, so he got caught up in all that crime bullshit. Guys liked him cause he was big. He can do stuff other guys can't."

Like what? Crush skulls with one hand while dribbling a basketball with the other? Pick fruit from the tops of trees without a ladder?

"How many people has he killed?" I asked.

"Ray!"

"Oh, come on. Don't act like he's some kind of innocent."

She stared at me. "I don't know what you mean."

"You know good and damn well what I mean."

"He's never hurt anyone that didn't deserve it."

"Oh, please!" I scoffed, shaking my head at her.

"So what if he beat a few guys up? Big deal, they should have paid their debts or should have had the good sense not to get involved with people like him in the first place."

"Beat up a few people? Is that all he's done now?"

"Yes," she said crisply. "That's all. He's not that bad, Ray."

60

"He is a mean motherfucker."

"When he needs to be, sure." She stared at me, a small smile playing on her lips. "Just think, once he was teeny, tiny baby in his Mommy's arms."

She pretended to be cradling a baby. I never even thought about a guy like that having a mother.

"Oh, please, Ray," she said, rolling her eyes. "We all have mothers and so does he."

"Ah ha!" I said and pointed my finger at her. "You're defending him!"

"So what if I am? What's it to you?"

"Everything!" I yelled.

"Oh, please." She rolled her eyes.

"So, he's never beat you?"

"Where the hell did that come from?" she asked, shaking her head.

"Has he?"

"You think I'd let some son of a bitch hit me and get away with it? Phil may be mean, but I'm vengeful, Ray."

She was contradicting herself, yet again. But what did it matter? All we ever went in were circles. That's all we ever did. We ran around in circles. Around and around, here we go, where we stop no one knows. Or cares. I suddenly felt tired.

"So did you like the porn?" she asked again.

I nodded, "Yeah, I liked it, Filthy Phil liked it and the delivery boy liked it, too."

She shot me a cross look.

"What is it now?" I asked.

"'The delivery boy'?" she asked. "He has a name, Ray. It's Zack."

"I didn't know. We weren't properly introduced."

"Well, he's a sweetie and you should get to know him. He's a good kid."

"And you saved him, right?"

"Ray, he was a poor kid on the street. What was I gonna do? Walk away and let him rot? Walk away and not help him? He was about to die!"

I shrugged. "You did a good thing."

"No, I did what was right, that's all."

"Oh."

"Anyway…"

I decided to test her. "So, how did you and Filthy Phil meet?"

"Why do you always call him Filthy Phil?"

"That's his name, isn't it?"

"Well, that's his professional name."

Professional? Even among the thugs, there was decorum. Nevertheless, I asked, "Wonder why they call him that? Filthy?"

"I have no idea, really. I could ask him."

"You don't have to ask him. You know."

She struggled to keep the frustration in her body. Her fists shook, then she grunted, "Okay fine! They started calling him that back in England. He was a really poor kid and after school, he worked on a sheep farm. And no bestiality jokes, please."

Damn! She was too quick!

"So, one day, he's rounding them up and he falls right into a hole stacked full of sheep shit. Alas, Filthy Phil. The name stuck. There, are you happy now?"

No, I was not. I asked, "How did you two meet?"

"At a bar," she said.

"He said you met at the track."

She pondered that. "Yeah, I guess he's right. We met at the track, then at the bar. I can't keep it straight. Hell that was a long time ago."

"And then what?"

I could tell she was getting a kick out of this interrogation. It was like a trip down memory lane for her.

She tried to hide her smile. "He bugged the hell out of me and wanted to take me to dinner."

"Oh. And then what?"

She shrugged. "We went to dinner and then I went home."

"You didn't fuck him?"

"Hell no! I never fuck on the first date."

"But you fucked me that first night we met," I told her.

"We met previously, asswipe, if you care to recall," she snapped. "And *we* weren't on a date."

"Oh," I muttered. "When did you fuck him?"

"Didn't he tell you?"

"He left that part out."

"Do you really want to know?" she asked and yawned.

"Why would I ask if I didn't?"

"Well, since I had already seen his massive dick, I really wasn't interested."

"Bullshit!"

"I thought it'd hurt."

"But it didn't, did it?"

She grinned, "No, it didn't. He knows how to move."

She was getting the best of me—again! I proceed, nonetheless, "So when did you fuck him?"

"It was about..." she considered, clucking her tongue. "A month later?"

"He waited a month on you?" I asked, hating myself.

"Well, I'm a helluva girl."

Duly noted. I asked, "And then?"

"We fucked. What more do you need to know?"

"Give me the details."

"Why?" she asked, perplexed.

"Well... I don't know! I just want details."

"We're stopping here," she said and started to stand.

"It wasn't good, was it?" I asked, hoping I was right.

"Do you really want to know, Ray?"

63

"Yes!"

"Fine," she said. "I'll tell you."

"And don't lie."

"I never lie."

Bullshit! I said, "Go on."

"It was good. He was gentle, passionate and damn near perfect. Sorry, but it's true. He's a very gifted lover."

Double damn him! Maybe this would get her, "Does he sleep around on you?"

"He better not."

"But at the bar that night you said he cheated on you."

"I thought he had, but he hadn't," she said. "I was wrong."

I could just tell it just about killed her to say that, too. She didn't like to be wrong about anything. I nodded for her to go on.

"There's this chick, okay?" she said. "She's a shop girl who works at the jewelry store and every time she gets a chance, she struts into his office. She likes him a lot. I get pissed off cause she's *such* a bitch. Anyway, I walk into the office one day and this bitch is bent over right in front of him. And are his eyes averted? Hell fucking no, they ain't."

"Go on."

"So, anyway, I was there to talk to him about something important. And there she is with her ass all hanging out, like she is somebody! See, I don't really mind that he's looking, I mean, he's a man, he's gonna look and that's okay."

"So what's the problem then?" I asked.

"He didn't notice that I came in."

I rolled my eyes. "But she's standing there with her ass hanging out!"

"Yeah, I know this already, Ray. It just pissed me off. I was standing there for a long time before he even noticed me. I didn't spend all this time training him just to let some other woman reap the benefits."

"What does that mean?"

"Exactly what it sounds like," she said. "You have to train men how to treat you. If not, they end up treating you like shit. And why do all the work if some other bitch is going to step in and take over? I don't *think* so."

I just stared at her, getting more and more confused.

"Besides" she said. "If he's going to do that sort of thing, I'm going to be in the room."

My ears pricked up. "What?"

"Nothing."

"No, tell me what that means," I said, my mind spinning. "Are you telling me that you had a…a threesome?"

"We tried it once, so what? Everyone does."

"No, they don't."

"Whatever," she said. "We're stopping this conversation."

I stared at her and nodded for her to give it up.

She sighed heavily. "It was his birthday, okay? He had never even mentioned it to me, alright? It was my idea. I have a very attractive girlfriend, alright? I felt like a damn fool asking her, but she agreed, okay? We did it."

"Was it Delores?"

She studied me with one raised eyebrow. "You like her or something?"

What man wouldn't? I measured my words very carefully, "She's okay, I guess."

"She's okay?" she asked, rolling her eyes. "She looks like a fucking playmate."

"Well, was it her?" I asked.

She shook her head. "No, it wasn't her, it was someone else."

"Who was she?"

"You do not know her," she said and took a pack of cigarettes off the table.

"Who was she, Kat?"

65

"Good God, Ray! She doesn't even live here anymore!"

"So, who was she?"

"Her name is Monique. She's French, really French, from France. She was an underwear model and we met when I was working as a photographer's assistant—"

"You were a photographer's assistant?"

"Yeah, I've had a lot of jobs, so what?"

"Nothing. Go on."

She lit a cigarette. "So, we met, we hit it off and...there was an...attraction—mutual—and I asked her one day if she would like to help me out. Phil's really hard to buy presents for. He has everything and he always says not to make a fuss and—"

"No."

"Huh?"

"I said no," I said. "You are not leaving out the good part."

"What good part?"

"The hot lesbian sex part."

She laughed. "There is no hot lesbian sex part."

"I think...you're lying."

"I am not!"

"Kat..."

She stared at me. "You want me to make it up or something?"

"No," I said. "Just tell me what happened."

"We had sex, that's all," she said and scratched her nose. "My nose is itching. Someone must be coming to see me."

"Come on!" I said and glared at her. "So you had sex with her?"

She eyed me curiously, then nodded. "Sure, we had hot lesbian sex all night long. Is that what you want to hear?"

"I just want to know what happened," I said.

"Nothing happened," she said.

"Come on," I said, feeling even more like a fool.

"Well, if you have to know," she said. "We had a threesome. I figured, why not? I've never done anything like that and I like to experience everything life has to offer."

"Did you get jealous?"

"If you're into *the situation*, jealousy doesn't equal in."

"Did he get jealous?"

She laughed, put her cigarette out. "No, he didn't."

"Did she?"

"No, we were both too into it to get jealous," she said.

"And you were into it?"

"What is this? A fucking cross-examination? Yeah, I got into it cause he got into it cause I got into it cause she got into it. It was a once in a lifetime thing. It was nice, we had some wild sex then it was over."

I stared at her.

"Besides, she was more into me than him, if you know what I mean."

Yeah. I knew. I figured as much anyway. I asked, "So that's the only time you did it?"

"He has a birthday once a year. You figure it out."

She just said that to get me. Even so, it pissed me off. I wanted to scream, I wanted to thrash about the apartment like a raving lunatic. But I was in pain and could barely move. Why did she do this to me? Why did I do it to myself?

"Would you do it with me?" I asked.

"Of course," she said. "I mean, if she would. It would be up to her, you know?"

I glared at her. It would never happen and I knew it. I was so pissed off knowing she had this great experience and Filthy Phil had been part of it and I hadn't. She had a whole world I knew nothing about. We didn't say anything for a very long time. She sat on one end of the couch and I sat on the other and we just stared into space.

"Why are you mad?" she asked, breaking the silence.

"You know why."

"Ray," she said and shook her head. "It wasn't that big a deal."

Sure it wasn't.

"Just calm down," she said.

"Calm down!" I roared. "Kat, we're supposed to—"

She held up one hand. "Shut up and I mean, shut up! I'm not fighting with you today."

"But—"

"Shut the fuck up, Ray!" she yelled. "Here we were having a good time and then you get pissed off for no reason."

Oh, I had a good reason. Jealousy is always a good reason to get pissed off.

She got up, sat in a chair and picked up her weights. "I forgot to do my triceps" she said and gave me an eat shit look. "If you don't mind."

I watched her as she lifted the weights over her head, then down. She kept at it for a while. We didn't say a word. Then Filthy Fucking Phil banged in carrying groceries and a bouquet of flowers.

"Hiya, baby!"

"Hey," she muttered, not looking at him. Or at me.

He stopped in front of her, holding out the flowers.

"I'm kinda busy!" she yelled.

He threw them on the coffee table, bent and kissed the tip of her nose and started off. On second thought, he plucked the weight right out of her hand like it was a feather. He walked on by and carried it off.

She gave me a look of consternation.

"The nosh will be ready soon!" he called. "And we're having grilled chicken!"

We didn't reply.

She sighed loudly, stood and said, "I'm going to take a shower."

I watched her leave the room, feeling like a trapped animal. Feeling loyalty to my owner—her—and resentment towards the other barn animal who divided her attention—him. I hated myself. But I hated him more.

I sat on the couch for a few minutes after they both disappeared from the room. I wanted to leave. I needed to leave. I needed to get up, walk out the door and never look back.

"Boy!" Filthy Phil yelled.

Now. I needed to go now.

He called, "Hey, Boy, come give me hand."

Shit. I glanced at the door and willed myself to walk through it. But I couldn't. I guess I was just a sucker for love. Sucker being the operative word.

"Boy! You hear me?"

I groaned, stood and hobbled into the kitchen. He was unpacking the groceries at an alarming pace. He had everything out and into the fancy cabinets in a matter of seconds. He had the refrigerator door open and was throwing shit in. One more bag was left. He picked it up, rummaged inside and pulled out a box of tampons.

I wondered what the people in the grocery store thought of him?

"Could you take these to Kat?" he asked.

He had to be kidding.

"Boy?"

I groaned, groaned again, grabbed the box and took off towards the bedroom.

"Kat?" I called and found her in the gigantic walk-in closet. She was on her hands and knees, pulling out something from the floorboard. When I came in, she glanced up but didn't try to conceal what she was doing, like most people would.

"What is it, Ray?"

I jerked then held out the tampons. "Oh, here's your...*things*."

She lifted one shoulder. "Just throw them on the bed."

"Alright," I said and turned to leave.

"Hey, Ray?"

"What?" I asked, not turning around.

"I'm sorry."

I turned to face her. "Yeah, me too."

We tried to smile at each other and pretend everything was okay. She went back to the floorboard and I skulked back to the kitchen to help Filthy Phil with the cooking.

"Now, the chicken is marinating," he said, slapping his hands together. "So that gives us time to chop up the veggies."

He was too weird. Why was he even cooking? Why was he here? Why didn't he go away?

"Time to get busy," he said and slapped me on the back. I nearly spit up a lung and tried not to say "ouch". The man did not know his own strength. The son of a bitch.

He laid out all kinds of veggies and ordered me to get to work. I started chopping the stupid vegetables, hitting them so hard a few flew into the air. He didn't notice. He was at the stove whistling as he stirred something in a pot.

The phone rang. Still whistling, he stepped over and peered at the caller ID. He groaned, "Shit, it's her mum. You take it, Boy."

I didn't argue and picked up the phone.

Kat's mother called about ten times a day. She was a very chatty woman who missed her only daughter. I had picked the phone up one day to call someone and she was on the line. I didn't know what to say or how to explain but she just went into conversation, talking about everything from the sun to the moon to the price of gasoline to the weather.

Kat later explained that she'd told her I was going through a bad divorce and needed somewhere to stay because I'd just had a terrible accident and couldn't work.

Through Mrs. Cumberland, I found out that Kat had two older brothers who she "fought with on a regular basis". I also found out the she hated Filthy Phil's guts, so we had a lot in common.

"Hello, sunshine!" she chirped.

"Hello, Mrs. Cumberland."

"How are you today, Ray?"

I said, "I'm fine, Mrs. Cumberland."

"Good, good. Where's my angel at?"

"She's in the shower."

"Oh. How's your leg?"

"It still hurts like hell," I said as Filthy Phil motioned for me to continue chopping.

"Too bad," she said. "Are you putting that salve I sent you on it?"

I wasn't, but I said, "Yes and it's helping, too."

"Great! Next time I send a package, I've got another surprise for you."

I should mention that Kat's mother was an herbalist. I asked, "More herbs?"

"Oh, no! This time I'm sending you some moonshine."

Moonshine?

"And don't get carried away with it. It will knock you out. I sent that ape some once and Katherine told me he drank about half, the idiot. Nearly put him in the hospital."

I smiled widely.

"It tastes good too," she muttered and I heard her drag on a cigarette. "Where did you say Katherine was?"

"In the shower."

"I don't know why she doesn't take her showers in the morning like everyone else," she muttered, then, "Y'all

71

coming down for spring break?"

For some reason, she acted like we were all in college, staying in dorms. It was always Christmas break, spring break, summer holiday.

"I'm not sure…" I said.

"Well, I wish you would," she said. "Since Old Hank passed, I sure get lonely."

Old Hank had been her fourth husband. Kat's father had been her first. I didn't know much about the other two and the only thing I knew about Kat's father was that he had left them when she was very little.

"Why don't you come to New York?" I asked.

Filthy Phil stood very still. I could tell the hairs on the back of his neck were standing up.

"Oh, I hate to travel all that way," she said. "And I'm old. Y'all are young. You could have an easier trip than me."

"That's true, but we'd love to have you."

Filthy Phil was almost shaking.

"I know you would, but I'd have to see that foreigner she lives with and I just don't think I'm up to it."

"Why do you feel that way?" I asked.

"I just think he's weird, honey."

Score one for the home team!

"Besides, I always thought Katherine would end up with someone like you, a college professor."

That's what Kat had told her I did. Taught college. What I "taught" was anyone's guess.

"All that education and I don't think *he* even graduated high school, if they even have such a thing over there where he's from. I don't know what they have and I don't care."

Kat entered in a bathrobe and with a towel wrapped around her head. She sat at the bar and lit a cigarette.

I mouthed, "It's your mom."

"Oh," she said and held her hand out for the phone.

"Mrs. Cumberland, Katherine's here now. Would you

ike to speak with her?"

"Oh, yes, sweetie, I would. You take care of yourself and look for that package."

"I will. Thank you. Here she is."

"Love you, sweetie!"

"Love you, too. Hold on." I handed the phone to Kat.

"Hey, Mommy!" she squealed.

Phil came up and peered over my shoulder at the vegetables. "Smaller slices, Boy."

I shrugged and started chopping.

"Oh, I think that's a fantastic idea," she said and stared at me. "You should come to New York."

Filthy Phil stood very still.

"You'd love it up here, that's why," she said and giggled.

Filthy Phil was getting agitated.

"Why not?" she asked and eyed him. "Well, I don't know about that. I just thought you'd enjoy yourself is all."

Filthy Phil was breathing a sigh of relief.

"Well, we could drive down and bring you up."

Filthy Phil was shaking again. His face was as pale as a glass of milk.

"Yes, we could. If Phil doesn't want to come, me and Ray'll come down and get you."

Filthy Phil shook his head and tossed the chicken in the pan. It simmered and smoked, much like he was now.

I chuckled to myself. I loved it when Kat's mom called, mostly because he hated it.

"We could do that," Kat said and stared at her cigarette then suddenly laughed. "Oh, yeah, I remember him, too. When'd you see him?"

Filthy Phil turned and stared at her. His face was now red.

"Tell him I said hi, too. God, I'd love to see old Bo again…. He did? When?" She stared at me, mouth open in astonishment. "That's terrible."

Filthy Phil was tapping his foot. Kat ignored him.

"Oh, Mommy, come on. He did love her, too." She rolled her eyes. "No, that's not true. All we had was puppy love."

Filthy Phil turned back to the stove and grunted.

She threw her head back and laughed loudly. "I'll tell him you said that."

She nodded at me, smiling. Filthy Phil was about to explode; he turned back and stared at her. She didn't seem to notice.

"Huh?" she said. "Oh, no. We're eating in tonight."

Filthy Phil turned back to the chicken.

"Grilled chicken and vegetables, I think," she said and peered over at the food. "Oh, and I made some tollhouse cookies."

Filthy Phil flipped the chicken.

"Okay, then. Yes, it is getting late. I love you, too."

Filthy Phil stared up at the ceiling and breathed a sigh of relief.

"Phil loves you, too," she said sweetly.

Filthy Phil groaned loudly.

"Uh huh. Bye, Mommy." She hung up and sighed.

"What was that all about?" he asked quietly.

"Nothing, just girl talk," she said sweetly. "I'll set the table."

She put her cigarette out, came around me and pulled some plates out of the cabinet, slapped me on the ass, went into the adjoining dining room and began to set the table.

"Is she coming here on holiday?" he called.

"I don't think so," she called back then came into the kitchen. "But I think it would be a great idea if she came up. We could take her to all the museums and do all that touristy bullshit we don't ever get to do cause, I mean, we live here and we're not supposed to do that kind of stuff."

He didn't reply.

"What do you think, Ray?" she asked excitedly.

"I think it's a great idea."

"Me too! I'll see if I can talk her into it. I'd love for you to meet her."

I was loving this. I said smugly, "Yes, I'd love to meet her, too, but, you know, I feel like I already know her. We've talked so much!"

She grinned. "She's great, isn't she?"

"She's really is."

Kat and I laughed a little, leaning in towards each other. Filthy Phil stomped over, grabbed the vegetables and threw them in a skillet, where they steamed and crackled.

"Cool," she said. "I'll call her back later and see."

She went back into the dining room and lit a few candles, then into the living room where she put on some Joan Jett. Kat loved hard rock music. Joan Jett, AC/DC, The Black Crows, Billy Squire and Loverboy were among her favorites. It was like she was still in high school, zooming down a dirt road as the stereo blasted in her Camero, her hair flying in the breeze from the T-Tops.

Soon, the food was finished and we were sitting down to eat. Filthy Phil poured the wine, while Kat bent over, threw off the towel, then ran her fingers through her wet hair.

"This is red," she said and stared at the wine.

"So?"

"You don't drink red with chicken, do you?"

He shrugged. "I don't know. I'm not French."

I noticed he wasn't even drinking wine. He was drinking beer. The bastard.

"I think I'll just have a coke," she said and went into the kitchen. "Ray, you want one, too?"

"Sure."

She brought us both a coke, sat down opposite me and

smiled. I smiled back and looked around the room. It was a very romantic setting or *would* have been if he hadn't been there. I'm more than sure he felt the same way about me.

She smiled at me. "Like the food?"

It was, actually, pretty damn good. Of course, I wasn't about to let him know it. I shrugged. "It's okay."

She turned to Phil, "It's really good, baby."

All of a sudden, he threw his fork down. "You know it drives me crazy when she calls!"

"What the hell are you talking about?"

"Your mother!"

Her mouth formed an "O".

He turned to me. "She hates me."

"She does not hate you, Phil," Kat said.

I so wanted to say, *Yes, yes she does, Kat, she hates him. She told me so.*

"She says she can't understand a bloody word I'm saying," he said to me.

"Well, she can't," Kat rebutted.

"Boy, can you understand me?"

Truly, I could. Of course, I wasn't about to let him know. I said, "Well, *some*times, I have a hard time."

A pained look crossed his face. He turned back to her. "Not that it matters if I say anything at all! She won't let anyone else get a word in edgewise. She's always yakking!"

"She likes to talk, big deal," she said, cutting her chicken in little pieces.

"That's all she does, talk, talk, talk. She'll die talking!"

Kat grinned mischievously, staring over at him through the corner of her eye, "At least she'll have the last word."

She glanced over at me. We both smiled broadly at the same time.

He dropped his head. Kat dropped her utensils, leaned over and touched his face gently with her hand. "Baby, she does so like you. She only pretends to hate you cause you're the reason I stay in New York. She wants me home with her."

He whimpered like a fucking child.

She stood, went over and pushed him away from the table. Then she sat in his lap and pulled his face to her bosom.

"There, there," she said sweetly, quietly. "Shh. You can't win 'em all, baby. Everyone else likes you."

Everyone else didn't like him! They were scared shitless of him, that's all! He perceived fear as admiration! That's how stupid he was!

"I know," he muttered and hugged her. "I know. It's alright."

She nodded and kissed the top of his head. "Poor baby."

I stared at them with such intense jealousy. I hated them both at that moment. Anytime I got the upper hand, it came right back down to smack me across the mouth.

Just then, she glanced over at me and smiled. Suddenly, I was filled with rage. I wanted to slap that smile right off her face. If I had been a violent man, I might have. She was playing me, just like a fucking fiddle. I wondered what she was getting out of it. Why was she doing this to me? Why did I do it to myself? I'd become a willing prisoner, though. I hated him and I was beginning to hate her. No, I didn't hate her. I couldn't. I wanted to, but it wasn't in me. Any animosity I felt was because of him, sitting there like a baby, making me sick to my stomach. He was what was standing between us and he wouldn't budge one fucking inch. I'd never win and I knew it.

I stood, threw my napkin on the table and hobbled to my room quietly. They didn't call after me. I was a stranger then, living in a strange, strange world.

I should just leave and get on with my fucking life.

In like Flint.

I was getting better and my other nurse Delores' visits were getting more and more sporadic. I *hated* that. But she was still occasionally coming by and she was here today. The sponge baths had stopped and they had me in the Jacuzzi. I was embarrassed at first, but, hell, when two beautiful women are soaping you up, you get over that shit quick. Oh, my God, this was so cool. I sat back and watched as they made a fuss over me. I couldn't take my eyes off their breasts which were right in my face. It was hard not to reach out and squeeze, they looked so good. Let me just say, there is nothing like a pair of tits. Nothing. Except, maybe, two pairs.

"Kat, when do you think I can…?" I began but stopped myself. Oh, shit, I couldn't ask her that.

"What Ray? Get a hard-on?"

I stared down at the bathwater. I wanted to hide under it.

It didn't faze her. "I dunno, Ray. I'm not a doctor. You'll have your big dick back soon enough, I'm sure."

Delores gave me a little smile. I looked away quickly.

I said, "I'm sorry, I didn't mean to…"

"What? Sound like a pervert?" Kat asked and winked at me. "It's cool, Ray. We're nurses. We hear this stuff all the time."

"Yeah," Delores said. "We're professionals. Stuff like that doesn't embarrass us."

They were professionals, all right, even if they didn't have the degrees to prove it. I liked them so much better than the doctor who came by a few times a week to check me out. He was the same one who'd removed my bullets. He looked like an old codger and would grunt orders at Kat who seemed a little sacred of him. His name was Dr. Harold and at one time, he'd been one of the top docs in New York but lost everything he had due to his gambling habits. From what I understood, he and Filthy Phil had worked out some "arrangement" and the old bastard was pretty much at Filthy Phil's beck and call. He even treated them for the flu and stuff, which he did grudgingly. I couldn't wait for his visits to stop altogether. But right now, I was so happy, I was grinning like a fool.

"Where's Phil?" Delores asked.

The bubble burst and a dark, dark cloud settled into the room.

"He's at work," Kat replied.

Work? Oh, so that's what he called it.

"He'll be home soon," Kat said and smiled at her. "Did you need him for something?"

She sighed and sat back on her heels, then stared at Kat with a look of incredible sadness. "It's Ricky."

"Oh, shit."

"Yeah," Delores muttered. "Kat, I just don't know what to do with him."

"Who's Ricky?" I asked.

Kat leaned in and pushed me forward and began washing my back. "Ricky is Delores's boyfriend."

Oh fucking shit! All these chicks had boyfriends! Didn't anyone stay single anymore? I know it sounds dumb, but I had this fantasy of Kat, Delores and I running off together. We would live in a doublewide trailer in Tennessee near Kat's mother. We'd make money by digging ginseng or selling crystal meth. Nah, we'd just live off the government and have wild sex all day and night. It was a stupid fantasy, and, apparently, that's all it would ever be now.

"So, how much?" Kat asked her.

Delores nearly cried.

"Oh, shit!" Kat exclaimed. "*That* much?"

She nodded, tears streaming down her cheeks.

"I'll talk to Phil," Kat said.

Delores sighed. "You did that last time. He won't help Ricky again."

"No, but he'll help you."

"I just hate to do that."

"Don't worry about it," she said and patted her back, then pulled her into a hug. Delores was quietly crying. Kat consoled her like a sister or like a... I watched them. Yeah, touch her shoulder, baby. Oh, umm... Yeah, squeeze her a little more, touch her cheek...stoke her—

All of a sudden, they were both staring a little suspiciously at me.

"Anyway..." Kat said. "You want to stay for supper?"

Delores nodded and wiped the tears from her face. "Sure, that would be great."

"BABY!"

All three of us jumped.

"I guess Phil's home," Kat said quietly.

"BABY!"

The son of a bitch was home all right. He had to spoil everything. You'd think he'd want to spend some time with his lackeys, but, no, everyday he came home right on time like he had a real job or something. I think he did it just to get on my nerves.

"BABY!" He was stomping towards the bathroom. "BABY!"

"SHUT THE FUCK UP, PHIL!"

He entered, saw us, stopped short and stared for a *looong* moment.

"Hey, Phil!" Delores squealed and grinned at him.

He shook himself then grinned back. "Hey, there," he said and leaned down to kiss the top of Kat's head. "Hey to you, too."

"Hey," she said. "Ray, you ready to get out?"

Phil was staring at me. "Need any help?"

Not from you.

"Eh?" he asked.

"No, I'm fine," I said but didn't move. I didn't have any intention of getting out until he left the room.

"We got him, Phil," Kat said, then stared up at him. "So, shoo!"

He shooed and Kat and Delores bent and pulled me out of the tub, then helped me dry off. Oh, good God! This was way better than a dream. Their hands rubbed me everywhere. I could see down their shirts. Their perfect breasts just heaved in the best way, as if they were waiting for someone to scoop them out and hold them and touch them and—

"Damn, would you look at that?" Delores said all of a sudden.

I looked down praying to God my erection hadn't decided to show up at that exact moment. Phew. She was talking about my stomach wound. It appeared to be healing at an alarming pace. I suddenly had a sinking feeling.

"Wow," Kat said. "You'll be up and at 'em in no time, Ray."

She was right. They helped me into my clothes then I hobbled out after them and into the kitchen where Filthy Phil was unpacking Chinese food. Kat gave him a little glare.

"Chinese food isn't that fattening," he said guiltily.

Delores laughed out loud. They stared at her. It was pretty funny when you got right down to it, though. I don't even know why Kat cared so much about what he ate. I liked to think she did it just to piss him off.

Kat set the table. Delores put on some music. Def Leppard. *Pour some sugar on me....* I sat down and stared into the kitchen. Kat had Phil backed up against the refrigerator and was speaking very quietly to him. He nodded ever so often, threw up his hands once, shook his head and sighed.

81

"Okay," he finally said and looked out at me.

I looked away quickly, then back. Kat smiled at me and came out with him close on her heels. Soon, everyone one else was seated and we began to eat.

"This is good," Delores said.

"It is," Filthy replied back and smiled at her.

Kat stared at him, didn't say a word, then turned to me. I smiled at her, she frowned and said, "I think I know what the problem with the world is."

"This ought to be good," Filthy Phil muttered.

"Men," she said. "Men don't take women seriously enough."

He stared at her, a smile playing on his lips, which he didn't dare reveal.

"Remember that movie *In Like Flint*?" she asked. "In it, these chicks are trying to take over the world, which is highly ambitious, just let me say. And they're doing it in a very tantalizing way."

Filthy Phil stared at her like she was crazy.

"But the men don't take them seriously. They're just so cute. Oh, look, she's piloting a helicopter, how adorable. Oh, wow, she's just kidnapped the president, ain't that sweet?"

"And what's the problem with that, love?" Filthy Phil asked cautiously.

"The problem is men don't take women seriously because all they're thinking about is fucking them. We could take over the world! If y'all would just start taking us seriously, we could do it!"

The problem was that, whether she or any other female would admit it, women like men to think they're hot and if they're thinking about how hot they are, they're not going to take them that seriously. Boobs get in the way of that. It was a good point, a good point that I made a point of keeping to myself.

Filthy Phil chucked her under the chin, "And you'd be

the leader."

"And you'd be my slave," she said and grinned wickedly.

Who was she kidding? He already was.

"Well, Kat," Delores said, sipping her drink. "If you want women to take over the world, you don't send a man as good looking as James Coburn in to stop them."

Kat stared at her. "You've got a point there."

Filthy Phil said, "Love, you don't realize this, but women do run the world."

Her entire face lit up.

"Why would we do anything if it weren't to attract females?"

She smiled so sweetly at him. Why hadn't I thought of that?!

"We build roads to get to the women," he continued stupidly. "We cross the ocean to do so; we build big buildings to show how strong we are. We go into outer space to see if we've missed any."

She threw her head back and laughed. "Oh, so that's what all those missions were about. Hot alien women."

He grinned at her. "Everything is done for women, because of women."

"You're so full of shit," she told him.

He shrugged. "Think of it this way, if it were left to women, would any of this have been done? No. And why is that? Because you don't have to. We do. To attract you."

He was such an idiot. Unfortunately for me, Kat and Delores were both eating it up.

She considered, "If you say so."

He nodded knowingly.

"But what about all the bad stuff?" Delores asked. "War and all that other stuff?"

He considered. "Same thing. We're brave. Look at us, we're strong for you, we'll fight."

Kat said, "There's nothing like a man in uniform."

"Or a woman dressed up like a nurse," I replied.

"Point taken," Delores told me.

Filthy Phil eyed me before turning back to Kat. "Didn't you say something about dessert?"

"Brownies a lá mode," she said and hopped up. "Help me, Delores?"

Delores smiled and followed her into the kitchen. I watched them, then saw Kat whisper something in her ear. Delores threw her arms around her and hugged her tight. Kat kissed her cheek and then they brought the brownies out.

"I think I'll pass on the brownies, Kat," Delores said. "Do you have a change of clothes for me?"

Kat nodded and they went into the bedroom. Filthy Phil gobbled his brownie up and I picked at mine until they came out. I noticed Delores was holding onto a thick manila envelope. She smiled at us and said, "I'll be going then."

"Tiny's out front," Filthy Phil told her. "He'll drive you home."

"Oh, thanks, sweetheart," she said and leaned over him and gave him a peck on the cheek.

He held her hand. "Delores, tell Ricky this is the last time."

She nodded, looking somewhat humiliated. "I will, Phil."

Kat shot him a glare then got up and hugged Delores, who then left quietly, her shoulders slumped. Kat turned on him as soon as she was out the door.

"Why did the hell did you do that?" she snapped.

"You know why."

"That wasn't nice," she snapped.

"Alright, that's enough."

"You son of a bitch. She can't help if she's in love with a bum."

"And that's what he is, Kat, a bum. He always will be. She'd be better off without him."

"Like I don't know that!"

"I won't let him slide again. The next time he comes in, he's cut off. No more. And if he takes his business somewhere else, then he'll have to deal with the consequences. You can't take care of everyone, love."

"I can try," she snapped.

He scoffed, shaking his head, which seemed to infuriate her. This was going to be good.

She glowered at him. "That's a crock of shit, ain't it, Ray?"

"Yes," I said. "I suppose."

"Stay out of this, Boy," he told me and stood to leave the room.

For some reason, that flew all over me. I saw red, I saw black. I saw me kicking his ass. I was so sick of him. Fuck him! I was so sick of him, of the whole situation. Before I could think, I stood, hobbled over to him and said, "She asked me a question, Filthy Phil and I think she deserved an answer."

He turned around and glared at me. "You better back off. Boy."

I stepped to him. "No, why don't you try to make me?"

"I won't warn you again."

Kat said, "Now boys!"

"I get sick of little punks like you always wanting to pick fights with me. You think you can take me?"

"Now Phil," Kat warned.

"They all want to pick fights with me! Every time I turn around some little punk is trying to pull some shit. Why do they think they can take me?"

"Phil—"

"I'll show you why," I said.

I stepped up to him and swung, but she just then

85

stepped between us and I hit her right in the eye. She howled with pain. I didn't have time to say I was sorry cause he put both of his mammoth hands on my chest and pushed me clean across the room. I landed against the bookshelf. A ton of books came down on my head. As they came down, "Ow, ow, ow, ow…"

She and Phil were staring at me. Then they cracked up. I guess it might have been a humorous sight if I hadn't been so humiliated.

"Here," Phil said. "Let me see your eye."

He studied her eye. She stood there like a child staring up at him. He made me sick.

"I'll get you some ice," he said, glaring at me, then took off.

She turned to me. "You shouldn't try that again."

"What?" I asked and threw a book off me.

"Try to fight him. He'll take it once, but the next time, he'll tear your ass apart."

"Well, he pissed me off."

She came over and helped me up. "And I have a feeling why, too."

No particular place to go.

It was true, I was recovering. In fact, I was well enough to move back into my old place. I didn't want to bring it up, but I felt it might be time. Yet, I liked being there. I liked waking up every morning and knowing I'd get to spend the greater part of the day with Kat. We got along great. We had fun. We laughed a lot and she took good care of me. I really didn't have any place else to go, and, if I did, I wouldn't have wanted to anyway.

There was one problem.

She was one of these, "Oh, God, oh, yes!" kind of girls. I could hear everything they were doing, when they were doing it. And they did it quite often. It drove me mad and, in addition to that, it hurt my feelings.

They always tried to be considerate when they were fucking by turning up the stereo—the Stones were a favorite—but Kat was very...*verbal.* She was also into the dirty talk, always moaning for him to do it "harder" or "faster". Sometimes to "slow down" or "make it last".

It drove me crazy, to sat the least. Their nightly sessions left me feeling so alone and abandoned. They were like two animals that couldn't get enough of each other.

Sometimes, they were quieter.

I didn't have to imagine what they were doing. One night as I made my way to the bathroom, their door was wide open and I saw what they were doing. They were making love. I tried to look away, leave. But, again, the train wreck mentality took over.

They were turned backwards on the bed, facing the door. She was on her stomach, raised up. He was on top of her, kissing her neck, her back, pawing her with his gigantic hands. They were both as naked as jaybirds. And as I saw them making love, cause that's what they were doing, I knew they were in love. She wouldn't admit it to me, but they were. She loved him, which meant, she didn't love me. He was so delicate with her, so gentle. And he had the bigger dick.

I felt like such a lowlife, such a pervert. I hated myself. How had I gotten here? What was I doing here? I didn't belong here. But what could I do? My life was fucked up over her.

She moaned and rolled over. He fell gently on top of her.

"We're all the same size in bed," floated into my mind. As I watched them, I knew it was true. It was like they were

87

meant to be. They were perfect for each other. He was kissing her. Then he looked up, straight at me. It was dark, though. I don't think he saw me. I wished he had. That way, they might have stopped.

"What is it?" she murmured.

"I thought I heard something," he said.

"Oh, come on," she said and began to move her hips. "Oh, come on!"

I walked back to my room and sat on the bed, realizing, I'd been had. I don't know what they got me on, but I'd been had. I just didn't know how to get out. I knew, deep down, that I was being lead, that I was being strung along. It pissed me off, sure, and sometimes when I thought about the pain I'd endured, both physically and emotionally, I wanted to hate her. Yet I couldn't. Instead, I hated him more. If he was out of the picture, I'd be in.

But if I left, I'd never see her again. And, besides, they treated me like family. Actually, they treated me better than family, as my family didn't know how to treat a dog. They moved me in after the "accident" without one word. I was never made to feel awkward or like I was in the way. Kat was kind, considerate and funny. She could lift a bad mood effortlessly. And did so often.

And Filthy Phil? Well, if I had to say something nice about him, I'd say this: He was a good cook. Well, maybe not good, but passable.

But I realized it was time to leave.

I studied her from the pod chair. She was plopped on the sofa on her belly with her legs swinging in the air. She didn't so much sit on furniture as she *lounged* on it. But who cared? She looked pretty damn good today. She had on this little, just right tight t-shirt and these men's pajama bottoms that were so big she had to keep pulling them up and re-tying the string. Her hair was up in rollers which were all on the verge of falling out. She looked fabulous.

I said, "Kat, do you think I should move out?"

She looked up from her magazine and eyed me. "What the hell does that mean?"

"I mean..." I sighed. "I'm getting better."

"Yes, you are," she said, flipping a page. "So do you want to leave or something?"

"No, I mean... I don't know."

"Ray, you are welcome here, you know that," she said.

"I just... I just feel like it's time."

She sighed like I was beginning to irritate her. "Don't worry about it, okay?"

"But I feel like me and Filthy Phil are starting to dislike each other. This is an awkward situation, you know?"

"It's only as awkward as you make it, Ray," she said. "He likes you, so you're the only one who feels that. You need to get to know him better."

"I don't want to know him!" I yelled. "I can't like a guy I'm supposed to kill, now can I?"

She ignored me as she always did. "You can go to work with him tomorrow. I've already arranged it."

She was out of her fucking mind. I told her that.

"Just do it, Ray," she said and rubbed her ear. "Someone must be talking about me. My ear's burning."

I didn't want to do it. What kind of "work" would I be expected to do? And I'd have to spend an entire day with him. The very thought made me nauseous. But I knew if I didn't do it, she'd give me a lot of hell. So, yeah, okay, I'd do it. But I didn't want to.

I started to say something, but the door buzzer went off. She threw the magazine to the side, got up and answered it. It was the delivery guy, so she buzzed him up. In no time, he was knocking on the door. He delivered so often he and Kat were on a first-name basis.

"Hey, Ron," Kat said, smiling at him.

"Hey, Kat," Ron said, then peered over at me. "Hey,

Boy."

I'm not even going there.

"What is it today?" Kat asked as he handed her a big box.

"Beats the hell out of me," he said.

"How's your mother?"

"She's good. Back on her feet now. Thanks for asking."

"No problem," she said. "Want a cup of joe?"

"Nah," he said. "I need to get back to work. You guys have a good day."

"You too, sweetie," she said and shut the door. "Now, Delores would be much better off with a guy like that."

What was I? Invisible? Delores, along with Kat, would be much better off with me, thank you very much.

She brought the package back to the coffee table where she tore it open. She said excitedly, "Whatever can this be?"

"Who's it from?" I asked.

"I dunno, but I have a feeling," she said and pulled out this beautiful, black mink coat.

Wow. It was probably from Filthy Phil. He was always sending her all kinds of great stuff—jewelry, books, baskets of fruit, flowers for "no reason at all" and "just because I love you". He'd have it delivered, he'd bring it home to her, he'd pull it out of his ass. She'd smile, act all thrilled. It was so annoying.

"Would you look at that?" she said, shaking her head before she slipped it on. "Ooh la la… I'm stylin', baby!"

"You are, indeed," I said and smiled at her. She looked absolutely ridiculous. Her hair was falling down and she had to keep pulling the pajama bottoms up. On top of this, she had on a mink coat.

She stuck her arm out. "Feel how soft it is."

I touched it and said, "It's nice."

"Yeah, but where would I wear it?"

I shrugged. "I dunno."

She smiled, twirled around happily. She could be so goofy sometimes. Truman, the cat, bounced after her, trying to grab the tail of the coat. She teased him for a little while, jumping over the coffee table, running around the room, doing stuff like that. The cat flew after her trying to get at the coat. Maybe he might have thought it was one of his relatives. The hair rollers were all but out of her hair.

"Stop it, Truman!" she yelled, turned and backed right into Filthy Phil's arms. She screamed and jumped away from him, then held her chest. "You scared the living hell out of me! You don't always have to sneak in here like you're trying to catch me doing something!"

Filthy Phil studied her, trying not to smile. "You're always doing something."

"Well, hell," she said and blew the hair out of her face.

"Pimping again?" he asked and tugged on the coat.

"Well, you know what they say," she said and strutted around like a pimp. "Pimps up, ho's down."

He laughed and pointed at the coat. "Where'd you get that?"

"You know where I got it," she said and tiptoed to kiss his cheek. "Thanks."

He grinned and carried yet another bag of groceries into the kitchen.

She sighed and pulled the coat open, like she was flashing me. I pretended to be shocked and covered my eyes with my hands. She giggled and walked over to me, stopping right in front of me. It took everything I had to keep my hands off her flat little tummy and from running them up to her breasts. She looked so good, I wanted to eat her. I might have tried if *he* hadn't decided to come home early. Bastard.

"Here, Ray, try it on."

"No, that's okay."

"Come on," she said and pulled me out of the chair.

I put the coat on. It was way too small. I heard the

91

stitching groan.

"Shit, be careful."

Filthy Phil walked in, saw us, shook his head, plopped down on the couch and turned on the TV. I handed the coat back to her. She put it on again.

"Let's go out to eat tonight," Kat said. "I want to show off my new coat."

"Oh," he said.

She sat down in his lap and began to take the remainder of the rollers out of her hair. He grimaced. She asked, "What is it?"

"Your bum's bony."

She slapped his face then threw a roller over her shoulder.

"Ow."

She slapped his face again. She threw a roller at me.

"Kat…"

She tried again. He grabbed her hand. She screamed, "Ow motherfucker! Let me go!"

"Say uncle."

"Fuck you!"

"Uncle…"

"I'm warning you, dickhead!" she hissed.

He wasn't letting go. She wormed around and grabbed him…*right in the balls*. I smiled, crossed my arms and leaned back. This should be good.

"Blimey!" he roared. "You're playing dirty!"

"Let me go and I'll let you go."

They stayed like that for a little while, staring at each other from the corner of their eyes. I watched them. All of a sudden, Truman began to jump at the tail of the coat. They leaned, very slowly, down and watched him. Kat kicked him off. He stumbled away and went right back in. She kicked him again.

"Don't kick me cat," Filthy Phil said.

"Your cat?"

"Me cat. Don't kick him."

"He's destroying *me* coat," she said. "This thing cost a fortune."

"Leave him be. He's just having a little fun."

She kicked him again.

"Kat!" he roared then his eyes grew wide. "Don't you dare."

She smiled at him. I could tell she was giving him a little more pressure. Good girl.

"Kat…"

"Let me go and we'll stop here."

He let her go. She jumped up and grabbed the cat. He swatted at her with his paws. She threw the cat at Phil, who ducked. The cat flew over his head. *Meeeooowwww…* He landed somewhere behind the sofa and then took off.

A moment of silence. Phil looked over the couch. He turned back around. "Need I ask why?"

"Oh, get over it. He's a very bouncy cat. Besides, he's got nine lives."

"It's no wonder he hates your guts."

She feigned sadness. "He hates me? No!" She fell down next to the couch and beat the cushions with her hands, wailing, "No no no!"

Phil tried not to laugh. He glanced over at me. "She's off her head."

I nodded. But in a good way. The cat didn't like me, either.

After dinner and a few pitchers of margaritas at a Mexican restaurant, Kat started getting goofy, drunk goofy, which meant she was louder than usual. Everyone on the street stopped to stare at her. It might have been the black mink coat she had on. But it might have just seemed that way because I was drunker than hell myself.

Kat slurred, "Anyway… What were we talking about? Oh! I know! We were talking about getting a dog."

Filthy Phil eyed her as we strolled up the street. "No, we were not."

She ignored him and turned to me, "Don't you just love dogs, Ray?"

"Yeah," I said. "They're cool."

"I mean, why not? Truman needs some company."

"You just want a dog to torment him," Phil said.

"I love Truman," she said with a little glare.

"You love tormenting him."

She sighed and said, "Anyway… Next subject."

"I mean it, Kat, no dog."

Which meant, go ahead and get a dog, Kat. Anytime you told her not to do something, she had to do it then. As I've said before, just to spite you.

We kept walking, not really in any particular direction. Damn. I couldn't ever remember having been this drunk. I should have paced myself better. I was about to just sit down on the sidewalk when Kat stopped and tapped Filthy Phil on the back.

"What is it?" he asked.

"Let me ride piggyback," she said and grinned drunkenly at him.

He didn't hesitate. He bent, placing his hands on his knees and waited. She started to hop up right then, but changed her mind. She backed up several feet and ran at him. Problem was, she forgot to jump or hop or whatever you're supposed to do when you're mounting another person. So, she ran straight into him and they both fell to the sidewalk.

All three of us began to laugh hysterically.

I bent down and hollered, "You should have seen your face, man!" and affected a look of shock befitting Filthy Phil. "Priceless!"

He grinned back. Kat had her face buried in his back. She was laughing so hard she was crying.

"Baby, wanna try it again?" he asked.

"Ohhhhh-kayyyy…"

They tried again. The scenario was repeated. I was laughing so hard, I had to sit down on the sidewalk with my head in my hands. They tried again and again. I watched them and wondered how this guy could be a gangster or a loan-shark or whatever he was calling himself these days. He just didn't act like a badass around her. He acted in part like a love-sick fool and dopey teenager. But then again, Kat said he used to be "caught up with the wrong crowd" and was now "doing well without them". I had no idea what that meant.

"Love," he said. "Try again."

"Okay," she muttered and took her position. "But stay still this time!"

He shot me a look and shook his head. "Will do."

Kat took three giant steps, stopped, went back three tiny steps, then ran like a bat out of hell and hopped right up on his back like she was jumping on a horse to get the hell out of Dodge. He held onto her and took off down the street.

Good riddance. They were giving me a headache. I think I must have passed out because the next thing I remember was that they were back and were pulling me into a cab, muttering something about a fight. I nodded off then Kat began to tickle me. I tried to hold her off, but she kept saying, "Come on, Ray, come on!"

"Where am I?" I asked when I opened my eyes.

"Beats the hell outta me," she said and hopped out of the cab. "But we've got a fight to go to. Hurry!"

I got out and followed her towards a warehouse, which

looked somewhat deserted and very scary. Suddenly, a pain shot through my stomach and I doubled over and vomited. Kat stared at me in disgust.

"Damn, Ray."

"Sorry."

She stared at me. "Are you okay?"

I nodded, held up one finger, and threw up again.

"Ugh!" she shouted. "How much did you drink?"

I shrugged. "I think that's the problem, Kat. I don't know."

"Come on," she said and took my hand. "Let's go over here and sit down for a minute."

"Where's Filthy Phil?" I asked as we sat on the curb.

"He went in already. Here," she said and pulled a piece of gum out of her pocket. "Chew this."

I popped it in my mouth. "Thanks."

"That's okay," she said and pulled a pack of cigarettes out of her jacket and lit us each one.

"Thanks," I said and stuck it in my mouth. "Aren't we going in to see the fight?"

She shrugged. "I dunno, you want to?"

"Nah, not really."

"Me either," she said and puffed on her cigarette. "Let's just sit here and vegetate."

I nodded. She squeezed my hand and smiled at me. I smiled back. We were together then, even if Filthy Phil was her boyfriend, it was just me and her. And our world. We had a world together that no one could take away. And that world was very important to me.

"I want us to run away together," I said out of nowhere.

She smiled widely. "Where would we go, Ray?"

"To Jamaica, like you mentioned that day."

"Oh, mon, that's a fantastic idea." She smiled. "Can we get a little beach house down there?"

"Yeah, in Runaway Bay."

"Can it be white and pretty and have wood floors?"

"Yeah, it does," I said. "It also has a huge bed."

She laughed. "And a mosquito net that covers the bed. We sleep in everyday, don't we? And we eat mangos and fish from the sea, right?"

"Wrong. We buy our fish from the locals."

"Oh, okay."

"And Bob Marley's *Legend* or UB40 is always playing wherever we go out for jerk chicken."

"UB40? Jerk chicken?" she asked. "Sounds like you've been there."

I shook my head. "No, I read up on it."

"It sounds really nice."

It did sound nice. I began to get excited. We could do it. We didn't need anything. I had some savings I could use. We could live on that for a little while.

"So let's do it," I told her excitedly. "Tonight. Let's forget everything that's happened."

She stared at me sadly and placed her hand on my cheek. I moved my face and kissed the back of her hand, then held it there with mine. I suddenly felt filled with hope, with love for her. I felt the future opening up and I felt at peace with the world.

"Please, Kat?" I asked.

She looked away. "Ray, we have some unfinished business here. You know that we can't have a future until we get it done."

And then I was right back at square one. I moved away from her and hissed, "Let's just leave all this shit, Kat! We don't have to do anything! We can go, we can leave. Tonight! He'd never know!"

She sighed and withdrew her hand. "Ray, leave it be."

"No, you leave it be!" I yelled. "I love you, Kat and I want to be with you."

She faced me. "You are with me, aren't you? You see

me everyday."

"It's not enough."

"It probably never will be with you, will it?" she asked.

"You don't love me," I said.

"No," she said. "You don't love yourself."

"What the hell does that mean?"

She stared over my shoulder at some people on the street. "I think you know what it means."

"I'm wasting my time," I grunted. "Aren't I?"

She shook her head. "No, Ray, you're not. One day you'll understand that, until then, shut the fuck up and be grateful for what you have."

"I don't have anything."

She shook her head. "You're drunk."

"So?"

"So you're getting belligerent."

"I just want—"

"Please, Ray," she said and stood. "Let's not get ugly."

I glowered at her. "Ugly? Ugly! How could it be anything else with him in the picture but ugly?! I thought you said you were miserable with him and—"

She pointed a finger at me and hissed, "Don't you talk to me like that! Don't you dare!"

"Why not?" I hissed back at her. "Why the fuck not?"

"Don't piss me off."

I stared at her. It was on her terms and on her terms only. That's the way she was. And that's why I loved her, why she drove me crazy. I couldn't figure her out. I couldn't allow myself to believe she loved me. Why would she love me when she had him?

"I'm going home," she said and pulled out her cell phone from her jacket. She made a call to a cab company and began to walk up the street. I watched her go. She could leave right now and really be gone. It would almost be okay if she did. Almost.

She turned back around and walked towards me. She didn't smile. She was too pissed off to smile. I looked away from her. She sat back down and we waited on the taxi without speaking. When it got there, she opened the door, got in, slid over and motioned me in.

"Let's go home," she snapped. "Phil can find his own ride."

I sat there for a moment and stared at her. Now. Now was the time to walk away. She stared at me almost as if she half-expected me to. I wanted to. I wanted to slam that door shut and leave. Leave all of it. But then what? I knew what. No more Kat. No more love. No more misery. No more dreams of happiness.

"You coming or not?" she asked quietly, staring me down.

I willed myself to walk away. I willed myself to say goodbye. Go, just go. Leave. Find something else. There had to be something else, maybe even something better. I knew there wasn't, though. And whatever chance I had with her was a whole helluva lot better than I had alone. I knew it. She knew it. We weren't pretending.

I groaned and got into the taxi and slammed the door shut. We didn't say a word until we got to the loft, then the only thing she said was "Goodnight" and that was to the cabbie.

Among the thugs.

Filthy Phil woke me up about six the next morning. "Boy, time to get up."

I jerked awake, startled. I'd been having an intense dream. I was chasing him with a knife but he wasn't running from me, only walking slightly ahead. The faster I ran, the more distance he put between us. Kat was bringing up the rear yelling, "Boy! Hold up, Boy!"

BOY!!!

So, I was sweaty and shaky. And a little freaked out.

"You up?" he asked.

"I'm kinda hung over, Filthy Phil."

"So?" he asked, leaving the room. "Time to get up."

I growled under my breath but got up anyway and dressed in the dark, then went out into the living room where he was watching cartoons and smoking a cigarette. I rolled my eyes and made my way into the bathroom then jumped away from my reflection. I looked like hell. I hurriedly brushed my teeth and washed my face, trying to avoid looking at myself in the mirror and decided against shaving. No need in shaving if I was going to hang around him all day. Or showering for that matter.

I went back out. Filthy Phil took the last drag of his cigarette and put it out.

"I'm ready," I said.

He nodded, motioned for me to sit. I sat and we watched some cartoon in its entirety.

"Kat still asleep?" I asked, thinking I'd like to talk to her before we left.

"Yes," he whispered. "Don't wake her. She had a hard day yesterday."

He always thought she had a hard day even if she just lazed around the apartment in her pajamas eating ice cream all day. Which was basically what she did yesterday.

I sighed and watched TV. Soon the cartoon was finished. He stood and went to the door. I rose, grimaced in pain as my leg began to act up and followed him out the door and down the stairs. His car, a sleek black Mercedes, was waiting on the curb. His driver, the guy named Tiny, jumped out and opened the back door. "Morning, boss."

"Morning, Tiny. Boy's joining us today. Take it easy

over the potholes. His leg still hurts."

Tiny nodded and I stared at him. Why was he being so nice? Then it dawned on me. He was taking me somewhere to kill me then they'd put me in the trunk and throw me in the river. Oh, holy shit! How could I get out of this? I looked up at the loft windows. They were all dark.

"Come on, Boy," he called to me from inside the car.

Tiny was staring at me. He jerked his head with agitation. I got in.

We drove through the sleepy streets. I stared out the window, watching shopkeepers spray off the sidewalks, watching men hurrying along and into the subways, watching women prancing along in their high-heel shoes. I almost cried. God, I was going to miss this. My New York, my city. I'd never see it again after today. I'd never see anything. I'd be dead.

"Tiny," Filthy Phil said. "Take us to Ben's first."

"You got it, boss."

Filthy Phil nodded and reached into his pocket. I nearly jumped out the window.

"What is it?" he asked and pulled out a pack of gum. "You're as jumpy as an old woman this morning."

"Oh…nothing…I thought…"

He popped a piece into his big mouth and offered me the pack. I shook my head. He tapped it on my chest. I took it.

"I didn't get much sleep," I said and put a piece of the gum in my mouth. Oh, shit. It was awful. I looked at the label. Blackjack. I hated Blackjack gum.

He nodded and stared out the window, chomping on his gum.

"Kat's mom has been sending me herbs," I said for some reason. I couldn't take it anymore. I rolled the window down and spit the gum out. "I don't like Blackjack."

He grunted.

101

"I think they might be making me nervous," I said. "The herbs, I mean."

"You have to watch that shit she sends. No telling what's in it," he said, giving me a look. "It could be making you paranoid."

"She said it was mostly ginseng. She digs it herself. There must be a lot of it down there."

He nodded. "Pretty country."

"You been there?"

"We went once."

"You like it?" I asked.

"Uh, yeah. Kat took me all over the place, in a four-wheel drive. She'd pull off on what looked like a deserted road, then we'd be in some sort of…community. I guess that's what you'd call it. Saw a pig get gutted."

"Really?" I asked.

"Yeah, he bled like a motherfucker, too." He and Tiny cracked up. "Almost made me sick, though."

I blinked. What was he getting at?

"Never seen anything like that."

"I thought you…" I stopped. I just couldn't say, *Killed people on a regular basis.*

He waited.

"…worked on a sheep farm," I finished.

"Eh, what's that? Oh, sheep farm," he said and smiled widely. "She tell you about that?"

"A little."

"Good times."

"You didn't see anything like that on the farm?" I asked.

"What?"

"Pigs being gutted."

"No, we didn't gut the sheeps," he said. "All we did was shear 'em."

"Sheep," I corrected, for some reason. "No plural."

"Oh, right," he said and smiled.

"She said you were in love with some girl." I regretted that as soon as the words were out of my mouth. For the life of me, I didn't know why I said it. It's not like I cared or anything.

"Some girl?" he chuckled. "Yeah, they were a lot of girls back then."

"She said—"

"Tiny, you need to take a left here," he said and pointed.

"Right, boss."

I started again, "She said—"

"I know what you said," he muttered. "She took it to be this big romantic thing, which it wasn't. That bird likes to romanticize things a bit too much."

"Really?"

"Really," he said. "But what are you gonna do?"

Indeed, what are you going to do?

"I was a kid then, didn't know what the fuck love meant," he said, then, "Right here, Tiny."

Tiny pulled up in front of a massive brown brick townhouse.

"Alright then," he said. "Let's go."

We got out and went to the front door where a maid greeted us, led us down a hall and into a huge dining room, where Ben, the guy we were seeing, was sitting at the head. He was older, maybe in his fifties, with graying temples. He stood and held out his hand to Filthy Phil and said in a crisp, New England accent, "Good to see you, Phillip."

Phillip?

"Nice to see you too, Ben," Filthy Phillip replied. "This here's Ray. I call him Boy."

"Ah, Boy," he said.

So, it shall be.

"Sit, sit," Ben said. "Shall we get started?"

"I don't see why not."

103

"Good, good," he said, then to me, "Would you like some coffee?"

"Sure."

He snapped his fingers and another maid brought in coffee. She served each and of us then disappeared through a door I hadn't noticed.

"Well, Phillip, I think it's all in order then." He opened a file and pushed it at Phillip, who took it, read with interest and nodded. He said to me, "Coffee alright?"

"It's really good," I said, sipping.

Filthy Phillip leaned over and pointed, "What's this all about?"

"That's just the real estate appraisal, Phillip."

"Oh. Right."

"Would you like me to call in my lawyer?"

"No, I trust you."

Ben smiled again and twiddled his thumbs, then jerked, held up his finger and pulled a set of keys out of his pocket. "You'll need those, too."

"Thanks," Phil said and slipped them into his pocket. He then signed the papers and slid them over to Ben who gave him a tight smile and said it was "all in order". Then we left.

As we got into the car, I asked Filthy Phil, "What was that all about?"

"He signed over his house in the Hamptons to me."

"Why?"

"Lost it," he said.

"Oh," I muttered and stared straight ahead.

"Ben isn't as good at business as he would like you to believe," he said, then, "Tiny, take us to the store."

I stared at him. Maybe he wasn't going to off me. Maybe he was just showing me the way things worked. Oddly enough, I was right. The day was pretty much straight forward after that. We checked into his various establishments which were filled with all kinds of people from all walks of life. I kept waiting for them to knock me off. Or for them to beat up some poor bastard or something. Nothing like that happened. It was, actually, very business-like. And normal. We even stopped at a nice restaurant for a big lunch of steak, potatoes and beer.

"I'm starving," Filthy Phil said and we sat down to eat. Halfway through, he turned to me. "Don't tell Kat."

And why wouldn't I? After we ate, we got back into the car and headed out again. His cell phone rang a few minutes later.

"Hallo? Oh, hiya, baby," he said cheerily, then to me, "It's Kat."

I nodded and looked out the window. I was having a good time, but wondered if and when I'd be offed. How long did I have? At least I had eaten well.

"What's that, love?" he asked, covering his other ear. "No, I can't hear you. We're about to enter a tunnel."

I stared up ahead. There was no tunnel in sight.

"Okay, hold on. I love you, too," he said and pushed the phone at me. "She wants to talk to you."

I took the phone. "Hello?"

"Hey, Ray, what's shaking?"

"Nothing much."

"Having a good time?" she asked.

"Uh, I guess."

"Are you really about to go into a tunnel?"

I didn't hesitate, "No."

"That's what I thought."

I smiled widely.

"Are we cool?" she asked.

"What?"

"Last night," she said and groaned. "It's just we never fight and when we do, it really upsets me."

"Me too."

"I mean, I'm sorry, okay?"

"I know and so am I."

I could sense her smile. I smiled. She just did that to me. I could be pissed off as hell at her, then she'd make me smile and everything would be good again.

"So are we cool?" she asked.

"We're cool," I said and actually let it stop bothering me.

"Good," she said. "What did Phil have to eat today? Was it greasy?"

"I hadn't thought about it, really."

"It was greasy then," she said. "Well, listen, I have to go now."

"Okay, bye," I said.

"Put Phil back on the line."

"Hold on." I handed him the phone. "She wants to talk to you again."

He took the phone, "Yes, baby." A slight pause. "I did not! No, I didn't!" He turned to glare at me. "Yeah, I'll see you later." He hung up, then hissed, "Why did you tell her what I ate today?"

"I didn't!"

"She said you did!"

"Well, I didn't."

He grumbled, then rolled down the window and tossed the phone out. "I hate that thing. It's like a bloody tracking device."

And on we rolled.

The bagel shop incident.

It was a very long day. I'd just given up the idea that they were going to kill me when we drove into Queens.

106

"Bagels," Filthy Phil said and got out in front of a bagel shop. "Come with me. I want your help."

"With what?" I asked and imagined myself carrying bags and bags of bagels out of the shop. Don't forget the cream cheese!

He ignored me and was almost to the door when I finally got out of the car. He held it open and we entered. It smelled very nice, just like fresh baked bread, as it should.

He strolled up to the counter and leaned on it. The female clerk glanced up. He told her, "You better leave."

She didn't hesitate. She grabbed a backpack from under the counter and headed out the front door. Not a second later, a big fat guy came out from the back. He stopped short when he saw us standing there.

"Good to see you, Albert," Filthy Phil said to the man.

I heard the door open. Tiny entered, stopped and stood in front of the door, with arms crossed.

"We can go in back," Albert said.

"Don't have to," Phil replied. "You got it?"

Albert was sweating. "No, I don't."

Phil nodded. "Well, then, you know what happens next."

"Oh, please, Phil, we go way back! You know I'm good for it!"

"If you're so good for it, then where is it?" Filthy Phil was getting agitated. Really agitated. I'd seen him get agitated with Kat and even with me, but never like this. His face flushed, his eyes narrowed and he looked...well, mean.

"Come on, Phil," Albert said. "Let's not do this."

"Tiny," Phil said, ignoring him. "Give Boy the knife."

Knife? What knife? What was I going to do with a knife? What the fuck was he talking about? *Give Boy the knife...* I got it. He was going to teach me the ropes. Normally, he wouldn't do this sort of thing as he didn't like to dirty his hands but today he wanted to show me how things *really* worked. Hell fucking no, I didn't want any part of this. I looked around. There was no escape in sight. Kat always said he didn't hurt anyone and you know what? He didn't. He got other people to do it for him and now I was one of the other people. I wasn't about to get this shit started. I wanted no part of it.

Tiny tapped a massive hunting knife on my shoulder. I reluctantly took it.

"You hold him," Filthy Phil said to Tiny. "Boy can do the rest."

There was no way I was going to do this. No way in hell.

"Uh, Phil—" I began.

He shot me one look that shut my mouth. See? This is what happens when you get caught up with people like this! It wasn't all fun and games and good food.

Tiny approached the man who was slowly dissolving into a quivering mass of nerves. He grabbed him and held his hand out towards me. I was going to throw up.

"Oh, please, Phil, for the love of God!" Albert wailed.

Phil didn't reply, only turned to me and jerked his head towards Albert. I was shaking. I was hesitating.

"For God's sake, Boy!" Filthy Phil hissed. "Get to it!"

Problem was I really didn't know what to do or how to do it. How *do* you chop off a finger? The very thought made me sick inside.

"Boy," Filthy Phil growled. "Now."

I was about to throw up. It could have been the herbs. It could have been that extra helping of meatloaf I'd had for dinner. It could be that I knew I'd never be able to look myself in the mirror after this.

Albert was staring at us. A glimmer of hope passed across his face and he almost smiled.

Then it all happened so quick.

Albert wiggled away from Tiny and ducked under the

108

counter and came back up in an instant. He held tightly onto a rifle and pointed it right at me. I thought, *THIS IS IT!* and he fired—the shot rang out—and Filthy Phil jumped in front of me, blocking the bullet. I hated to even think about it, but he had just saved my life. What the hell was up with that? Just when I thought it was over, Filthy Phil fell back on me, we crashed to the floor and I heard my arm snap in half. I let out a holler as we hit.

Tiny got shot, too, in the ass, but not before he let off a round at Albert, who went down crying like a girl, "I'll get you for this!"

Then...

It was very quiet, very still. I looked around at the gun smoke, then Tiny, who held tightly to his extra large ass and howled with pain. Albert was wailing behind the counter and Filthy Phil was coughing up blood.

I could, simply, get up and walk away. I didn't have anything to do with this. Then I thought about Kat. If I walked away, she'd never forgive me, even though she said she wanted him dead which by now I knew was a big fat lie. All of it was a lie. And now Filthy Phil needed me to help him. I didn't want to, but I had to do the right thing.

I hobbled over to the phone, picked up and dialed 9-1-1.

Filthy Phil coughed out, "What are you doing?"

"Calling an ambulance!"

He shook his head. "No, no! You help us."

He had to be kidding. In addition to being a weakling, I was also recovering from my own bullet wounds. And now I had a bone coming out of my fucking arm!

"Shit!" I yelled and slammed the phone down.

How in the hell could I do this? I couldn't heave-ho them up. I cursed under my breath. If I was going to do it, I'd have to do it quick. I don't think I could come up with a hasty excuse for some New York cop. Tiny would go first.

I bent down next to him. "Can you walk?"

"No, I can't!" he wailed.

Motherfucker!

"Here, at least get to your feet," I said and pulled him up. Then I half-carried, half-dragged him to the car. And wouldn't you know it? The fucking doors were locked.

"Bad area," he groaned and eyed me.

"Where's the fucking keys?!"

"In my pocket."

I found them and shoved him in the car. He let out an "OWWW!" that rattled my ears, then I limped back in and stared at Phil. Now this would be tricky. Why did he have to be so damn big?

"Filthy Phil?" I asked and slapped his face. "You there?"

He mumbled something incoherent then fell back unconscious.

I stood, grabbed one of his arms and tugged. He didn't give. I leaned back on both feet and pulled with my "good" arm as hard as I could. He gave and I nearly fell to the floor. I did this all the way to the car, opened the back door up, then got in the car, pulled and, miraculously, he slid in. I sat him up so he didn't choke on his own blood, then jumped out, slammed the door shut, got in the drivers seat and peeled away just as I heard sirens.

I wondered what explanation Albert would give them. I had a feeling Filthy Phil's name wouldn't be mentioned.

Kat was asleep on the couch. Truman was sleeping on her head. I screamed, "KAT!"

She didn't move.

"KAT!"

She jumped up all of a sudden and stared at me a little wild-eyed. "Fuck! You scared the shit out of me, Ray. I was having the weirdest dream."

"Kat," I began and pointed to the door.

She looked me over good. "Why do you have blood all over your shirt?"

"The bagel shop!"

She walked over to me. "What happened to your arm?"

"Kat, the bagel shop...Albert..." I was in so much pain I didn't know what I was saying. Neither did she.

"What is it?" she asked.

"In Queens!" I finally got out. "This fat guy shot Tiny and Phil!"

She was registering the information. She grew very quiet, very still. Calm even. "Where are they?"

"In the car. Downstairs."

"Okay," she said. "Go into the kitchen and call Dr. Harold."

I nodded but didn't move.

"His number is on the fridge! Go!" she yelled and raced out of the apartment quicker than a jack rabbit on a date.

I jumped back to life, raced/hobbled to the kitchen and found the number dialed Dr. Harold. I told him hastily what had happened and he said he'd be right over with a few guys. I limped back outside and noticed that she already had Filthy Phil on the sidewalk. She slapped his face several times and I could tell she was holding her tears back.

"Baby, can you hear me! Baby, can you hear me!"

She put her ear to his chest, breathed a sigh of relief then gave him CPR. She repeated this several times and ripped off her shirt. Why in the hell did she do that? After a couple of seconds, he suddenly came to life and began to cough up blood. She held the shirt to his mouth and nodded.

"That's good, baby, keep it coming," she said gently.

She repeated this process a few times and turned to me. Tiny moaned in the car. She glanced towards him, then back at me. She said, "They're both okay. Is Dr. Harold coming?"

"Yeah," I said. "He'll be here."

"Good," she said and smiled at me.

A few minutes later, a gigantic old Caddy crawled up the street. It came to a slow halt behind the Mercedes. And out jumped Dr. Harold and four big guys.

I stepped away from the car and they picked Filthy Phil and Tiny up like they were sacks of potatoes and carried them upstairs. In no time, Dr. Harold had the bullet out of Filthy Phil then out of Tiny. Then he turned to me, popped my arm back in place and it was, miraculously, as good as new. During all this, Kat helped and was so calm it was almost unnerving. Not once did she break down and cry though I did see her wipe at her eyes ever so often. She was so strong, probably the strongest person I'd ever known. I wondered how many times she'd been through this.

When Dr. Harold left, after giving strict orders for their care, Kat turned to me and said, "You did a good thing, Ray, I'm really proud of you. Thank you so much."

I stared at her, thinking about bringing up the fact that she wanted him killed not too long ago but it wasn't the time or the place. But if he'd died, I would have gotten what I wanted. But it seemed like a selfish thing to point out at that time. So, I said, "You're welcome."

She nodded. "As soon as all this is over, Ray, we'll do something."

I felt hope then. It felt so good, too.

"Let's just give it time, okay?" she said. "We'll figure out a way to, you know. We just have to be patient and play it safe."

I nodded and smiled at her. I'd gone this far, hadn't I? What were a few more weeks, or months? Nothing if it meant I could have her all to myself.

Who do you love?

Filthy Phil recovered in no time flat. Within a week, he was up and at 'em. Kat yelled and stomped her foot and demanded he get back in bed. He ignored her and walked out of the bathroom about the same time as I walked in.

"Morning, Boy."

"Morning, Filthy Phil."

It was almost as if we were passing each other at a factory on our way to punch the clock.

I shut the door, turned the water on and started to brush my teeth. Then I heard a little commotion outside the door. I turned the water off and listened.

"Phil, I mean it!" she hollered. "Get back in bed!"

A slight pause then I heard smooching noises. I groaned.

"You shouldn't be kissing me just yet," she muttered.

Oh, good God!

"I wasn't kissing you," he muttered. "I was whispering in your mouth."

I could tell she was about to smile.

"Come, on," he muttered. "Give us a kiss."

"Get out of here!"

"Ow!" he roared.

"Oh! I'm sorry! You okay?"

"Blimey!"

"Shh, let's see...ohh...ohh...Phil...really?"

She seemed excited. You had to be kidding me! It took me two months! Two months to get my dick back in working order and he got it back in a week? The son of a bitch beat me at everything.

"Really," he said. "You wanna try?"

Just say no! Say no!

"I dunno," she said. "I mean, can you?"

113

He can't!

"I can try," he said.

Bastard!

I heard them rush off. I banged my head on the wall a few times, groaned and turned the shower on. I stayed in there a long time but still heard the stereo come on. This time it was Van Morrison. I pushed my fingers in my ears.

After I had finished dressing, Filthy Phil called to me, "Hey, Boy! Come watch telly with me."

I groaned but went into the living room anyway. He was watching cartoons. I'd already seen this one—twice. Kat smiled at me. She looked…flushed. Damn, damn, damn. I sat down in a huff. She was lying to me again. I was being strung along. I should just leave. What the fuck was wrong with me? Didn't I have any balls?

She said, "Phil, I'll get a TV for the bedroom if you'll go back to bed."

"No, don't," he said pleasantly, smiling at her. "There's no need."

He held her gaze and they stared at each other as if entranced. I coughed loudly and she jumped a little.

"Hey, Boy!" Tiny called from the bedroom.

He called me Boy now, too. Him and the rest of the damn world. I yelled back, "What?"

"Care for a game of poker?"

I shook my head and stared at Kat.

She smiled and yelled, "Ray doesn't feel like it, Tiny!"

A pause, then he yelled, "Who's Ray?"

She shook her finger at Phil. "You should have never started that."

He shrugged. "You don't mind it, do you, Boy?"

"Well," I began. "It's just—"

"See, he doesn't mind, doesn't mind at all."

She rolled her eyes and laid out the Wall Street Journal on the coffee table. She liked to dabble in the stock market.

As she dabbled, we sat there and watched TV until the door buzzer went off. I sat up a little taller and smiled. Today Kat was getting something special from me.

"You gonna get that, Kat?" I asked.

"Oh," she said and raced to the buzzer.

In a few minutes, Ron knocked on the door. She opened it, smiled and he said, "Special delivery."

She nodded. "What is it?"

"I dunno," he said. "But I have to wait until you open it."

She stared at him then at the box, which suddenly moved. A little whimper came out. She jumped back. She stared at Ron, then at the box. "What is it?"

"Why don't you open it?" he asked.

"Maybe I will," she said and sat down on the floor, pulled the box to her and tore it open. Then she squealed, "Ohhhh! My God! How cute!"

And she pulled out a puppy. A beautiful white and black English mastiff.

"Phil, you didn't!"

He was eyeing me. "No, I didn't."

She glanced over at us and squealed, "Ray, did you buy me a puppy?"

"Yeah," I said and sat up taller. "I did."

"Oh, Ray! Thank you! You bought me the cutest dog in the whole wide world!"

I grinned. Yeah, I knew how to pick 'em. I explained to Filthy Phil, relishing rubbing it in, "You know, she works so hard and everything, I just thought she deserved something special."

He didn't respond. I left it at that.

Ron said, "What are you going to name him?"

She didn't hesitate, "Shazam!"

"Shazam?"

She nodded. "Yeah, I think so. Is it a boy or a girl?"

"It's a boy," I told her.

"Really? Then Shazam it is!" She held the puppy up and touched its nose to hers. "I love you, Shazam!"

"I gotta go," Ron said.

"Want some lunch?"

"Nah. I'm meeting a friend later."

"A friend or a *friend*?" she asked.

He blushed and stammered, "A girl."

"Good for you. What's her name?"

"Hilary."

"Oh, that's a beautiful name."

"Yeah, I know," he said and started out the door. "You guys have a good one."

"You too, sweetie," she called after him. "I told Delores someone would snap him up." She shook her head in dismay and turned to the puppy. "You're just the cutest little thing and I love you so much."

She held it to her chest and squeezed it gently. The puppy got real excited and began to lick her face. She smiled over at me. "You are too cool, Ray."

Yeah. I know.

Filthy Phil said, "You can clean up after him, Boy."

Filthy Phil was recovering rapidly but he still couldn't go back to "work". So, he conducted most of his "business" from the kitchen table, much to the chagrin of Kat. He also had several small TVs installed all over the place, which were constantly tuned to sports channels, so he could keep up with the "business". He also set up a computer to watch over his internet enterprise, whatever-the-fuck that was. The son of a bitch had his hands in everything. I hated him so much.

In addition to that, the place was constantly being bombarded with all kinds of people. In and out they came at all hours of the day.

This was about to drive Kat crazy. "Good God, Phil, this is my house."

"And this," he said and spread his hands over a bunch of papers. "Is your bread and butter."

She rolled her eyes and tapped her finger on the table.

He glanced up and asked, "What?"

"I was thinking…"

"Here it comes," he muttered.

"That we should take a road trip."

He went back to his papers.

"You know, drive," she said and lowered her voice, "Down south…"

"Hell fucking no," he muttered.

"And see Mommy," she said and perked up again. "Ray, don't you think that's a good idea?"

I sighed. "Yeah, you know, it is."

She nodded. "See? Ray wants to go."

"Then you and Ray sashay along."

She and I glanced at each other. We cracked up. He cracked a smile too.

"Anyway…" she said, then yelled at the puppy, "Shazam, get out of that! Now, boy!"

Shazam ignored her and continued to tear apart the garbage.

"He's thick-headed, just like someone else I know." She smiled at Filthy Phil. "Anyway, I can't leave you or Tiny here. Or Shazam."

"Why not?" he asked, got up, grabbed the puppy by the scruff of the neck and plopped him in her lap.

"Damn you," she said. "You hurt him."

"Now you know how Truman feels."

"Where is Truman?" I asked.

"He's pouting cause he's got some competition now," Kat said, then, "You are going with us, Phil."

"Why?"

"You're sick. I have to look after you," she said and set the dog on the table where he began to tear Filthy Phil's papers apart.

He nodded, took the puppy off the table and sat him on the floor, where he began to chew on his pants leg. "Yes, I am sick and that's a good reason not to come in contact with your mother. Move, dog!" He kicked at the dog who went skidding across the floor.

"He's got a fucking name," she snapped and picked the dog up.

"Yeah, that he does."

"Come on, Phil," she whined. "As soon as you get better, you'll be back at work and won't have the time or at least that's what you tell me."

He threw his pencil down. "Woman, I am trying to do some calculations here! You're breaking my concentration."

She leaned over, took the pencil and broke it in half, then threw the pieces at him. "We're going whether you like it or not."

"But—"

She ignored him, prancing off.

He glowered at me. "Why did you have to buy that damn dog?"

Southern comfort.

We started out the next afternoon. The Mercedes had been cleaned up and Kat took the wheel, Filthy Phil rode shotgun, and I got in the back with Tiny and Shazam. To an onlooker, I'm sure it looked downright odd. It certainly felt odd anyway.

"Why don't we just fly?" I asked.

"What's the fun in that?" Kat asked.

"Well, you get drinks and peanuts."

"God, Ray, where's your sense of adventure?" she asked.

It wasn't that. It was the presence of Filthy Phil and Tiny. What good is a sense of adventure when you're locked up in a car with them? Shazam could stay, of course.

She drove through the New York traffic like a New York cabbie. Filthy Phil, Tiny and I held on for dear life. Shazam sat up and barked occasionally.

"AHHHH! Watch that old lady!" Phil screamed.

She stopped just in time and began to tap the steering wheel impatiently. "Hurry up, grandma."

"Let me drive," Filthy Phil said.

"You're in no condition to drive."

"And you're in no state of mind."

She scoffed, "Good one, jerkass."

He cracked a smile.

That was just a sampling of the nearly twelve-hour drive. They bickered back and forth and he demanded once that she stop the car and let him out.

"It was not my fault!" she screeched. "That guy nearly hit me!"

"You didn't have to swerve back at him!" he yelled.

"Well, he pissed me off!"

"That's no reason to get us all killed!"

"I wasn't—"

"Stop the car!" he roared.

"No."

"STOP THE CAR!"

"NO!"

"STOP THE FUCKING CAR!"

She didn't.

And that was just the first half of the drive.

We stopped off at a hotel that night somewhere in Kentucky and got separate rooms. She and Filthy Phil in one, Tiny in one, Shazam and I in the other. After a meal in a greasy diner that Kat called, "quaint", we said goodnight and split up.

I had trouble falling asleep as I could hear through the wall the goings on in the next room. The headboard was banging up against the wall. It was like we were back in the apartment before the "accident" at the bagel shop. The reprieve was over. Now they were at it again and didn't seem to think—or mind—that anyone could hear them through the paper-thin walls.

I covered my head with the pillow and groaned. I hated Filthy Fucking Phil!

I couldn't take it anymore. I got up, slipped on my clothes and headed out the door. I don't know where I was going, but I couldn't stand the noise anymore, especially since I wasn't getting any.

As I walked across the courtyard, I heard a door slam. I glanced over my shoulder to see Kat standing in front of her door wearing a pair of shorts and a long t-shirt, which was obviously Filthy Phil's. She was holding onto an ice bucket.

She spotted me and waved. I didn't wave back.

"Hey!" she called.

"What!"

"Wait up!"

She was racing across the wet grass towards me. I looked down at her feet. She wasn't wearing any shoes. "Where you goin'?"

"Nowhere," I said. "The noise was keeping me up."

"What noise?"

I didn't answer.

"Hey, let's go over there and get a drink," she said and pointed to a little blockhouse tavern that was lit up like a firecracker.

"That's a redneck joint."

"So?" She rolled her eyes, tossed the ice bucket to the side and put her arm in mine. "You gonna buy me a drink or not?"

"Okay."

We strolled along quietly.

"Oh, Ray, look at all the stars," she gasped.

I looked up. The night was black and covered with twinkling stars. It was beautiful even if the romance of it was lost on us.

"I love…" she began but stopped.

"Filthy Phil," I said.

"You," she said and tiptoed to kiss my cheek. "Ah, hell, I love the whole world!"

She was too happy. I couldn't help but smile. I thought again about how God put people like her on earth, not only to confuse us, but to amaze us, too. She could see things the rest of us didn't. She could see beyond. She was mesmerized by life and because of that, I was mesmerized by her. I wasn't the only one.

A few days ago, I'd been instructed to change Filthy Phil's bandages because she'd had to go out. I hadn't wanted to, but what choice did I really have? We sat at the kitchen table as I did the best job I could.

"Kat does this so much better," I muttered.

He chuckled. "You're right. She does. She's great at a lot of things."

"Really," I said though I didn't want him to go on. I didn't want to hear from him, of all people, about how great she was.

"Yeah," he kept on anyway. "You know why I love her so much, Boy?"

This Boy shit was really getting old. I snapped, "Why's that, Filthy Phil?"

He chuckled again. "Because she doesn't pretend to be

innocent, but she really is. Innocent."

I had stopped what I was doing and stared at him.

He nodded good-naturedly. "You know, I love her so much, it scares the shit out of me sometimes."

How could I compete with that?

Now she was with me and we were standing on the stoop of the tavern. The music was so loud, it hurt my ears. It was aptly called "Pop-A-Top".

"Are you sure about this?" I asked.

"Come on, don't be a pussy," she said and leaned on the door. "There's just probably a bunch of good old boys in there."

"That's what I mean. Think they'd be afraid of someone like me?"

She shook her head. "Well, let's just say, southerners aren't afraid of other people, other people are afraid of southerners. It's that Scots-Irish/hillbilly thing."

"Oh," I said and glanced at her feet. "You don't have any shoes on."

She stared at her bare feet and said, "Think I can get away with it?"

Was she kidding? She had the kind of face that let her get away with anything. Filthy Phil would stare at her from time to time with a look that said, "How did I get so lucky?" I wondered the same thing myself. How *did* he get so lucky?

"Ah, hell, let's give it a try," she said and proceeded in.

I followed her. No one took notice of us. She took a twenty from me and got us a pitcher of beer, two frosted mugs and two shots of Jack. We sat down at a table in the back and she poured us one. Then she picked up the shot.

"Here's mud in your eye," she said and tapped my shot glass. We drank them and she said, "Good God, speaking of mud. Look how dirty my feet are."

She showed them to me.

"Dirty feet...dirty mind," I said.

She threw her head back and laughed loudly. "I've certainly got that."

"You sure do."

"You've never complained about it before."

"I'm not complaining now," I said.

"Touché!"

I grinned and was suddenly glad we came in here.

She put her elbows on the table. "You know when I was in first grade, I got a new pair of shoes."

"Is this some kind of joke?"

"No, but it is kinda funny. See, we were real poor and all I had was this awful looking pair of sneakers. I was little so I didn't notice how bad they were."

I nodded and lit a cigarette. She took it from me. I lit another one.

"And one day, my teacher, her name was Ms. Connors... I'll never forget her. Anyway, she called me out of the classroom and took me into the principal's office. I thought I might be in trouble."

"Were you?"

"No," she said and smiled sadly. "I thought I might have been, though, cause I was always getting in trouble. For talking and laughing and being loud. Why do they frown on that in school so much? Then you grow up and turn out to be an asshole who never laughs and they wonder what went wrong with you."

"I never thought about it like that."

"Anyway, I went in there and she sat me down, and the principal, Mr. French, smiled at me. Ms. Connors went to a closet and pulled out a brand new pair of shoes. She brought them to me, took them out of the box and helped me put them on." She wiped a tear from her cheek. "I didn't even think about it, you know? I was just so happy to have a new pair of shoes."

"That's an extremely depressing story," I said.

She slapped my arm. "No, it's not! I don't know what made me think about that."

"What does Filthy Phil think of that story?"

"I dunno. I never told him," she said. "Oh, hell, I had it a lot better than a lot of other kids. Mommy fed me, clothed me, did the best she could. And she had my brothers to worry about, too."

"What about them?" I asked.

"Well, Johnny joined a rock band, yes he really did! Listen! And he's pretty successful; they do a lot of covers and stuff and are really good. They were in New York not too long ago. Call themselves The Fifth Business. I thought of it for them."

"Cool," I said.

"And then there is Jake. He lives out West, in Las Vegas. He's a professional gambler, travels everywhere and good looking—you'll never meet a better looking man in your life! And I'm not just saying that causes he's my brother."

"Of course not," I said and smiled at her.

"Well, I'm not. He and Phil get along real well, you can imagine, because they're in the same kind of business. They practically do the same thing."

Not quite, but practically.

"I only see him every once in a while," she said with a sigh and looked into her beer. "He's a loner. Always has been."

Lynyrd Skynard's *Gimme Three Steps* came on just then.

Her head jerked up and her mouth fell open. "Oh, my God, I'm back home, baby! I'm really back home!"

I grinned at her. But she was at home wherever she went; it didn't matter if it was a redneck joint in the middle of the south or a five-star restaurant in the middle of Midtown Manhattan. She fit in where ever she went and she fit in because she knew who she was. If only the rest of us could be so lucky.

Who's the man?

"Only three more hours," Kat said and yawned.

"You said that three fucking hours ago," Filthy Phil muttered.

She ignored him. Shazam barked. She ignored him, too.

"What time did you get in last night?" he asked.

I sunk behind a newspaper.

"I dunno," she said. "You remember, Ray?"

"Nope," I muttered.

"Are we even headed in the right direction?" he snapped.

"You wanna fucking drive?"

"Yes!"

"Shh…hush, now," she said and turned up the radio.

He grunted.

"Listen, I got mixed up on the bypass in Lexington, okay! Sorry! We were heading to Louisville, which was wrong, but I figured it out, and now we're headed towards home, which is right." She smiled widely at him. "That Lexington bypass gets me every time."

He smiled back, momentarily mesmerized by her, then stared ahead and screamed, "WATCH OUT! YOU'RE IN THE CENTRAL RESERVATION!"

"The what?"

I was just asking myself the same thing. Then I stared ahead and nearly jumped out of my skin.

She shot him one look before turning her attention back to road, where it should have been in the first fucking place. She had somehow—don't ask me how—gotten into the median and was now driving into the oncoming traffic.

"Son of a bitch!" she yelled with a trace of calm, as though, while this was not the best situation to be in, it could be worse. It could be worse if, perhaps, there wasn't an eighteen-wheeler coming right at us. The driver bore down on the horn.

I began to pray, remembering that there are no atheists in hell, just as she cut the wheel sharp and the whole fucking car just turned and turned until we were facing the right way again. She punched the gas and we barely missed getting rammed in the ass by the eighteen-wheeler as she sped away. He honked at her for a long time. She hauled ass and soon he was a distant memory.

Filthy Phil was white as a sheet. Tiny and I had almost shit our pants. Shazam had retreated under the seat. He whimpered. I pulled him out and scratched him behind his ears.

"Well, I'll be damned… Phew!" she said pleasantly and turned to Filthy Phil and gave him a big old happy grin. "What you think of that Mr. Hotshot? I did good, didn't I?"

Calmly, he said, "Please pull the car over."

"Why?" she said and pulled off at an exit ramp.

"I think I'm going to be sick."

"Okay, hold on. I have to get us going back in the right direction," she said and stopped at the stop sign then pulled through, turning left twice until we were back on the interstate and going in the right direction again.

"Kat," Filthy Phil said. "I said to pull the car over."

"Are you still feeling sick?" she asked.

"I am."

She shrugged and pulled the car over to the shoulder. "Are you okay now?"

"Could you please get out of the car?" he asked.

She smiled suspiciously. "Why?"

"Please."

126

She sighed and turned to us, "Y'all okay?"

We nodded feebly.

"Would you please?" Filthy Phil asked.

"Okay, okay," she said. "I'll leave the air on."

We nodded.

"You coming?" he asked.

She shrugged happily and got out of the car. Filthy Phil was out too. He went to a guard rail and sat down. He motioned her over. She went to him smiling. I noticed he wasn't smiling back.

Tiny and I glanced at each other. Tiny rolled his window down.

"What is it, Phil?" she asked.

"Come here," he said, not unpleasantly.

She went to him.

"Turn round, please."

"Why?"

"Please?"

She complied. In one quick motion, he had her on her belly over his knee and was whaling the hell out of her ass. We watched in horror. He gave her a good twenty or thirty whacks, too, right there in front of God and everybody.

I reached to open the door to rescue her. Tiny held me back and shook his head. And rolled up the window. Shazam was furious, too. He barked and barked.

"Let me out!" I yelled. "He's hurting her!"

"More like he's embarrassing her."

"Get your hands off, motherfucker!" I yelled. "I am going out there to kick his ass!"

He pulled his gun out and held it to my head. "Don't think so. That's between them, not you and not me."

"You fucker," I seethed.

She was screaming, "LET ME GO! LET ME GO! YOU MOTHERFUCKING ASSWIPE LIMEY SON OF A BITCH COCKSUCKER PUSSY CUNT PRICK SHITHEAD DILDO!"

She wriggled this way and that, trying to get away. He wouldn't let her.

"Let me out, asshole!" I yelled at Tiny.

"None doing."

I glared at Tiny. She was suddenly at the window, banging on it. We both jerked back.

"Tiny! Give me your gun!"

Tiny ducked behind the seat. With his gun.

"You little shit, Tiny!" she yelled. "I'll get you for this!"

She turned around. Filthy Phil was still sitting on the guardrail waiting patiently for her to calm down. She snarled, found a rock and hurled it at him. He dodged it. She found a stick, ran at him and hit him over the head. It broke in half. She kicked his shin. He hopped up and down. Then she did the unmentionable. She kicked him right in the balls. *As hard as she could.*

Even I winched.

As soon as he doubled over, obviously in too much pain to move, she raced to the car, got in, put it in drive and peeled out.

"That motherfucker!" she roared. "*Motherfucker!* I'll kill the son of a bitch!"

Tiny cleared his throat to indicate that he was still in the car. She didn't give a shit.

"Oh, I forgot something," she said and pulled back over. "Get out, Tiny!"

"What!"

"Now you little worm! Get the fuck out of my car!" She turned and gave him a hellacious look. He got the fuck out—he was probably better off anyway—she threw it in drive and we peeled away. "Wouldn't give me his gun, I'll show them both! The motherfuckers."

I had never been happier. Kat went on and on planning

the demise of Filthy Phil.

"I'm gonna get him," she said as if she were possessed. "What do you think about what he did?"

"I think it was downright barbaric," I said and I did. Who did he think he was? No wonder she wanted him dead. I saw it more clearly than ever before.

"You're damn right it was! Beating me like I'm some...I dunno, some little girl! The fuckhead!"

Three hours later—exactly—we pulled off into a long, tree lined drive.

"Where we going?" I asked.

"Home, Ray," she said. "And this time I'm staying! That cocksucker can suck his own dick from now on!"

I didn't venture a comment, for obvious reasons.

The place was beautiful and that was just the grounds. We finally pulled up in front of a sprawling *Gone with the Wind*-type mansion. It took my breath away. For some reason, I thought her mother lived in a trailer or, at the very least, a shack.

"Is this your house?" I asked.

She stared at me. "No, Ray, we're here to rob it. That was the plan. Then we'll go on to Mommy's."

My mouth fell open.

"Of course it's my fucking house," she said, glowering. "Why would I pull up to it if it weren't?"

"Sorry," I muttered. But what about the sob story about the shoes? Did she make that up or something? What the hell was going on here?

"If you don't watch it," she told me. "You can walk back, too."

I shut my mouth.

She slammed the car in park and got out grumbling, "Fucking men, fucking cocksucking sonsofbitches..."

I turned to watch her race up the steps crying "Mommy" all the way. She was about to the top when a lady who had to be her mother was on the porch. She ran into her arms crying.

"There, there, baby, what's wrong?" she asked and patted her head.

"Mommy, I want him dead," she bawled. "This time I mean it!"

"I can take care of that."

"He bent me over and spanked me on the side of the interstate!"

Mrs. Cumberland was livid. "That son of a bitch!"

She cried, burying her face into her mother's enormous bosom. Damn, Dolly Parton had nothing on this woman. Kat's tits were nice, but they weren't…quite as mammoth.

"We'll get him, baby," Mommy said. "Hush now, no sense crying over his sorry ass."

I opened the door and Shazam flew out after her. I got out of the car and made my way over to them.

"Oh, is that Ray?" she said cheerily.

"Hi, it's me," I said and gave her a cautious smile.

She smiled at me and said with a twinkle in her eye, "We'll get him this time. Hopefully, he'll have sense enough to stay away."

That would have just been too easy, though, wouldn't it?

Kat took a baseball bat to the Mercedes. If Filthy Phil had been around, she'd have taken it to him. In about an hour's time, Kat had the exterior destroyed, then she started on the engine, tearing out wires, pipes, hoses, anything she could get her hands on.

"German engineering, my ass!" she yelled and glanced over at us. Mrs. Cumberland and I smiled and waved to her from the porch, then continued rocking on the swing. She went back to work.

Mrs. Cumberland called, "Baby, make sure you get the taillights."

She did. I smiled at her and gave a thumb's up. She glanced over at me and smiled back. Then I turned to Mrs. Cumberland and smiled at her. She smiled back, staring at me.

"Ray, you're more handsome than I imagined," she said.

"Thank you, ma'am," I said and then laid it on, "You're more lovely than I could have ever thought."

"Oh, you're not blowing smoke up my ass now, are you?"

"Oh, no," I said. "Definitely not."

"People still mistake Katharine and me for sisters," she said with a smile.

"I can see why," I said. And for an older lady, she looked hot. She was not the grandmother type at all. She was petite and slender, like Kat. Her shoulder length (bleached) blonde hair was styled perfectly. And, then there was the matter of her tits…

"This is a nice place you got here," I said.

"Sure is," she said.

"Umm," I said and gave a little smile. "So, what happened? You win the lottery or something?"

She threw her head back and laughed loudly. She definitely had a coarse, smoker's laugh. "No, baby, I didn't hit the lottery."

I nodded. "So…"

"Old Hank was a rich son of a bitch."

"Old Hank? Your fourth husband, right?"

"Yes, my husband, Lord rest his soul," she said sadly.

"I'm sorry to hear about that."

"Honey, he's been dead near ten years now."

"Oh," I said.

"Old Hank Cumberland was a good man," she said. "And he loved Katherine better than anything. Adopted her and my boys cause he never had any kids on his own, you know? Gave her anything and everything she wanted, even his name."

I nodded, then realized I'd nodded at her tits. I looked up quickly.

"Treated her better than her own daddy, that sonofabitch," she said, then flicked cigarette ash on the porch. "You wonder what makes men so mean sometimes, don'cha?"

I nodded and averted my eyes. Again.

"I'm glad he left, myself," she said, nodding. "Didn't miss him much when he did. But then I had to go through two more before I got Old Hank. But he was worth waiting for."

I almost laughed. But looking around the place, I'd have to agree with her. She'd hit the jackpot and I never had a problem with gold-diggers. More power to them.

"Of course, it wasn't enough for Miss Katherine. She's never been one to care about money much." She paused and shook her head at her daughter's foolishness. "That child always got a wild hair about something and then one day, she announces that she's going to New York City! After all the work I had to do to get all this, it wasn't enough for her. She wanted to 'explore' the world, whatever the hell that means."

I nodded.

"Better places to start than New York, if you ask me," she said and took a drag off her cigarette. "So, I sent her with a suitcase of money and she went through it in no time at all, calling home to me, begging me for more. I told her to get her ass back home. 'But, Mommy, I'm having so much fun!'"

I didn't want to hear this. Especially since I hoped I

132

wouldn't have to deal with Filthy Phil for a while.

She scoffed, "Then she met that son of a bitch. He thought she was some poor old...something. Damn it, if I had known, I'd sent her anything she wanted. Ending up with that low-life bastard!"

"Why do you hate him so much, if you don't mind me asking," I said.

She didn't mind me asking at all. "Well, she brought his sorry ass down here one summer and I asked him how did he do, you know, being polite and all and he said, 'I don't quite understand.' It all went to hell from there."

"I know what you mean."

"Then I asked him if he's ever met the Queen. I mean he's from over there someplace and he says, 'Commoners don't usually meet the Queen'. Oohh, la la. Shithead. I was just being polite, that's all. Like I would expect the Queen to know a scumbag like him."

"Ray," Kat called. "Come help me."

I excused myself and we got into the car and tore it to pieces. It was fun, too. We ripped the upholstery and kicked the dash in. We stopped and I stared at her. Her face was covered with grease and oil and dirt. Her hair was falling down in her face. She never looked more beautiful. Fresh hope filled me and I leaned in and gave her a kiss. She kissed back and we laughed with glee. I glanced over my shoulder. Her mother was watching us, smiling. See! It could work! It would work! If you can get the mother on your side, you've got it made.

We stopped for supper. Kat didn't even wash her hands. She ran into the dining room sat down, gobbled a few bites said to her mother, "Can I go now?"

She nodded and Kat ran out. I stood to go after her.

"Ray, this is something she needs to do on her own, sweetheart. And I'd like a little company for dinner."

I wasn't the only company. The maid, the gardener and

some guy who was there to work on the water heater joined us.

"Okay," I said happily and we conversed about this and about that and did I ever get to Churchill Downs and things like that. Everyone was so nice and polite. Now this was southern hospitality. And the food? It was so good it nearly melted in my mouth.

After supper, we went back outside. Kat was finally finished destroying the car. Shame, really. But what did I care? It wasn't my car.

Mrs. Cumberland clapped her hands together with glee. "Oh, you got him good, baby!"

Kat grinned mischievously. "There's eighty-thousand bucks he won't be getting back."

She gave me a high-five and we hugged each other and jumped up and down. Then we heard the car. We turned to see a big black Cadillac crawling up the drive. Oh, fuck.

"Oh, no, he don't," Mrs. Cumberland said.

"Yeah, he does," Kat replied. "He got some fucking nerve."

"Watch your filthy fucking mouth, young lady!" Mrs. Cumberland snapped.

Kat merely eyed her and turned her attention to the car.

The car pulled up and neither Filthy Phil nor Tiny got out. Kat and her mother stepped back and leaned against the now demolished Mercedes. His mouth fell open.

Kat smiled and pretended to be a game show host by moving her hands up and down in front of the car. *Isn't it beautiful?*

Filthy Phil was not happy. You could just tell by the look on his face. His face turned red and his eyes nearly popped out of his head. This was going to be good. Maybe he'd finally get the hint and move along.

I glanced over at Kat who was now standing with arms

crossed and giving him his look back.

"Let's go inside," I told her.

"If he's got something to say," she said, going over to the car, then shouting, "He needs to get his sorry ass out and say it!"

Tiny rolled down the window. "What's that?"

"Well, Phil, looks like you're a day late and dollar short."

And he wasn't too happy about it, either.

"What's that?" Tiny said again.

"You heard me," she snarled.

Filthy Phil said, "Why did you wreck my car?"

"I didn't wreck it, baby, I tore it apart."

"And why did you do that?" he asked, obviously baffled and a more than a little pissed off.

"Why did you beat me like a red-headed stepchild on the side of the road?!"

"Oh," he said, then shook his head at the car. "But why do that?"

"Why did you beat me?"

"I did not beat you."

"Oh, really!" she scoffed. "Ray did he or did he not beat me?"

I only nodded.

"You need to get going," Mrs. Cumberland said.

"Hold on a minute, Mommy," Kat said. "Let's see what the bastard has to say for himself."

"Oh, hallo!" Filthy Phil said and waved weakly at her.

It was so out of character, but Mrs. Cumberland flipped him a bird. I tried to contain my laughter.

Filthy Phil was now exiting the car. Cautiously. Kat walked over to him, rather she stomped, almost daring him to do something.

"I'm sorry," he said. "But you—"

One hand was up, out and now landed on the side of

his cheek with a loud *SMACK!*

Tiny winced. Phil did not.

"Kat, please, don't," he said.

The other hand was up, out, and intercepted by Filthy Phil. That's when I had a feeling this was not going according to plan.

"I will tell you once, not twice, to let me go," she snarled.

He let her go. Her hand went up and again, he intercepted it. She almost cracked a smile. Ah hell, here it is. I knew what this was leading. I'd seen them showdown against each other before. And I knew how it always ended. But one can only hope, right? No, one shouldn't. Not in cases like this.

"You fucking asshole," she said.

"Kat—"

"You could at least let me spank you back."

"Whatever that means."

"I hate you."

He nodded.

"I wish you'd die."

He looked away.

"Get out of my yard!"

He shifted his feet.

"Go!" she yelled.

Yes, GO! Get out! LEAVE! You're not wanted here!

This time she kicked his shin. He didn't howl with pain, he only grimaced.

"I'm warning you," he grunted.

"Warn away."

"Kat, please, let's get in the car and take a drive and talk this out." He took her arm. She wriggled away. He stepped to her. She stepped back. "Come on, Kat. Tiny can stay here. All I need is ten minutes."

And I knew what he'd do in those ten minutes, too!

I stepped forward, but someone held my arm. It was that fat bastard Tiny, who I hadn't noticed standing there before. When did he get out of the car? I looked back at them and noticed everyone else was watching with rapt attention as well.

Again, the train wreck mentality.

"No, Phil, let go of me!"

He wasn't about to. She twisted this way and that. Then she wrung free and took off across the enormous yard. He took off after her; it didn't take any time for him to catch up, but I noticed he slowed just as he got to her. He was teasing her.

I felt sick.

"PHIL NO!" she screamed.

He chased her around the yard for a good three or four minutes. Shazam ran after them, barking at their heels. I tried to break free but that fucking Tiny held my arm tight. All I could do was watch as she tried to climb up a tree. He grabbed her ankle; she kicked him in the head and slid back down. Then she took off again.

"Phil, stop it!" she said just as he grabbed her in the middle and threw her over his shoulder. She wiggled and squirmed and tried to get down but he wasn't about to let her. She beat his back with her hands. And then a terrible thing happened. She started laughing.

He was laughing, too. He threw her down under the big oak tree. She yelped, tried to hold him off, but he was on top of her, holding her to the ground. It was no use. She cried and laughed and spat and… He kissed her. And she melted, just like that. She threw her arms around his neck and pulled him closer. He was so close to her, closer than I could ever hope to get. They kissed and kissed and kissed…

I realized then that I could be anyone. I could be prince fucking charming. I could be a rock star, Dean Martin. And it wouldn't have mattered. She would never see me. All she saw was him. To her, no other man existed. Least of all a loser like me, who was none of the aforementioned. Then why did she keep me hanging on? Why did she do that? Why did she tell me those things about being patient? I couldn't do this any longer. I couldn't keep getting used.

The maid said, "I'll be. Would you look at that?"

I wish I had never seen it.

"Son of a bitch," Mrs. Cumberland muttered.

I couldn't have said it better myself.

They took off, hand in hand. They took off down the long drive alone. Just before they were out of sight, he threw her up on his shoulder again like a fucking Neanderthal.

No one went after them or even called out. I sadly watched them go. Everyone else, including Mrs. Cumberland and excluding me, were trying to hide their smiles.

I don't know where they went, but I knew what they went to do. Oh, and it made me sick. Every time I thought I had her, he was back in the picture. Maybe he was a better man than me. Maybe it was that simple.

I hated him more than ever.

Kat and the drunk.

It was past midnight when she came out onto the porch. I tried not to look at her and rocked quietly in the swing. She plopped down beside me and tried to take my hand. I jerked it back.

"What's wrong?" she asked.

I didn't respond.

"Ray?"

"I'm sick of it, Kat," I said.

"Sick of what?"

"You know," I said.

She rolled her eyes. She was beginning to get agitated. So what? I was beyond agitation with her.

"What do you want?" I asked.

"I just wanted to make sure you were okay."

"Yeah, I'm okay," I nearly spat. "Why wouldn't I be okay?"

"Come on, Ray."

"You don't want him dead," I said accusingly. "You love him."

"No, he caught me on a bad day."

"Everyday must be a bad day for you."

"Come now."

"Kat, I can't do this any more." I turned and looked her square in the eye. "You love him, don't you?"

"Why are you asking me this now?"

"I need to know."

She stared at me. "Ray, I don't know what to say."

"He has you wrapped around his little finger. Everyone thinks it's you that has him, but I know better."

She sighed.

"Isn't that right?" I hissed.

"I don't know. Maybe we both got each other."

I scowled and looked away.

"What do you want me to say?" she asked quietly.

Tell me you love me. Tell me this was all a bad dream. Put an end to all this hurt in my heart. It triggered off so many other hurts. It hurt me to see her so in love with him. It hurt me to see him give back that emotion with the full abandon he did.

Yes, this was a love triangle, indeed it was. I loved her, he loved her, she loved...she loved him. There wasn't room for me.

I said, "Just tell me to leave, Katherine."

She looked away quickly. "But I love you, Ray. You're

one of my best friends now."

"Why do you say that when you know you're lying?" I asked. "Don't do me like that."

"I'm not lying. I do love you, Ray," she said. "I need you."

"Bullshit," I said. "Don't do this to me, please don't. I can't take it anymore. Just let me go."

She stared back at me, her eyes filling with tears. I wanted to reach out and touch her face, tell her not to cry but I couldn't. Instead I told my heart to go on and break, that it was over, that it had never really began. It had been a game, a ruse but never love. I was tired of trying to fool myself into believing in something that wasn't there to begin with.

She mumbled, "Is that what you want?"

I nodded. It hurt like hell, but I had to be freed. I couldn't take it anymore.

She stared at me. "Then what do you want from me?"

"I want you to run away with me. Tonight."

She smiled sadly. "No. I have too many things to do here. I've got people to see, places to go. I won't leave tonight."

"No, not tonight or any other night."

She sighed. "Ray—"

"I get the hint, Katherine," I snapped and jumped up and made a hasty departure. She called after me. But she didn't run.

"Light dawns on marble head," Kat's cheery voice drifted into my dreams. "Wakey, wakey."

She was standing next to the huge four-poster bed I was sleeping in with a large silver tray piled high with steaming

140

breakfast food. She grinned from ear to ear. Her long hair was in pigtails. She had on a cute little gingham shirt with a pair of short-short jean shorts. She looked like a cross between Ellie Maye and Daisy Duke. And she was barefoot.

I couldn't help but smile back. She looked good enough to eat. And I was starving.

"Hungry?" She held the tray out.

"Uh, yeah," I said, sitting up.

She put the tray on the bed, climbed in with me and we began to eat. I watched as she put some dark, syrupy substance on a biscuit.

"What is the hell is that?" I asked.

"Molasses," she said and held the biscuit under my nose. "Try a bite. Come on, it might make you sweeter."

I tasted. "Oh, that's not so bad. Let me have another," I said and leaned over. She gave me another bite. I smacked my lips. "It grows on you.

"Yup," she said, nodding. "So, I was thinking we could go riding today."

"Riding?"

"Yeah, horses. Where's Shazam?"

"I dunno," I said and stared around the room. "Maybe someone let him out."

"Oh," she said and scratched the palm of her hand. "Damn! My hand's itching like crazy! Maybe I'm going to get some money!"

Like she needed any. I watched as she rubbed her palm against her pocket and smiled at her. She was so ridiculous. That's when I realized why I stayed around. It was for her. I needed her so bad I'd do anything, suffer any humiliation, let her use me just to be near her. I was pathetic and I knew it. But I couldn't tell myself no when it came to her.

"So, anyway, you wanna go riding or not?" she asked.

"Sure, it sounds like fun."

"And tonight, Mommy's having a party for me."

"Cool," I said and smiled at her. God, it was so hard to be mad at her and I shouldn't be mad at her. I should be mad at Filthy Phil. If he'd just drop dead everything would be perfect. She loved me, I knew that, but she loved me like a friend and I didn't know if that was any better than not being loved at all. If he was gone, that love would turn into the real thing.

"What attracted you to Filthy Phil?" I asked.

She eyed me. "You're very fascinated with Phil, aren't you?"

God, that offended me. The animosity I'd felt last night was coming back and coming back strong. Why did she have to say that?! I hissed, "I am not."

"Yes, you are," she said, lighting a cigarette. "Look, I think it's cool. It's funny, but you two are almost like brothers."

"We are not!" I half-yelled.

"Yes, you are," she said, shaking her head at me. "You're always watching him and—"

"Because I'm afraid he'll find out about us and kill me!"

"Ray," she said and laid a hand on my shoulder. "He knows about us, sorta kinda."

"Holy shit!" I exclaimed, shocked. "You told him?"

"Yes, I did."

"Why the fuck did you tell him?" I asked, aghast.

"He suspected it."

"So, what did he say?" I asked. "Did he get mad?"

She nodded. "Yeah, he got mad."

"And?"

"And he wanted to kill you," she said and put the cigarette out. "But he calmed down. I told him I had a weak moment."

"A weak moment?" I asked. "I don't believe you."

"Why?"

"Because I don't," I said and crossed my arms. "That guy

142

is jealous if you *look* at another guy and you fuck someone else and he forgets and forgives?"

"Well, that's what I did, didn't I?" she said. "It wasn't like I could take it back. Besides, he suspected it and asked me and… Well, you know how compulsively honest I am. It gets me into a lot of trouble, but I can't help it."

"What did he say?"

"See?" she said. "You are fascinated with him."

"I am not!"

"Listen, it's okay," she said. "You were an only child, right? So, you probably, on a subconscious level, always wanted a sibling. I bet you even had an imaginary friend."

She was very intuitive. She was also right. My imaginary friend's name was Conrad and he had red hair, freckles and a mean streak. He got me into a lot of trouble.

"Children who have imaginary friends are very creative," she said, eying me. "And you're a Cancer, right?"

"What?" I asked, baffled. "I mean, yeah, that's my sign. What does that have to do with anything?"

"Cancer's are super sensitive."

"I am *not* super sensitive," I huffed.

"Yes, you are." She smiled at me. "I'm a Sagittarius, and we have big mouths, which means sometimes we hurt poor little Cancer's feelings without knowing why."

I just stared at her. Maybe that was my trouble, I was a Cancer. No, that was bullshit. She began to jab me in the ribs. I squirmed away. "Ow! Stop it! Tell me something I don't know."

She stopped, considered and said, "Phil's a Gemini and that's the symbol of the twin."

"What does that mean? That he has two personalities?"

She laughed out loud. "Sometimes I wonder…but no, it doesn't mean he has two personalities."

But he did. He was good and sweet to her and mean as hell to the rest of the world. I asked, "So, you like him because he's a Gemini?"

"No. When I found out, I almost broke up with him," she said. "Gemini and Sagittarius are polar opposites. We're as far away from each other as we can get on the astrological chart."

I could see it. "So is that why you two fight all the time?"

She considered. "Maybe. But, really, fighting isn't so bad, is it? You don't know how passionate you are about someone until you argue with them."

"You two don't argue," I told her. "You wage war."

She giggled and said, "Yeah, that's what we do."

I cracked up and shook my head at her. "Anyway… What about Cancer and Sagittarius?"

She ignored me and lit another cigarette.

"Kat?" I said. "What about Cancer and Sagittarius?"

"I don't know. I never looked it up."

"Oh," I said. "Can we get back on the subject now?"

"Which was?" she asked and ashed on the tray.

"The reason you were attracted to him. And the other thing, too."

"Oh. I like bad boys."

Well, there you go.

"And the back of his neck is just so wonderful." She touched the back of my neck. "Here. I love the way the back of some men's neck's look. That's why I hate long hair on men. I like to see the backs of their necks. I think it's so sexy, the back of the neck. That was what attracted me to him."

That's probably because she hadn't seen his face yet. I stared at her and asked, "You fell in love with him because of the back of his neck?"

"Well, that had a little to do with it but I liked the whole package."

"Good grief," I said. "That is so weird."

"It is not weird," she chirped. "Anyway, the thing about us sleeping together, he just let it go. Besides, I never said it was you."

I just stared at her.

"He likes you a lot. He tells me all the time how much he admires you. He said he never saw anyone take a shot to the stomach like you before."

I rolled my eyes. "So that's why he admires me? Not because I'm a loser?"

"You are not a loser," she said and touched my face. "You're a wonderful man, Ray, and I am honored to know you. I think you're the shit."

She was so full of it. I stared at her. She was sincere, but she was still full of shit. I rolled my eyes. "Yeah, and look where it got me. It got me shot."

She just stared at me then said, "Yeah, look. I mean, you're shit out of luck, ain't ya? You got me here trying to be your friend. You're sitting in a mansion eating good food. You're about to go horseback riding. You got the time to do that, that's the most important thing, but you'd rather sit around and feel sorry for yourself."

I shook my head and rolled my eyes.

"You got Filthy Phil on your side," she said. "You don't know how many men would love to be in your position."

"Right. Just cause he isn't scared of me doesn't mean he's on my side."

"He's not scared of anyone, Ray."

"And, I do not feel sorry for myself," I said. "I'm just afraid Filthy Phil is going to jump my ass, okay? You never know what a guy like that is thinking."

Actually, this didn't really scare me. More like it puzzled me. Why didn't he do something? If Kat were my girl, I mean, *really* my girl, I'd kill any son of a bitch that dared touch her. Sorry, but I would. Maybe he was just waiting for the opportunity. Maybe he was waiting for me to try it again. Maybe he didn't give a shit. But I knew that wasn't true, either.

I remembered that once back in New York we were in a bar and Kat excused herself to the ladies' room. Five minutes went by, then ten. Filthy Phil became worried. "Where is she, Boy?"

"I dunno," I said and sipped my beer. "Want me to go look for her?"

"Nah, I'll go," he said and left.

I had to use the john myself, so I followed him. Kat was in the little hallway that led to the bathrooms. She was talking to some guy. She didn't see us. The guy was being aggressive, you could just tell. He was drunk and a drunk won't take no for an answer. He tried to grab her arm, she pulled it back.

"I'm warning you," she hissed. "Now get the fuck out of my way."

Filthy Phil was watching them. I started towards her, knowing this guy could hurt her, but Filthy Phil held up one arm and halted me. I glared at him for a moment, then stared back at Kat and the drunk.

"Come on, baby," the drunk slurred. "With pretty lips like those, you've got to give good head."

"Get out of my way," she said. "I mean it."

He licked his lips. "You're a southern girl, ain't ya? I like that. Why don't you tell me what it's like to fuck in a trailer park?"

Just then, she glanced over his shoulder and spotted Filthy Phil. She gave a wry smile and said, "Why don't you tell him, Phil?"

The guy looked over his shoulder only to be greeted by Filthy Phil's fist. He fell to the floor on his ass, then tried to squirm away but Filthy Phil grabbed him up, twisted his arm behind his back and hissed in his ear, "What that's motherfucker? What'd you say?"

146

The drunk howled in pain. "Nothing!"

Filthy Phil was livid. He pushed the guy up against the wall and began to beat him in the face. Soon he was a bloody mess. The guy tried to fall to the floor. Filthy Phil grabbed him by the back of the head and turned him to face Kat.

"Tell the lady you're sorry!" he hissed.

The guy mumbled something.

"TELL THE LADY YOU'RE SORRY!"

"Sorry," the guy said and passed out, collapsing to the floor.

Filthy Phil started to reach for him to do more damage, but Kat took his hand and said, "He's not worth it," and led him away.

So, why didn't he have the same reaction to me? Why? I had actually fucked her.

She was saying, "I just said you were 'some guy'. He suspected it was you, but I never confirmed it. And then, he got to know you and decided it wasn't you after all, he said you weren't my type and he forgot about it."

It was forgotten because I was no threat to him. And that pissed me off. Who did he think he was? He'd beat up some drunk in a bar but not a man having sex with his girlfriend?

"You ready to go riding now?" she asked and headed to the door.

"I'm going to die alone," I told her. "I'll be in a room by myself, alone."

"No you won't, Ray," she said. "I'll get you a bird to keep you company."

I stared at her. "What the hell does that mean?"

She stared at me and shook her head. "I don't know. It just popped in my head."

We stared at each other for a moment, then we cracked up.

White lightning.

After she slipped on a pair of cowboy boots, she saddled up two horses. A beautiful black stallion for herself, she liked bad boys, after all, and a shorter mare for me.

"Now, this old mare is gentle, but she's fast too. So, when you want her to go faster, kick her with the side of your foot but not your heel." She demonstrated. "She's very sensitive. If you kick her the other way, you better hold on for dear life."

"Why isn't Filthy Phil going riding?" I asked, looking around the stable.

"He's afraid of horses."

"Really?"

"Hell, Ray, I don't know. It's just not his thing."

As soon as the words were out of her mouth, Filthy Phil strolled into the barn. He stopped short when he saw her. He tried to hide his smile.

"What is it?" she growled.

"I like your boots."

"Fuck you," she said and looked down at them. "I think they're cute."

"Oh, they are cute, love," he said and walked over to her, slipped his hand around her waist and gave her a little kiss. "How's it going, Boy?"

I was so sick of that. I looked away.

"What are you doing?" he asked.

"We're going riding," she said and expertly mounted the horse.

"Oh, be careful then," he said and slapped the stallion's ass.

The horse, obviously spooked by his presence, whinnied and reared back on its hind legs.

"You fucking asshole!" she screamed as the horse tried

to buck her.

"Shit! I'm sorry!" He jumped away from the horse, looking almost terrified.

She calmed the horse down and headed out of the barn, but not before slapping the back of Filthy Phil's head with her riding crop. He ducked and held his head.

"Blimey," he muttered under his breath and stared at me. "You going with her?"

I glared at him and took off after her. I saw her galloping towards an open pasture. I kicked the old mare with my heel instead of the side of my foot and just like Kat said, she gave a snort and took off like a bat out of hell. I had to hold on for life.

"Kat!" I hollered. "Hold up!"

By then, she was already out of sight.

I held back on the reins like she'd instructed but it was no use. The damned horse kept going. Soon the house was out of sight and we were headed into the woods. I didn't know where the fuck I was. The horse finally stopped at a creek and took a drink of water. I jumped down and caught my breath. When I tried to get back on, she moved and sidestepped me several times, not letting me on. Hell, I wouldn't want anyone riding around on my back either. I gave up and began the long haul back to the house.

I was walking behind the small guest house when I heard a voice, "Hey, Boy!"

I looked around. Where the hell was it coming from?

"Hey, Boy!" Filthy Phil called. "Over here!"

I walked around to see him standing in the doorway of the guest house. I asked, "What's up?"

He jerked his head. "Come in."

"Actually, I'm going to go—"

"Come on in," he said and disappeared into the house.

"Motherfucker," I muttered under my breath. I entered and looked the place over. It was nice, comfortably furnished. A bear skin rug was on the wood floor. A nice kitchenette off to the side. A big stone fireplace in the center of the room. I noticed the wood was still smoking a little. I went into the kitchenette. He was holding two Mason jars.

"What happened to your horse?" he asked and handed me a jar.

"I got off and it wouldn't let me back on." I took the jar and sniffed. "What's this?"

"Try it, Boy," he said excitedly. His eyes were sparkling and he was shaking with excitement. "Go on now."

"Is this poison?" I asked.

"I got the same stuff here," he said and held up the other jar. "We'll do it at the same time."

"Let's exchange jars," I said.

He shrugged and we exchanged jars. But *this* one could be the one with poison in it, just like in all the cartoons. Which one? I stared at his jar, then at mine. Oh, fuck it. Why not put an end to all this misery?

We held up our jars and at the same time, threw them back. OH HOLY MOTHER OF GOD! What was that?! My throat burned. My senses began to leave me. My eyes watered. I was out of breath. I was blinded momentarily. I could have breathed fire. I tried. Almost.

He was having the same reaction.

"What the fuck was that?" I croaked.

"Moonshine," he said and held the jar up, admiring it. "Good old white lightning."

"Shit. Really?"

"Boy," he said and motioned me to sit with him at the little table. "This is the best stuff. The old hag won't give me any, so I snooped round earlier and found some. Like it?"

I nodded. Actually, it did have a certain flavor. I smacked my lips. "Let's do another."

"Okay," he said. "But only one more. This shit will knock you on your arse."

I'd like to knock him on his arse. But first, another shot. He poured us each one and we shot it. Soon, everything was so warm and fuzzy. He even seemed warm and fuzzy. I still hated him. And I wanted to test him. Now was as good a time as any. With as much nonchalance as I could muster, I said, "I fucked Kat."

He glanced over at me. "I know."

No malice, no nothing. Uh uh. I wasn't about to let him get away with that. "She told me she didn't tell you it was me," I said, trying to affect an intimidating look. "But it was. Me."

"She was just trying to confuse you," he said and held up his jar. "Just like she tries to confuse me. But if you listen, she'll eventually give it away."

"So you knew it was me all along?"

"I did."

I leaned in. "I don't give a shit about that. Just tell me why you didn't beat me up."

He sighed and tapped his jar against mine. "This is our last shot."

We threw them back. Damn! But it was getting easier. And much, much better. I said, "Listen, Filthy Phil, I want to know why."

"Why what?"

"You know what! You're not threatened by me, are you?"

He laughed. "How could I be? You're what? One-sixty soaking wet?"

"One seventy-one, completely dry."

"Yeah, okay."

"And I fucked your girlfriend," I said.

He sighed. "Do you really want to get this started?"

I rolled my eyes, "I want to know why you don't care."

"I do care."

"Then why don't you defend her honor or something?"

He cracked up, slapped his hand on the table several times. "What is this? The middle fucking ages?"

"Remember that time you annihilated that guy in the bar cause he said something rude to her? And he didn't even touch her."

"He was disrespectful, Boy," he said. "No one is disrespectful to Kat. I won't let them be."

Fair enough, but I proceeded nonetheless, "He made one rude comment and you almost beat him to death."

He shrugged. "He caught me on a bad day."

"Oh, please," I said, trying to piss him off. "And besides, Kat can take care of herself. You had no right to be so pissed off."

This got him. In an instant, he had me grabbed me by the shirt and pulled nose to nose. "She thinks she can take care of herself, but she can't. She is a physically small woman who thinks she's bigger than she really is. There are a lot of creeps out there who would like nothing better than to hurt her. And, that, Boy, pisses me off. I take one of them out here or there, then it gives them the idea that they can't do it, period, to Kat or some other poor girl who happens to cross their path."

Sarcastically, I said, "So, you're trying to make the world a better place?"

"I can't make it better, but I can make sure she's safe. And if that means I have to beat the shit out of a few guys along the way, then that's what it means."

"Then why not beat the shit out of me?" I asked.

He released me. "Have you ever disrespected her? Have you ever gotten out of line with her?"

"Not that I recall," I said, but thought, *she's done it to me.*

"Have you ever physically attacked her?" he asked.

"Hell fucking no!"

He nodded. "So, why should I beat you up, then?"

152

"Because I fucked her, that's why!"

He chuckled. "Right. You fucked her, yeah, Boy, I know. You trying to rub me nose in it?"

"Yes, I am!"

He laughed this time, shaking his head. "It's no wonder Kat likes you so much. You're just like her. You'd rather die than say what's really on your mind."

"This is what's really on my mind."

"No, it isn't," he said. "Tell me, Boy, why you, of all people, hate me guts?"

I didn't know what to say.

He nodded. "That's what I thought. You don't hate me. You're just—"

"Oh, shut up!" I said, trying to come up with something. "What if I told you she came on to me last night?"

"So, did you do it?" he asked almost suspiciously.

Now we were getting somewhere. There was a little agitation in his voice. He was daring me to reply in the affirmative. I said, "Yeah, I did."

He stared at me. "You're worse than Kat. I can tell you're lying."

"What the hell are you talking about?"

"Number one, your eye twitches when you lie and you've lied to me before. Number two, she was too sore last night."

"You motherfucker!" I roared, my face flushing.

"I got you, didn't I?" he said.

He always got me. That was the fucking problem.

"Listen," he said and leaned in again. "I don't know what you think, I don't much care. I like you, Boy, for some reason, I do. And Kat loves you."

"Yeah, she told me she did," I said.

"She doesn't love you like that."

"Why not?" I asked.

"Cause she loves me."

I glared at him. "If you two are so in love, why aren't you married?"

He shot me a look, leaned back and put his paws behind his head. "Who says we aren't?"

I stared at him and got that sinking feeling. "Well, are you?"

"No." He shook his head and sighed. "She won't do it. She said it would ruin our relationship. I want to, but she doesn't."

"Do you think it would?"

He shook his head. "No, not at all. I'm not going to stop loving her because of a piece of paper."

No, he wouldn't ever stop loving her. I could see that. But would she ever stop loving him? That's all I had to bet on and it was a longshot.

"And I love her so much, probably too much," he said. "I put up with a lot of shit from her. You don't get to see her other side that much. She has a fury in her that you don't know."

"I saw it yesterday," I said. "I don't think she loves you as much as you think."

"Now why would she tear me car apart like that if she doesn't?" he asked.

"Cause she's crazy?"

We stared at each other. The moonshine got the best of us. We cracked up and laughed for what seemed like forever.

"Boy, let's have another drink," he said. "We'll call this one our last."

I matched him. I was at least going to drink him under the table if nothing else. "You better watch it, Filthy Phil or you might get sick on this stuff like you did the last time."

"Kat tell you about that, did she?"

"No, her mother did."

154

"Oh," he said, then his eyes widened and he got that goofy look on his face again. "Have you seen her tits? Blimey! What torpedoes!"

He held his hands out. We cracked up again.

"Shit," he continued. "The first time we came down here, I couldn't keep my eyes off them. And she was asking me all these stupid questions and I don't even know what came out of me mouth, then she suddenly hated me guts and Kat wanted to know why."

I chuckled.

"And I couldn't very well tell her, now, could I?"

"I think you should," I said.

"No, I can't do that."

We took another shot. Yee dawgy! He lit us both a cigarette. I smoked and said, "Tell me, Filthy Phil, what you think of me fucking your girlfriend?"

He shot me a look that said, *Now you're crossing the line*. He didn't know I was well over it. He muttered, "I think we covered that."

"You know, I think we didn't."

"What do you want me to say, Boy? That I think it's fantastic? Well, I don't. It pissed me off so much, I wanted to beat you to a bloody pulp. Then I saw you and I understood."

"Well, I am a good looking guy," I said proudly.

"Yes, you are, I suppose."

Well, now we were getting somewhere. I smoked and eyed him.

"But, alas, that's not what I meant," he said. "Kat likes to take care of people. You look like you need taking care of."

"It never crossed your mind that she would be attracted to me?" I snapped.

"No," he said.

"Of course not! What if I told you she wanted me to kill

you? Would that be good enough reason?"

He sighed. "Listen, that's all over now."

"So, you know about that, too?" I asked and put my cigarette in the ashtray.

"I know about it, yes."

"Is there anything that you don't know?"

He shrugged, "Not much."

"You son of a bitch!"

"Now, now."

"You motherfucker!" I yelled and stood, putting up my dukes. "Come on then! Let's have it!"

He scratched the side of his neck and said, "Boy, this is really getting tiresome."

"What?"

"Your jealousy."

"My what?!"

He smoked and stared up at me. "Your jealousy. Of me."

"I am not jealous of you! I hate you!"

"Yes, you are jealous of me and, no, you don't hate me."

"Shut up and stand up like a man!" I roared.

"No, you sit down."

I groaned. But I didn't sit down.

"Boy, I have everything you want," he said. "The cars, the clothes, the money, the undeniable good looks."

"Shut up!"

"But most of all, I have Kat. You can't stand that I have all this and her too, can you?"

Unfortunately, he hit the nail on the head. Why did someone like him get it all while the rest of us losers ate shit? Why? He didn't deserve her. Maybe I didn't either, but he sure as hell didn't. Guys like him always got what they wanted no matter what and there was nothing the rest of us, especially someone like me, could do about it. All we ever got was their fucking leftovers. I was sick of it, too.

"Boy, Kat is mine. She always will be. She may tell you

stories about how she hates me and wants me dead, but she crawls into my bed every night. Now, why do you think that is?"

I smirked. "Because of your big dick?"

"What does a big dick have to do with it? Nothing, that's what. She comes home to me because she loves me, Boy. And that's what you can't stand. That she loves me, which means, she'll never love you."

"She hates you," I said.

"Well, she's like that sometimes."

"I hate you."

"No," he said. "No, you don't."

"No," I said, nodding. "No, I do."

"Boy, jealousy is a very destructive emotion. And it's useless. Once you let it go, you'll be fine."

I didn't know what to say. I could have broken down and cried. I could have started to befriend him, like he was always trying to befriend me, for whatever reason. However, if I did that, there would be no more Kat. She'd just be some chick some other guy had to hold over my head. I could stare at her, I could fantasize about the two of us, but that would be it. Besides, I had enough friends, even if I didn't see them much since I'd met her.

"If she loves you so much," I said. "Why is she fucking around on you?"

"She isn't fucking round on me."

He was right. We hadn't had sex in…well, a long damn time. I said, "She fucked me a few times. Well, more than a few."

"Don't embellish."

"I'm not!"

"I know why she did it," he said. "And that's all you need to know."

"What if she doesn't really love you?"

"There's no question in my mind."

I sat down and leaned in towards him. "But what if one day you wake up and she's gone? I mean really gone?"

"That's not going to happen."

"Please. People fall in and out of love everyday."

"If people are really and truly in love, they don't fall out of it, Boy. And Kat and I are, really and truly in love."

He was just too smug.

"But I don't own her. She doesn't own me. We're together because we chose to be together. We may fight, we may want to kill each other, and yes, there's been times when that woman gets under my skin so much that I could... I couldn't have done a thing to her."

He stared up at the ceiling and smiled like a goofball.

"I could, however, break a few plates," he said and stared back at me.

I rolled my eyes.

"And she just stood there like I was baking a cake. That's why I love her. She's got no fear."

"Whatever."

"Boy, don't put so much into this whole thing, alright? It's just fun and games, that's all it is."

"Oh, really?"

"Next time she asks you to kill me, remember that."

"What does that mean?" I asked.

"It means..." And he smiled broadly. Every tooth in his big fucking head showed and seemed to be glaring at me. "That we get to have some really wild sex."

That did it. I jumped up and before he could blink, I punched him right in the eye.

"Ow," he said and held his head. "Why'd you do that?"

"You know why! Now get up!"

He chuckled and, still holding his eye, got up and grabbed my head. What was he going to do? Kiss me? Yes, but not like that. He head-butted me into oblivion. And as I went down, I knew I'd never win.

Long time no see.

Somehow, I managed to stumble to my room, where I laid down and closed my eyes, hoping the pain would go away. I slept the afternoon away. Isn't that what you do when you're depressed? Sleep? That's what I did. I don't know when I woke up, but it was dark outside. I sat up, held my spinning head and looked around wildly. I could hear a party going on downstairs.

What time was it? After seven. In the p.m. Damn, how long had I been out?

I got up, slipped on my shoes and went downstairs. Everyone and their mother was in there. Tiny sat in the corner by himself. He gave me a little wave. I gave him one back.

"Oh, it's Ray!" Mrs. Cumberland squealed and pulled me into the room. "Everyone, this is Ray!"

Everyone in the room hooted and hollered and I was suddenly surrounded by all these different people slapping me on the back and pushing drinks in my hand. I have never heard so many "how-do's" in my life.

I stayed there for a few minutes, looking around for Kat or even Filthy Phil. I didn't see either of them. But everyone else was having one hell of a good time. It looked like a really good party. But I didn't feel much like celebrating.

"Mrs. Cumberland," I said, trying not to look at her tits. "Have you seen Phil?"

"No, and I don't want to," she replied curtly.

I excused myself politely and slid out of the room. He was probably still pissed at me, but I was going to face him like a man. I was going to face him and tell him... I don't know what I was going to tell him. I'd gauge his reaction. Then I'd say whatever came out of my mouth.

I walked out of the house and looked around. About

thirty Caddys were parked everywhere, even on the lawn. I headed out towards the guest house, kicking pebbles as I went.

When I got there, I peered through the open door. The TV was on but no one was in the room. I called "hello" several times but there was no answer. I was about to give up when I heard a noise coming from the barn. The lights were on. Maybe he was in there. I just wanted to get this over with.

I went to the barn door, pushed it open and there—oh dear God, would I never learn! There they were! Everyone have a look! They were fucking just like the animals in the barn fucked, just like in some sleazy dime store novel.

He had her up against the stable. She bounced up and down, her legs wrapped tightly around his waist. She bounced up and down moaning, having the time of her life, hanging onto him and taking what he was giving. Taking it so much she gasped from time to time. She still had her cowboy boots on, but other than that she was completely naked. His pants were around his ankles, his shirt undone. His hands were in her hair, pulling it ever so slightly. His mouth sucked at her throat. He was giving it to her rough. And she was loving it.

The animals ignored them and they ignored the animals, just like they ignored everybody else in the whole fucking world. It wasn't Frank's world, after all. It was Katherine and Phillip's world. We just lived in it! They didn't care about anyone else. They only cared about each other and about fucking. They would never get enough of each other. They didn't care whose feelings they hurt or whose hearts they stomped on; it was just them, partners in crime, them against the world, them, them, them. There was not room for anyone else, no matter what she said.

I turned on my heel and I walked away from them and from their love and from their fucking. Let them have each other. I was done. Besides, I had been happier when I was miserable. At least I had that to go back to.

I had been with them for over six months. That was six months of my life I'd never get back. At least I wasn't limping anymore.

I resumed my empty life. I was over everything— women, money, everything. Nothing mattered anymore. I got a job as a bartender in some bar that was just like the other one, only busier.

I don't suppose I was depressed. Well, I was, a little. More like part of my life had just stopped and I had nothing to fill that void. Before I always had something to do, something to look forward to. Now, I had nothing. I looked at the future and saw a big empty space. I looked at the past and saw even less. I looked to the now and saw Kat. And that meant everything. And that meant nothing. She was gone now. She was gone to me. I'd never get her back. More importantly, I'd never get her.

I sometimes wondered why she didn't call me. Then I'd remember my number was unlisted. I wondered why she didn't come by the bar. Then I remembered that I was working at a different one. I would walk by their loft, stare up at the window and hope she would be looking out at the exact same time. She never was.

I could hear her now, "Good God, Ray, I don't have time to look out windows for you! You know my phone number, you know where I live, so stop acting like some dumbass and come over. Phil misses you."

Ugh! Even though I hadn't seen him in a long time, my hatred of him had not dissipated one fucking iota.

I knew New York was a big city. I knew, also, that if

she wanted to find me, she could. She knew people who could find other people. So, why didn't she find me?

Maybe, just maybe she didn't want to find me. That killed me, but not enough to pick up the phone. If I picked it up and dialed her number, what would I say?

"Hello? Kat? That you?"

"Uh, Ray? Ray! Why haven't you called me?"

"Well, I've been stupid, you know, and jealous and other stuff like that."

"Ray," she would say. "You are one stubborn son of a bitch."

Oh, and by the way, I found out about our signs, Cancer and Sagittarius. Get this: Cancer is a water sign, Sagittarius is a fire sign. Water puts out fire. They are two of the most incompatible signs in the zodiac! So, it was just as well.

Not that I believed in any of that crap.

A month passed, six, then a year. Then I was hailing a cab one day, and wouldn't you know it, she got out as soon as I opened the door. We stood there for a long moment staring at each other before she broke out into a big smile and threw her arms around my neck.

"Oh, Ray," she said and squeezed me tight. "How have you been?"

I pulled away from her and said, "No."

She smiled. "Where you been?"

"No."

"Oh, come on," she said. "Don't you have a kiss for your old friend?"

"Kat, no," I said and tried to push her off. But she wasn't having it. She leaned into me and gave me a kiss that sent shivers up my spine. God, I had missed her so much. My entire body began to ache for her. I pulled away first.

"Uh...no," I stammered.

"Ray..."

162

"Fuck!" I roared. "No, no and no!"

"Ray," she said. "I've missed you."

She leaned in for another kiss. She pulled away first. I stared at her, long and hard. Damn, damn, damn.

She tiptoed and whispered in my ear, "Let's forget all that. It doesn't matter anymore."

I stared at her. She seemed sincere but she had a knack for doing that.

"What do you say?" she whispered. "You wanna go somewhere?"

"Sure," I said and grabbed her, pushing my tongue into her mouth, tasting her sweet taste and allowing the love I felt for her creep back into my heart. I kissed her, knowing I would never let her go. I kissed her knowing she'd never be mine. But that was just as well. I was back in. And this time, it was going to be on my terms.

The cabbie said, "You getting in or not? I've not got all day!"

"No," I said. "We're gonna walk."

But we didn't walk. We ran. We ran all the way to my apartment and there we fell on the bed kissing and didn't stop all afternoon. This went on for months, just me and her with no mention of Filthy Phil, which was the way I had wanted it all along. Sure, she left me at night but I knew she'd be back the next day. That's all I had but it was good enough.

"I love you," I told her one day.

"Love you, too," she replied and kissed me. "Let's fuck."

So we did. I squeezed her tit and she moaned. I loved that sound so much. I slipped my hand down her pants and pushed her back on the bed. She lay back but kept her eyes on me as I rubbed her. Her hips raised a little and I bent down, pulling her pants off. I dove in and licked and ate at her until she grabbed my hair and pulled me to her.

"Oh, God," she moaned and kissed my face. "I can't take

it. Put it in! Oh, baby, put it in!"

I put it in and she grabbed onto me.

"I want a big one," she said, staring into my eyes. "Give me a big one."

I did my best, holding back as she ground against me but soon she was coming. I sucked on her nipple and bit it a little. She let out a wail and rose up and dug her teeth into my shoulder. I almost yelled with pain, but it felt so good when she did that.

"Harder, baby," she moaned. "Give me all you got."

I gave her all I had and then some. When we were done, I gasped for air. She was wearing me out. She wanted it almost everyday. She was always on top of me, wanting me. I let her have at it. She was insatiable. She'd come over to my apartment dressed only in a raincoat. She'd stop by the bar and take me into the stockroom. We were always fucking. I loved every minute of it and didn't try to figure out what she was doing or why she was doing it. This was all I had. But I knew why I was doing it and that's all that mattered.

Let me go.

Kat called me one day. "Let's go to the park."

"Kat, it's freezing outside," I said and pulled back the curtain in my tiny apartment.

"Come on, it's not that cold," she said.

"Okay," I said and hung up, got dressed and raced to meet her. She was sitting on a bench, staring out at the pond. Shazam sat at her feet. He was fully grown now and beautiful. They both looked up when they heard me.

"You're late," she said.

"I don't live near here," I said and scratched Shazam

behind the ear. "How you doing, buddy?"

We started walking. Shazam trotted ahead of us.

"Are you working today?" she asked.

"Nope."

"You wanna get some supper later?" she asked.

"Sure, why not?"

She smiled at me. "Cool."

"Is there something you want to talk about?"

She stepped on an acorn, which popped, smiled up at me and said, "Ray, do you want kids?"

I looked away.

"Ray?"

"Yeah, someday, sure, why not?" I said. "Why do you ask?"

"Just wondering."

"Oh." I sighed, stared at her for a moment. "You know, I almost had a kid once."

She stopped and asked, "What do you mean?"

I pointed to a bench and we sat down. "I knocked up a girl I used to date in high school. She had an abortion."

She stared at me, looking puzzled for a moment, then she shook herself and said, "That really sucks."

"Her name was Elise," I said for some reason, then a flood of memory came at me. I had really loved her. She didn't tell me until after she did it, the bitch. And then she told me not to call her house ever again. That had stung like a motherfucker, too. She had pushed out of her life. I got this sick feeling at the pit of my stomach that never went away.

I couldn't get close to any girl after that, to any woman. Except Kat. Then it occurred to me. Shortly thereafter, Elise had started going out with some jock, some big guy. She hadn't given me a second glance after that. She just tossed me to the side like a piece of trash. When Kat had appeared, it was like my second chance. Even if I had to kill, I wanted that second chance. I wanted to show the whole world that I was, for once, the better man. I wanted to show Elise she hadn't gotten to me.

All of a sudden, I saw everything so clearly. Was this why I had agreed to do all this? Oh, good Lord! Thank God I hadn't succeeded! What an idiot I was! All because of a girl who had hurt me. All because I wanted to show the world that I was better than they thought. It wasn't that I'd let it beat me. It's just that it had become a habit, the misery. It kept me afloat, aloof, out of touch with everything in a place where nothing mattered. In that place I couldn't get hurt, I couldn't be touched. I had let it fester inside me until it turned me completely sour.

It was simply the drug of unrequited love. It kept me from moving forward, from getting hurt. From doing anything with my life. But this wasn't just about the abortion. Or Elise. That had been the excuse I needed not to get things done, not to take risks. Not to live my life the way I wanted. My excuse not to get hurt again. I'd lived by it, but now, I wouldn't die by it. I suddenly felt free then. I felt like a weight had been lifted off my shoulders.

"Oh, God," I muttered.

"What is it?" she asked.

"Nothing," I muttered. I didn't want to share this. It was too much.

"Ray, is this why you haven't been married or whatever?"

"Yeah," I said. "It hurt me, okay? It fucked me up. I just didn't realize how much."

"Strange how people can hurt us like that, isn't it?" she said softly. "You know when my dad left, I hurt a lot."

I nodded at her.

"And every man I saw, I looked for my daddy. I looked for a man who would leave me, who would treat me like shit, like he did my mother. And I found them, plenty of

166

them. A few of them almost broke me, Ray."

I nodded that I understood.

"I'd given up finding anyone," she said and cracked a smile, then took my hand. "One day my friend Sissy and I were talking about New York and how we'd like to go. And I suddenly thought, today is the day! It was like my guardian angel was pushing me towards here."

"Yeah," I said.

"I begged her to go with me but she wouldn't," she said. "She dared me to go alone. Well, that was that. And I got in my car and I drove all the way here. Alone."

"I thought you took a bus."

"No, I drove," she said. "And I was scared shitless. I mean, you hear all these stories about how bad it is. Anyway, I got here and I met some really nice people. We had a really good time with all the money Mommy sent me up here with. In fact, those people stole most of it from me."

"That sucks," I said.

"Yeah, it did. I called home and Mommy wouldn't send anymore. She told me to get back in that car and come home. I knew it was about time, too. So, I packed my stuff up, carried it out of the hotel and guess what? My car had been stolen."

"Shit!"

She nodded. "So, here I am, alone, broke and without a car. I'm lugging this big suitcase around, too. I felt like such a dumbass. Then I thought, why not go to the track?"

I knew where this was going but for some reason, I didn't mind hearing it.

"So I went. I didn't know what I was doing. I didn't know a trifecta from a box bet, so I put everything I had on a horse called Sunshine. She lost, of course." Her eyes watered. "It just killed me and I started crying. I looked up and there he was."

She looked away, lost in memory. I stared off into the

distance with her.

"And there I was, a hick without a clue, and we just stared at each other. The whole world stopped for a minute. All I saw was him. Do you believe in love at first sight?"

"I guess I do now," I said and smiled a little.

"It certainly happens a lot, Ray," she said, smiling broadly. "I didn't believe in it, either but after I saw Phil for that first time, I knew it existed. And he walked over, picked up my suitcase and told me he was taking me to dinner."

I nodded and squeezed her hand. She squeezed back.

"And I stayed a little longer, having the time of my life and you know what? I'm still having the time of my life."

I smiled at her. I was, actually, very happy for her, oddly enough.

"And Phil accepts me, totally accepts me," she said. "I couldn't ask for anything more."

"He's dangerous, though, isn't he?"

"Not to me, no. He's no teddy bear but he's not a meanie, either."

Meanie? And then it occurred to me. She didn't see Filthy Phil as the rest of us saw him. He wasn't a thug or a barbarian or a menace to society to her. She just saw him as another person in the world, as she saw everyone else. She saw him as this great guy. She accepted him as she accepted everyone. He was no threat to her, so why should she worry?

I had to ask, "Why did you pick me, Kat? I mean, why me? Out of all the guys around, why me?"

She patted me on the back. "Cause you are so good looking, that's why."

We stared at each other for a long moment. Then we cracked up and we couldn't keep from it. We sat there in the freezing cold and we laughed. We couldn't help but laugh because we both letting go of something that had tainted us. And it was good to let it go.

She stood and said, "Come on, let's stop acting like a couple of pussies and go get a burger."

Compensation.

It was just after New Year's when Filthy Phil came into the bar. It was around two in the morning. I hadn't seen him but a few times since I'd been back with Kat, but I wasn't surprised when he sat down.

"Hey," I said.

"Hallo, Boy," he replied.

It was like we were old friends.

"You seen Kat today?" he asked.

I shook my head.

"She's not been home all day," he said, looking around. "I'm starting to get worried."

"I haven't seen her," I said knowing she was probably just pissed off at him about something and decided to make him miserable by her absence. But then I thought about it. I hadn't seen her since that day in the park, nearly a week ago. She'd called me to say she was "busy" once. But I didn't worry about it. I figured she'd call soon enough.

"Close up, Boy," he said and stood. "And help me find her."

I didn't argue. The last of the drunks were still lingering. I kicked them out without a second thought and followed him to his car.

"Hey, Boy," Tiny said.

"Hey, Tiny," I said and got into the backseat.

Filthy Phil took the front seat for some reason. I soon realized he was riding shotgun so he could look out onto the street for her.

We drove and drove and drove. A few times, he made

Tiny stop the car and he jumped out and ran up to some girl who resembled Kat from the back. He'd come back to the car, his head down, get in and tell Tiny, "It wasn't her."

This process was repeated over and over.

"If somebody's hurt her..." he muttered, shaking his head.

"No one's hurt her," I told him. "We'll find her. She's probably just mad about something. Don't worry."

"Don't worry? She's never done anything like this before."

I didn't respond, but I remembered the first time I met him he was looking for her. This was the sort of stunt she pulled. She liked to make people worry.

"Where to now, boss?" Tiny asked quietly.

Phil turned in the seat and stared at me.

"Have you checked the apartment?" I asked.

"I've called a billion times."

"Yeah, but if she's mad, she won't pick up."

"He's right," he said, turning back around. "Take us home, Tiny."

We arrived at the loft a few minutes later. He raced up the stairs, taking them not two, but three at a time. He threw the door open and yelled, "Baby?"

No answer. She wasn't there.

"Where the fuck is she?" he growled and looked around.

I shrugged. "I dunno."

We sat in the living room. He didn't turn on the TV, but just sat there staring at it. Soon, the sun came up and I was yawning.

"Go get some sleep, Boy," he said.

"You sure?"

"Yeah, I'll wait on her."

I started to the door.

"No, I mean here. Take your old room."

I stared at him.

"Please. Just in case I need you."

I nodded and went to my old room. It looked the same, though there was a new patchwork quilt on the bed and new curtains.

I got into bed. I heard him pacing in the living room. I smelled a cigarette. I heard him come to the door and crack it open. I shut my eyes. He peered in, sighed, then turned and left the door half-open. Now I could see him in the living room. He had a terribly anxious look on his face. He was sick with worry. I felt kinda bad for him. Kinda.

I glanced out the window. It was morning now, early morning. I closed my eyes and fell asleep then was suddenly awakened by the slamming of the front door. I bolted up. The door to my room was now almost completely open. Shazam was sitting at my feet. He must have let himself in. I scratched his head and looked through the open door and sighed with relief. She was home. She looked fine to me. Great. I could leave now.

I started to get out of the bed, but she was glaring at Filthy Phil. I fell back down and cursed under my breath. This would probably take forever and a fucking day.

"Hallo, baby," he said, smiling. "I'm glad you're home."

"Don't start with me," she said, crossing her arms.

Shazam, upon hearing her voice, leapt off the bed and raced into the living room. She patted him on the head once and said, "Sit". He sat.

"Good to see that you're alright," he said. "Where you been?"

"What's it to you?" she snapped.

He sighed, looked up at her. "It's just that I couldn't find you."

"I didn't want to be found."

"I was worried," he said.

"And it didn't do you a damn bit of good, did it?"

"Tell me where you were," he said softly, with no threat in his voice, only genuine concern. He really just wanted to know. Tell him so I can fucking leave.

"None of your fucking business." She started off. "I'm going to bed."

"Tell me."

"Fuck you, Phil," she said and wheeled around. "Fuck you."

"What's wrong?" he asked.

"Not a damn thing. Now shut up and let me go to bed."

He stood, looking at her. "Have you been crying?"

She scoffed like a child trying to conceal her emotions and tried to shrug it off.

"Did someone hurt you?" he asked.

I realized he said that because then he could find that person and settle the score. I rolled my eyes. Hurry up, hurry up!

"What's the matter?" he said anxiously.

"Nothing. Why won't you leave me alone?"

"I was worried about you, that's why. And now you come home at ten in the morning with a tear-stained face and I want to know why." He stepped in close to her. "Did someone hurt you?"

She stared up at him, her eyes full of tears, full of hurt. She shook her head.

"Then what?" he asked. "Did you get a ticket or something?"

She laughed. Not a happy laugh. A sad, resentful laugh. A coarse laugh. It was very unbecoming of her.

"Come on, baby, tell me what's the matter."

"What's the matter? I'll tell you. It's not you, it's me. That's what's the matter." She pulled a tiny, folded piece of paper out of the back pocket of her jeans and flipped it at him. He caught it with his right hand. "It says so right there, Phil."

"What's this?" he asked and unfolded it.

"Read it," she said then added, "Read it and weep just like I did."

He had it unfolded and began to read. (I didn't even know he could.) What he read made him stumble back and fall on the couch. He looked up at her with sheer hopelessness. "Oh, baby," he said and reached out for her. "I'm so sorry."

"Don't touch me," she snarled and stepped back, holding up her hands. "I don't wanna be touched right now."

His head fell to his chest. He looked like he was about to cry.

"See, Phil, it's not you. It's me."

"I'm sorry," he muttered. "I am so sorry."

"You're sorry?" she asked and bit her bottom lip. The tears escaped her eyes and ran down her cheeks. Her face flushed bright red. "No, I'm sorry. I'm so very sorry. I am so *SORRY!*

She wasn't sorry for him. She was sorry for herself. Shazam whimpered and left the room. He'd seen this all before. He knew where it was heading.

"Oh, baby," he said and stood. He leaned out for her.

She jumped back as though he'd slapped her. "I said not to touch me!"

He dropped his hand.

"It's over now, isn't it?" she asked. "I can't give you what you want. You'll find someone who can and you'll leave me."

He stared at her in disbelief. "I will never leave you."

"Yes, you will!" she said and hit her stomach with a balled up fist. "I'm a loser! I'm shit, Phil! That's what I am! I'm a piece of shit!"

What the hell was she talking about?

"No, you are not," he said and tried to take her in his

173

arms.

"Let me go!" she wailed and pushed him away. "You won't love me anymore."

"I love you more than anything. I'll always love you. No matter what."

"Didn't you read it?" she asked and picked it up, pretending to read. "I'll skip the medical jargon, I don't understand it anyway. It says, 'Katherine Cumberland is a barren piece of shit who can't have kids.'"

I sat up, my head reeling. *What?* Then it occurred to me. So, that's why she…yeah. I held my head as I grasped this. She wanted me to father her child. *Holy shit!* Was this what it was all about all along? Huh. I guess she had been serious when she said she thought I was good looking.

"You are not a piece of shit," he said. "It'll be okay, baby."

She rolled her eyes then took the paper and began to shred it into tiny pieces. "'It'll be okay?' Ha! Okay my ass! Wanna know why my mother hates your guts? Cause she thinks you can't give me a kid. She wants a house full of grandchildren. I'm her only hope cause neither of my brothers are interested. But she didn't realize I've got something wrong with me."

He sighed.

"You wanna know how? I'll tell you how. I was fourteen and was riding horses with Sissy. My horse jumped over a log and then skidded to a halt. I went flying over his head and…" She stopped and stared at him so sadly. "That's why. Mommy told me not to go riding that day."

"I'm so sorry," he said.

"Yeah, whatever," she said. She had the paper shredded. She threw it up into the air. The pieces caught in the air from the vent and hung airborne for a moment, then fell slowly to the floor.

"It was easier to blame you, I guess," she said, staring at

174

him, then, "I've been sleeping with Ray for the last six months."

The hair on the back of my head jumped up. I glanced over at the window, which was, unfortunately, painted shut. I mean, I know he knew, but we'd been drunk when I told him and that'd been a long time ago.

"I had a feeling," he said.

"I thought he might be able to…you know, help me," she said. "That's what I thought all along. But after a while, I knew something was wrong. I knew it was me. I just couldn't accept it. That's how in denial I was."

He didn't respond.

"I started thinking the same thing about him as I thought about you, that there was something wrong with him," she said. "But the doctor tells me it's just me." She paused and stared at him. "Did you think it was me that had the problem?"

"What's that?"

"Did you think it was me?"

"No," he said.

"Liar."

He shook his head. "I'm not lying to you."

"Ray told me," she said and licked the tears at the corner of her mouth. "That he knocked some girl up in high school. She had an abortion. What I wouldn't give for that baby. Why did she do that?"

"You know why."

"Yeah, I do," she muttered. "But, shit, what's wrong with me? I thought it was you. And then I thought it was Ray. But it was neither of you. It was me that had the problem all along."

"Baby, I'm sorry."

"Phil, that's all I ever wanted in my whole life. That's all I ever wanted!" She stomped her foot, then kicked something off the coffee table. "I never wanted any of this shit! I don't care about this shit! It doesn't matter! I want kids! I want a baby!"

"So do I!"

"All I ever wanted was a baby and I can't have it!" She looked over at him, wild-eyed, as if the realization had sunk in and she finally believed her own words. "I can't have it, can I?"

"Yes, you can. There are things—"

She laughed again. "You don't know shit, Phil. I can't have it!"

"Yes, you can! We can adopt."

She doubled over with menacing laughter. "Adopt! Oh, yes, they'll give us a baby right away! Filthy Phil and his loser girlfriend! Here you go! Want another one? This one's got blue eyes!"

"Listen—"

She glared at him, her nostrils flaring. "I could get as far away from New York as possible but still no one in their right mind would give me a kid."

"Yes, they will," he said and stepped over to her. "I'll buy one for you if I have to."

"Please," she hissed as he reached out for her, pulling her into his lap. She tried to get away, but this time he wasn't going to let her. He took her into his big arms and held her tight. She shook with sobs that would have waked the dead. She cried for about ten solid minutes. And he held her, let her spit and slobber all over his expensive clothes. He held her like he loved her, like she was the only person on earth.

And she held onto him for dear life.

That's when I realized, this wasn't my love story. It was their love story. As sick and deluded and as bittersweet as it was, it belonged to them. And everybody loves a love story, right?

He was kissing her then and she held onto him, kissing

176

his lips, opening herself up to him so he could console her, make her feel better. That's what love is. Right there. It was right there in front of my face. But it didn't make me feel sad. It was too beautiful to make anyone in their right mind sad.

"I love you," he whispered and kissed her eyelids, her forehead, the tip of her nose.

"I love you, too," she muttered back and let herself be kissed. "I love you so much."

"Shh, baby…"

She pulled back suddenly and laughed. "God, this was so stupid, wasn't it? What was I thinking?"

He grinned. "Only God knows that, baby."

She smiled, kissed him again then held his face in her hands. "I don't want you to ever leave me."

"I won't ever leave you."

"Promise?"

"I promise."

"Oh, Phil," she said. "Baby, I'm so sorry."

"It's over now. Shh."

She was kissing him more passionately. She stopped all of a sudden. She stopped cause she saw me standing in the doorway. We stared at each other for a long moment. She nodded slightly, tried to smile and muttered, "Hi, Ray."

I didn't know what to say. I just stood there, like a bump on a log, staring at her, wishing I could be the one to hold her, to make her feel better. Knowing I never would. She was never mine. She never would be. And, really, we both knew all along that she wasn't. But it didn't matter anymore.

Phil cleared his throat. Kat let out a long breath. I didn't move.

"I'll make us some coffee," he offered and tried to stand.

She held him tight, not letting him move and shook her head. "No. He needs to know."

"Know what?" I croaked then cleared my throat. "Know what?"

She didn't answer. She got up off his lap and sat down on the floor, Indian style. She reached for a cigarette, lit it, inhaled, exhaled and said, "Sit down, Ray. You can tell him now, Phil."

"Tell me what?" I asked and sat down.

He stared at me uncomfortably, then back at her. She nodded so he said, "Uh, Boy, I don't know how to say this, but it was a test."

"What?" I asked. "What was a test?"

"You killing me," he said. "That was a test."

I was flabbergasted. "What the hell are you talking about?"

"I wanted to see what you were made of," he said. "And then I wanted you to join my team."

I stared at him. "Your team?"

Kat interjected, "It's like this, Ray. When you first started working at the bar Phil noticed how the register was never short. He also noticed that you were never late and you never closed early."

I nodded. "Okay."

"And then one day someone left a bag of money there, do you remember that?"

I nodded again. It had been a small grocery bag full of money. It had been tempting to take it, but it wasn't mine, so I handed it over to the management guy I saw every few weeks.

"Well, that was Phil's." she said. "Tiny got drunk and accidentally left it."

"And I have to say, Boy," Filthy Phil said. "I was impressed that there wasn't one dollar missing. So I started thinking that maybe you were the kind of guy I would like to have work for me. That was when I decided to give you a little test."

"And what test was that?"

"You killing me," he said.

I still wasn't following. "What?"

"I wanted to see what you were made of," he said.

My head was spinning but I managed to get out, "So you wanted to see if I'd murder you?"

"No," he said. "I wanted to see what you were made of. If you could go through with it, I knew you'd be able to...go through other things."

"Okay," I said. "But why that? Why not just ask me directly?"

"I knew if I approached you, you'd turn me down," he said. "But if Kat approached you, I knew you'd consider it. She has a way of persuading people. Obviously it didn't go to plan."

"Because you shot me!" I shouted.

"Sorry about that," he said. "I mean, I really felt bad over it, still do. And the fact is, I was trying to shoot around you but you went the wrong way and..."

I just stared at him, then said, "Wait a minute. Let me get this straight. You wanted me to join your team but instead of just asking me, you sent Kat in?"

"Yeah," Filthy Phil said. "You see, the business was growing and I needed some help but I can't just hire anyone. I needed someone trustworthy, someone like you."

"I'm trustworthy?"

"Yeah," he said, then glanced at Kat then back at me. "You're loyal to a fault."

Not to him, to her.

"But that's also your greatest fault," he said.

"So did I pass the test?" I asked.

He shook his head. "No..."

I rolled my eyes. My head was spinning with scenarios. She hadn't picked me, he had picked me. I hated that. Of course, she didn't have to fuck me, but she did. I guess she did think I was special. Then it dawned on me. All fun and games—he had told me that. I was just too stupid to get it. Damn. What a damned idiot I was. Well, it all made perfect sense now.

"I'm really sorry about that, too," he told me. "But you're not cut out for the business. You're just not a criminal."

That was the greatest compliment I'd ever received. So he had wanted me to work for him and she had wanted my sperm. What the fuck?!

"But why didn't you tell me?" I asked but I knew. Kat couldn't tell me what was really going on or she wouldn't end up getting what she really wanted—a baby. I was just an added bonus. Me and my sperm. That's why she went along with it, why she'd told me those lies and strung me along. Why she kept saying how special I was. She believed I was special because he believed it. If Filthy Phil liked me then I would be the kind of guy who could father her baby. She needed me. She'd told me that a million times, "I need you, Ray." If Filthy Phil knew she was having sex with me, it'd be over. She had played a very tight game, keeping both him and me in the dark.

I started to say something to her about using me to knock her up, but looking at her tear-stained face, I couldn't. She was really hurting and I knew as soon as I left, she'd start crying again. And she wouldn't mention it to me because she had played a fool's game. She'd be too embarrassed. So, I let it slide.

"What's the fun in that?" she asked and rolled her eyes. "I've always said it and I'll say it again, you're not one for adventure, Ray."

She was one hundred percent crazy. God, if only she could be mine. But, alas, no, she would never be.

"You're crazy," I muttered.

"I never said I wasn't," she scoffed and stared at Filthy

Phil. They both cracked up.

I didn't know what to say.

She sighed and puffed on her cigarette. "It's a win-win situation for everyone."

"It's a win-win situation for everyone but me!" I roared. "What kind of sick people are you?"

"What kind of sick person would agree to go along with it!" she shot back.

She had a point. But that's what I thought people like him did. I went along with it cause it made sense to. I just got caught up. Besides I didn't think I had a choice. Hell, she never gave me a choice.

I glared at her. "I could have been killed!"

"He would *never* hurt you."

"He nearly killed me when I tried to…uh…uh…kill him! And the guns were real!"

"Oh," she said as if she'd forgotten about that. "Oh, no, your gun had blanks, Ray."

I rolled my eyes.

"Well, it doesn't matter anymore," she said. "It's over and I'm sorry, Ray, but it wasn't my idea, you know?"

"Sorry" was not going to cut it. Not in this case. I was almost livid but then I wasn't. I was just glad it was done.

Kat said, "It's time to get the envelope, baby."

Filthy Phil got up and retrieved a thick red envelope from the hall table and tossed it into my lap. He said, "Your compensation."

"My what?" I asked.

"Well, we need to pay you, don't we?" Kat said, then excitedly, "If it had worked out, we were going to surprise you with it. But it didn't and things got fucked up and… Anyway, see how much is in there!"

I stared at them, shook my head and opened the envelope. There was a fucking lot of cash in there. I said, "You both are fucking sick."

They shrugged simultaneously.

I stood ready to get the fuck out of there. I mean, fuck them. I went to the front door; they followed me.

"Ray, don't be mad at me," Kat said. "We're still friends, aren't we?"

I guess we were. That's all I had ever been to her. A friend, someone she could lean on, someone to help her out with her problems. A potential sperm donor. A would-be "hitman". A possible member of Filthy Phil's "team". But most of all, I had been her fool. I hated that most. But it was my own damn fault.

She leaned back into his arms. He hugged her. They stared at me. It was friendly stare. They didn't want me to go with any hard feelings. I stared at them, then for the first time, I realized it was true, they were meant for each other. They would be together forever. If they didn't kill each other first.

"Goodbye," I said and meant it.

"Ray…" she said.

I turned to her and said, "Just let me ask you one question, okay? If I'd been about to…_help_ you…"

"We'll never know Ray," she said sadly. "We'll never know."

She was right. But that was good enough for me.

She smiled at me. I wanted to smile back but there was no need. The smile, bit by bit disappeared. We stared at each and our looks said goodbye. And we meant it. It was really over now.

As I left, I heard him say, "I always said you should have told him."

"Shut it, Phil."

He shut it.

Close. But no cigar.

I walked all the way home, knowing I had to get out of New York, knowing I could now that I'd been "compensated". Compensated for what? For ruining my life?

But they hadn't ruined my life; in fact, they'd made it better. Even I had to admit that. I knew I was better off knowing them. They had shown me the way. They had showed me how to live. I hadn't realized before how lonely my life had been until they stepped into it. But I had to find my own someone. There was no sharing in matters of love.

And, through them, I knew that a deep, intense love was possible. If you were brave enough to surrender to it. Like they were. They were two of the bravest people in the world. That bastard had even saved my life in the bagel shop, hadn't he? And he hadn't hesitated to do so.

I shook my head, recounting the events as they happened. This was too fucking bizarre. But then I smiled. Yeah. Bizarre. That's what life is anyway, isn't it? Bizarre. I fell in love with a girl but she'd been the wrong girl at the wrong time. And then... I stood a little taller. I guess I was a pretty good guy if she wanted me to knock her up. Even if I hadn't theoretically won, she'd picked me out of everyone else and I guess that meant I had been the better man for once in my life. And it was good to know, I suppose, that Filthy Phil thought so highly of me that he'd go to those extreme measures to ask me to join his team. I guess I was a special guy even if I'd never believed it. I guess I could start to believe it now.

Fuck, what did it matter? I wasn't ever going to work for him. I felt the envelope. I'd earned every fucking cent of that. And I was going to have a helluva time spending it.

I knew I'd leave New York. Probably. Definitely. I mean, maybe.

And I'd sit somewhere, maybe on a sandy, white beach and stare up at an empty blue sky as empty as my heart would be then. I'd sit and rot and know that somewhere Filthy Phil was pulling Katherine Cumberland into his lap. He was showering her with love and affection and gifts. He would give her everything she wanted. Everything, that is, except her freedom. And a baby. But that could have been a lie, too, couldn't it?

I still hated his guts.

ROLLING IN THE DOUGH

RAISED AND GLAZED COZY MYSTERIES,
BOOK 29

EMMA AINSLEY

SUMMER PRESCOTT BOOKS PUBLISHING

MW01602853

CHAPTER ONE

"Don't talk to me yet," Orson Hawley mumbled over his steaming mug. "I haven't had nearly enough coffee this morning to deal with people."

"What's the matter with you today?" Maggie Sharpe looked over her oldest and sometimes favorite employee, despite his rough edges.

"Nothing," Orson said, waving her off. "I'm just an old man with an attitude."

"You're old enough to have earned the right," Myra Sawyer Macklin commented from behind the counter. As another Dogwood Donuts employee, Myra had plenty to say about Orson's demeanor. As the person he lived with, Maggie was content to let her have the last say.

Maggie left both of her employees out front and

retreated to the back to speak with her best friend and business partner, Ruby Cobb. With Valentine's Day just two weeks away, Maggie feared they would not be ready for the changes to the menu to celebrate the holiday all month long. She blamed herself and her upcoming wedding as the reason for the distraction.

"Sounds like Orson is right on track for a Monday morning," Ruby said. She stood over the prep table and massaged her neck and shoulders. "I don't know why, but I woke up with the worst knot in my neck this morning."

"I woke up with a headache," Maggie said. "For this being the season of love, it sure feels like the season of pains in the neck." She moved beside Ruby and began working at slicing up tomatoes for her Caprese salad.

"Why does this stuff have to smell so good?" Naomi asked as she passed by the prep table. She headed to the baker's area with the ingredients for her menu offering for the month of February. She had made her case with Maggie and Ruby to pick a new variety for the Month of Love.

Naomi assembled her dry ingredients. She measured the flour, baking soda, baking powder, salt, and sugar in a large bowl. She mixed eggs, almond extract, vanilla bean paste, and sour cream in a sepa-

rate bowl. Slowly, she added melted butter to the dry ingredients in the extra-large food processor, then poured the egg mixture in a little at a time. She added dried cherries into the mixture and formed the scones on the floured table top with her hands.

"Those look so good," Maggie said. She moved to the side of the baker's table and watched as Naomi's hands moved quickly. After the scones were formed and cut out, Naomi made a vanilla cream spread to be served with each scone.

"I hope so," Naomi said. "Unlike the two of you, I am a little out of my element here."

"Bologna," Ruby said from the prep table. "You're a pro at this by now. I'm very much in awe of you."

Naomi stopped what she was doing and looked straight at Ruby. "Thank you," she managed to say, blinking back tears.

"Well, I for one am in a great big hurry to try them because they look delicious," Maggie said. "Did you find the cherry jam I ordered? I think it's in the store room."

Naomi nodded. "I did find it, and I may or may not have already tried it out."

"What are you ladies carrying on about back here?" Orson asked. He pushed his way through the

swinging door into the kitchen and stood glaring at them with his arms folded over his chest.

"Orson, what's the matter?" Maggie asked him. "Is something wrong out front?"

"Well, if you gals must know, there is a crowd forming out there and Myra is doing her level best to handle it all by herself," Orson said. "All the while the three of you are back here gabbing about something or another."

"I'm on it," Maggie said. She set her knife down on the prep table and followed Orson out into the dining room. When she pushed through the door she stopped behind Myra, who was at the register waiting on a grand total of two customers.

"Maggie," Myra said when she saw her. "Is everything okay?"

Maggie dropped her shoulders and sighed. "I just thought I would check with you and make sure you didn't need any help."

Myra smiled at the two customers and assured them that she would be right out with their order. She turned to Maggie. "Did Orson go back there to fetch you so you could come up here and help me?"

"He did, but I don't want to make a big deal about it. He seems preoccupied about something," she whispered.

Myra glanced over Maggie's shoulder at the kitchen door. "I don't know what's wrong with him right now, but he hasn't been the same since yesterday."

"What happened yesterday?"

"I don't exactly know," Myra said. "Right after Brooks brought in the mail, Orson started in with his attitude. I don't know what he might have gotten in the mail or who it was from, but it upset him something awful."

"Have you tried to talk to him?" Maggie asked.

"Yup, and Brooks even tried," Myra said, shaking her head. "When Brooks can't get through to him, we know there's a real problem. He's even driving Gretchen nuts. She called me last night and asked if there was anything she could do to help."

"What are we going to do about this?" Maggie asked.

"I think we need an intervention of sorts," Myra said. "What do you think?"

"Lunch with the guys?"

Myra smiled. "I'll text Brooks."

"I'll text Brett," Maggie said. "It's his day off anyway." She headed back to the kitchen and went straight to her office after her phone. She scooped it

up off of her desk and sent a quick text to him. "You busy, Sheriff?"

"Just hanging out with the guys," Brett texted back. As county sheriff, days off were rare. "What's up?"

"Do you have time to hang out with another guy?" Maggie replied.

"Who do you have in mind?" Brett asked.

"Orson. Something is eating at him," Maggie wrote. "No one can get through to him. Maybe you can stop by here and see what you can do."

"Can I bring a friend?"

Maggie smiled as she texted. "The more the merrier. I think Myra is trying to get Brooks here, too."

"Do I get lunch if I come?" Brett asked adding a winky face emoji to his text.

"Of course, you do," Maggie responded. "I'll put your order in to the chef right away. How many are we feeding?"

"Two," Brett wrote back, with no further explanation.

Just before noon, Brooks arrived at the donut shop in his uniform. As police chief, his days off were also few and far between. Maggie held the door open for him when he came in. She directed him to the Old

Timer's table where Orson was already seated. Two more old men sat across from him. Brooks said nothing when he took a seat.

Maggie headed back to the kitchen and returned with a boxed lunch for him. She said nothing when she set it down in front of him. Orson eyed them and sipped his coffee. A second later, she spotted Brett's pickup truck in the parking lot. She watched with curiosity as he shut the driver's door and rushed around to the other side. He opened the rear passenger door. A second later, he stepped out. Wyatt, Maggie's grandson, was in his arms.

"Well, look at that," Brooks said. He sat back in his seat. "We've got ourselves a special guest for lunch." When they arrived inside, Brett retrieved a booster seat from the stack in the corner and carried Wyatt to the table. He pulled out a seat next to Brooks. Together, they secured the seat to the chair.

"What are you up to, buddy?" Orson asked the little boy. No matter what was on his mind, he was unable to resist eliciting a smile from one of the little ones.

Wyatt glanced up at Maggie once. She watched the interaction from behind the counter. He pointed his little finger at Brett. "Papa," he said.

Maggie had to turn around. She felt her insides

melt a little. When she did steal a glance back at the table, she caught Brett swiping a tear from his eye. It was the first time the small boy had addressed Brett as his "papa."

"Did you just hear that?" Brooks leaned over and hugged the little boy. "Is that your papa, Wyatt?"

"So, what's going on today, fellas?" Orson asked Brett. Myra said nothing as she set two boxed lunches in front of Brett and Wyatt. She returned a second later with a carton of chocolate milk for Wyatt.

"What's going on with you, Orson?" Brett asked. He carefully opened the carton for the small boy and arranged his lunch.

Orson glanced over at the counter, and then back at Brett and Brooks. "Oh, okay," he said, shaking his head. "I think I get what's going on here. You two guys are here because these ladies think I'm having a bad day, so they decided to bring you in here. Is that what it is?"

Maggie held her breath. Orson was onto her scheme, and he was less than impressed with it. She raised her head up in time to see him stand up from his chair and head out the door. Brooks and Brett turned around and watched as well. Orson walked slowly across the parking lot and climbed into his car to leave.

CHAPTER TWO

"That was a wasted effort," Myra said a half hour later. She was seated at the counter on one of the bar stools flicking sprinkles on a napkin she had unfolded.

"Agreed," Maggie said. She folded her hands beneath her chin and closed her eyes. She could hear Wyatt squeal with delight behind her. Brett had just revealed Wyatt's treat to him, his favorite chocolate sprinkle donut. Despite the fact that his grandmother and his father owned donut shops, the tot was not often given the chance to indulge in the pastries.

"Looks like we've got someone coming in," Myra said when the front door chimed.

"I've got it," Maggie said. "You just sit there and continue your game."

Myra chuckled and wadded the napkin up with the sprinkles inside it. Maggie rose from her seat and walked around the counter. She stopped in front of the iPad and faked her best customer service smile. Her mind was still on Orson and whatever was eating at him.

"Can I help you?" she asked the tall and lanky man in front of her. He was her age, maybe a little older, with a thick shock of gray hair standing up on his head. There was something about him that was familiar to her, even just slightly.

"I'm, um, looking for someone," he said. "And I heard he works here."

The man's words caught the attention of the two law enforcement officers behind him. Maggie watched as Brett's eyes went up and he glanced at Brooks.

"Okay, who are you looking for?" Maggie asked.

"My father," the man said. "Orson Hawley."

Maggie gasped. The breath went out of her, and she blinked rapidly. "I beg your pardon," she said. "Orson is your father?" It dawned on her that was the familiarity she noticed in the man's appearance.

"That's what I've been told," he said. He smiled weakly and extended his hand across the counter to her. "Toby Hawley. I have just recently come across

this information, and I would like to meet my father." Maggie looked past him at Brooks. Her eyes pleaded for help. Brooks stood and made his way across the dining room and stopped in front of the man.

"I'm Chief Macklin," Brooks said. He extended his hand to the man. Toby turned around to face him with his hands behind his back. After a moment, he extended his hand slowly and shook with Brooks.

"I don't want any trouble, sir," Toby said. He kept his eyes averted slightly.

Brooks smiled broadly and released his hand after a few shakes. "I'm not saying that you are," Brooks said. "But I know Orson very well. As a matter of fact, he lives with my wife and me."

Toby took an entire step back. "Orson lives with you? Is he retired now?" he asked.

"Oh, no, nothing like that," Brooks said. "We invited him to move in with us when he got a little older, you know, just so he wouldn't be by himself in that old house of his all alone when the water heater went out or some other appliance decided not to work."

Maggie was puzzled at the choice of words Brooks spoke. To her knowledge, the water heater had never been a problem for Orson in his old house.

She wondered why Myra had not stepped forward yet, either.

"Orson's house was that bad off?" Toby asked.

Maggie opened her mouth to speak but caught a stern shake of the head from Brett, who was watching the entire scene with keen interest. She was even more shocked when Brett whispered a few words to Delbert, one of the regulars at the Old Timer's table. The old man rose swiftly and took a seat next to Wyatt. Brett stood and walked across the dining room and leaned against the counter just a couple of feet from Maggie. "Go get Wyatt," he mouthed to her.

Maggie rushed around the counter and walked quickly to Wyatt. She unbuckled the booster seat restraint and scooped him up, then headed around the other side of the counter toward the back.

"Here," Naomi said just inside the swinging door. "I've got him. You might be needed out there." Maggie nodded and passed the baby off to her.

"How are you, Sheriff?" Brooks said. He made it clear who Brett was, despite his street clothes. "You enjoying your day off?"

"Just hanging out here with my grandson," Brett said. He looked at Toby, "So, you're Orson's son? I don't recall him ever saying that he had a son."

Every muscle in the man's body tensed when

Brett spoke. "Look," he said, holding a finger in front of him about hip level. "I'm just here to speak to my dad. I don't want any trouble with the cops. I just want to talk to my father. He owes me that much."

Maggie felt inclined to add her thoughts. "Mr. Hawley. Toby," she said. "You have to understand that Orson is family to all of us. The sheriff and the chief of police are close friends of his and they watch out for him. So, when a stranger wanders into his place of employment asking questions about him, we tend to want to circle the wagons around him." She caught an approving nod from Brett as she spoke.

"So, that's it? That's all I get? You're not going to tell me where he is?" Toby said. He stopped closer to the counter and pushed a stack of napkins over.

"Okay," Brett said. "That's about enough of that." He took a step toward the man.

"Hold up a second, Sheriff," Brooks said. He raised his hands up and approached the man. "This doesn't have to go like this, okay, Toby? Why don't we all just take a deep breath here for a second and relax."

"I don't want any trouble," Toby said again. Maggie bit her tongue to prevent herself from uttering a snarky reply about her napkins.

"Then why don't we do this," Brooks said. "You

give me your contact information and I will make sure Orson gets it. If he is agreeable to it, maybe this nice lady here will let us come back later tonight and use her restaurant as a meeting place. You can talk to your father, and we can make sure everything is fine and dandy."

Toby turned back to look at Maggie. "Fine, but I don't want donuts for dinner," he said.

"Maybe you could show a little bit of cooperation by picking up the mess you just made and thanking this nice woman for even being open to having us here in the first place," Brooks said. His words had an edge of warning in them.

"We could order pizzas," Brett offered. "But that's only if everyone is going to play nice."

"And if Orson agrees to it," Brooks repeated.

Toby nodded. He looked at the napkins on the floor and smirked. "Yeah, okay," he said. "If that's the way we're going to do this, that's fine." He turned on his heels and headed back out the way he came.

Brett walked to the windows and watched him leave. Maggie began cleaning up the mess. Her heart raced as she picked up the pile of napkins from the floor.

"Let's go back to the kitchen and talk," Brooks suggested.

Ruby met them at the kitchen door and nodded. "You go on back there, Myra," she said. "You're as involved in this as anyone." Naomi followed her out front with Wyatt.

"What in the heck was that all about?" Maggie asked.

"That was probably what has Orson so tied up in knots right now," Brooks observed. "I think he got a letter or something from this guy and that's why he has been so much fun to live with."

"Do you think this guy is legit?" Myra asked. Her eyes brimmed with tears.

"I don't know," Brooks said. He hugged his wife reassuringly. "I think the first thing we need to do is fill Orson in on what's happening. He has the right to know what happened here."

"Orson is back," Ruby called from out front.

"Looks like we're not going to have to wait very long," Maggie said.

"We need to be honest and lay everything out in the open," Brooks reminded them just before Ruby directed Orson into the kitchen.

He stopped just inside of the door and stared at each of them. "What's going on here?" he asked. "Did I just sprout a second head?"

"We just had a visitor, Orson," Brooks said. "He

said his name is Toby Hawley and he claims he is your son."

Orson hung his head and shook it side to side. "I know who he is. I just didn't think he was going to show up here."

"Is this guy legit? Because he shows some concerning signs," Brett said.

He shrugged. "He might be my son. I honestly don't know whether he is or not. I knew his mother. We dated once or twice fifty years ago, but she never once mentioned a pregnancy."

"What signs are you worried about?" Maggie asked.

"Well, smacking the napkins off the counter, for one thing," Brett said.

"He did that? I'm so sorry, Maggie," Orson said.

"It wasn't your fault," she said. "You're not to blame for anything."

"I have to say there was something in the way he stood," Brooks said. "He kept his hands behind his back like he was used to them being in handcuffs."

"I picked up on that too," Brett said.

"What does that mean?" Myra asked.

"Probably that he has served time in prison," Brooks said.

"This day just keeps getting better and better,"

Orson grumbled.

"Here's the thing," Brett said. "Brooks suggested a meeting, here tonight. We can order in pizzas and sit around and talk. If you're up to it."

"Meet him here? All of us?" Orson asked.

"Unless you don't want all of us involved," Maggie spoke up. "We're concerned about you, but we will all back off if you don't want our help."

Orson folded his hands in front of him and gritted his teeth. He began to shake his head back and forth. "No! I don't want you all involved," he said. "This is my problem to deal with and I would appreciate it if the rest of you would let me handle things on my own."

Shortly after, Maggie waved to Wyatt as Brett carried him back outside to his pickup truck. He had promised to return the little boy to his father in Hunter Springs. Despite the distraction from Orson's situation, she was still delighted with the visit from her small grandson and his relationship with Brett. She planned to call her son later to gush about the experience.

Naomi produced the first trays of her cherry vanilla cream scones around ten. Their debut had been pushed back with the dramatics of the morning. Maggie helped her carry more trays to the display

case and watched as the customers in the dining room flocked to see the new addition.

The trays were sold out before noon. "I think that ranks as a success," Ruby said when she sat with Maggie for their lunch break.

"The only problem I see with the cherry vanilla cream scones is the amount of extra work it takes to give the customer the jam and vanilla cream when they order one."

"Why don't we prep the jam and vanilla cream separately tomorrow?" Ruby asked. "We do have plenty of those one ounce cups with lids. I ordered a bunch of them several months back thinking we could use them for some of my boxed lunch ideas."

"Why didn't we ever use them?" Maggie asked. She tried to think back to when Ruby had ordered them.

"I found a divided container that worked better," Ruby said. "Anyway, we have a bunch of them just sitting in boxes back there in the store room."

"This is why we have such a good partnership," Maggie said. "Because at least you know what you're doing."

"And you don't? Maggie, you have made this place a raging success," Ruby said.

"Thank you for saying that." Maggie blushed. "I

was just kidding around, but that is really nice of you to say."

Orson stood in front of the counter arranging the stack of napkins in front of the register and cleared his throat. He glanced twice in their direction, then cleared his throat again.

"If there's something you want to talk about, just come on over," Ruby said. Orson folded his arms and headed into the kitchen.

"What do you suppose that's about?" Maggie asked.

Before Ruby could answer, Orson pushed through the swinging door again and made a beeline for their booth. "I want to say something," Orson said.

"Okay," Ruby said. "We're all ears."

He cleared his throat again. "I may have been too hasty earlier," he said. "And far too rude about the subject. Heck, I have been rude all morning, and I apologize for it."

"You don't have to apologize, Orson," Maggie said. "We're all family here."

"She's right, old man," Ruby said with a wink.

"That is more kind than the two of you have to be to me," Orson continued. "But as much as I love this little family we have here, I am running out of time in my life to connect to any of my own family. So, if it is

alright with you, I would like to arrange that dinner with Toby tonight."

"Okay," Maggie nodded. "We can make that happen. The question is, who do you want to be here?"

"I think it's a good idea to have at least Brooks and Myra here," Ruby chimed in.

Orson agreed. "I'd like to have the two of you and Brett around as well. I'll ask Naomi if she would mind sitting with Lexi while her parents are here."

"Okay, then," Maggie said. "Why don't you contact Toby and set it all up?"

"And we'll take care of the pizzas," Ruby said. "You just let me know what you want, and I will arrange to have them delivered."

"Thanks," Orson said. He turned to leave, then stopped and faced them again. "You have to know how hard this is for a man like me. Making apologies and amends has never been a talent of mine. But I am trying."

"That's all anyone can ever ask for," Maggie said. She stood up and embraced the gruff older man.

"Alright, alright," Orson said, smiling. "Enough of that. You two finish up here so I can take a break. All you do is sit here and eat." He muttered to himself all the way back to the kitchen.

CHAPTER THREE

Maggie carried a small box from the backseat of her car through the doorway into the kitchen just after six that night. Ruby held the door for her. "What are those?" she asked Maggie.

"Wine glasses," Maggie said. "I bought a couple of bottles of wine to go with our pizza."

Ruby chuckled. "I made a couple of cheesecakes when I got home from work," she said.

"We're too much sometimes."

"Who's too much?" Myra asked from the store room. She appeared with a stack of napkins for the front.

"The two of us," Maggie said. "I brought wine and wine glasses, and Ruby made a couple of cheese-cakes for dessert."

Myra cackled. "Then I don't feel so bad for baking garlic bread sticks," she said. They laughed together.

"What's so funny?" Orson asked from the kitchen doorway.

"Just the fact that the three of us aren't satisfied with simply ordering pizza," Maggie said.

"Whatever you say." Orson shrugged and headed back out into the dining area. Toby was expected to arrive by seven. The pizzas had been ordered and scheduled to arrive shortly afterward.

"Did you notice what he's wearing?" Myra asked quietly.

"His suit? I saw that the moment I got here," Ruby said.

"It's the third thing he tried on," Myra said. "He's so nervous about all of this."

"I'm nervous for him," Ruby said.

"I wonder what Brett and Brooks found out about Toby," Maggie said. Myra's eyes widened. "What? Do you honestly think the two of them haven't run that man's name through every database available to them? I bet they show up here with his entire legal and credit history."

"Printed out, in triplicate," Ruby added.

Maggie shook her head and picked up the wine

bottles to place in the cooler until dinner. Ruby searched the storage room for dinner plates and cutlery while Myra texted Brooks. He had gone to pick up Brett, explaining that the two of them had police matters to discuss before the visit. All three of the women joked that they were sure who the subject of their discussion was.

Shortly before seven, Maggie heard two car doors closing just outside of the back door. Brooks and Brett had arrived at last with very little time to spare. She hoped that it was the two of them, because allowing Toby to walk through the back of her business was not something she wanted to do.

"About time," Myra said to her husband when he walked into the kitchen. Maggie smiled at Brett and noted the grim look on his face.

"You look like the cat who ate the canary," she said when he made his way up to her. "Why do I think you have some information about this Toby person?"

"Because I do," Brett whispered. "And so does Brooks."

"Someone just pulled up out front," Ruby announced. She walked back out into the kitchen from the office where she had just been to check the cameras to watch for Toby.

"Well, if that's the pizza, they're early," Myra said.

Maggie headed to the front and found Orson watching out the front windows. He turned to look at them, pale faced, as they all filed in from the kitchen. "I think that's him," he said.

She watched as Toby stepped out of his car. He moved around behind the car and approached the passenger door. He opened it and a woman stepped out. She continued to watch as they made their way up the sidewalk and to the front door.

The woman entered first. She looked around the room and spotted Orson. "Well, if it isn't the absentee father, in the flesh," she said. Her voice had the quality of a yelping chihuahua.

"Hey," Myra said. "Let's be nice to each other."

Orson turned toward Toby. He inhaled and stepped toward him. "I'm Orson Hawley," he said, extending his hand.

"Why don't you explain yourself first," the woman said.

"I can speak for myself, Kara." Toby moved ahead of the woman. "I'm Toby." He held out his hand and moved toward Orson.

"It's not that easy," Kara said. She stepped

between them and pushed Toby's hand back. She placed herself in front of Orson and folded her arms over her chest. She was dressed in a pair of ill-fitting jeans, tight and slung low on her hips. Her abdomen hung over the waistband, and she was barely covered by the button-up flannel shirt she wore over a tank top.

Maggie felt her ire rise like bile in her throat. "Why don't we all take a seat and calm down?" she said. "The pizzas will be here in just a few minutes. We can eat together and let the conversation flow."

Kara turned to look at her. "Who are these people, Toby? Why are they even a part of this?"

Maggie waited for Toby to answer the question. When he failed to respond, she decided to weigh in again.

"Well, I'm Maggie Sharpe, owner of this place you're standing in," she said. "And that's my business partner, Ruby Cobb."

Toby turned to his companion. "I told you, these people set up this meeting," he said. "Let's just please have a seat so I can talk to my father." He held out his arm to the woman. Kara grumbled as they walked to the table Ruby had arranged in the middle of the dining room.

"So, where is this pizza anyway?" Kara said when she sat down.

"It is on its way," Myra said with a smile. "By the way, my name is Myra Macklin, and this is my husband, Brooks."

"And you two are the ones sponging off of him and living in his house?" Kara snapped. Toby sat back in his chair and remained silent.

"Well, the truth is, they do not live with me," Orson spoke up at last. "I live with them. It's their house and they created a room for me there."

"Oh, really," Kara said. "Well, you do know that a lawyer might see that differently. Why would a young couple take in an old man, anyway? If what you're saying has any truth in it, I think that's fishy."

"Kara," Toby said weakly.

"No, I want to know," Kara said. She raised her voice. "Why do you even have to work? Don't you receive some sort of retirement money?"

"I work because I enjoy being around these people," Orson said. "And I would really like to have this conversation with Toby."

Kara's mouth fell open. She looked over at Toby and smacked him hard on the leg. "Are you going to let this jerk speak to me this way?"

"Hey," Brett said. "Name calling is not okay."

"And just who are you?" Kara fired at Brett.

"Kara, stop," Toby urged her.

"I'm the county sheriff, and he's the chief of police." He pointed at Brooks.

Kara turned to Toby. "You are being harassed by the cops now? That's just wonderful."

Maggie stood up and headed to the door to meet the pizza delivery driver. She could hear more murmuring between Toby and Kara behind her while she paid for the pizzas. Brett appeared behind her to help carry the boxes back to the table.

"Finally," Kara said. She stood up and made her way to the pizza boxes before Maggie and Brett set them down.

"Let's hang on a second," Orson said. Maggie looked over at him. His face was reddening and sweat dripped down his forehead. "Why don't we all have a seat and let the two of them set the pizzas down before we jump in?"

"Are you serious right now?" Kara asked. "You abandoned him for all these years, and you want me to step back from the pizza boxes?"

"We don't even know if I'm Toby's father," Orson muttered. His patience was clearing wearing thin.

"Yes, we do." Kara turned to Toby. "Tell him! Tell him what you found online."

Toby sighed and cleared his throat. Kara pushed Maggie out of her way and began opening the pizza boxes. "When I submitted my DNA to the genetic search website, it matched with Orson's and said he was a close relative or a parent," Toby said.

"Orson, did you take a DNA test?"

Orson shook his head slowly. "I have never submitted my DNA for testing to anybody," he said. "I don't have any clue what you're talking about."

"Oh, come on," Kara said. "One look at the two of you and it's easy to see that you're father and son."

"You did know my mother, didn't you?" Toby asked. "Gladys."

Orson nodded his head. "I did know her, and we went on two dates," he said.

"So, you clearly could be the father." Kara smirked.

Orson shook his head. "To my memory, I'm not so sure that's possible."

"I've heard about enough of this," Kara said. She carried her plate stacked high with pizza back to her chair. "What are you going to do to make up for this? You owe Toby back child support."

Brett chuckled and shook his head. "Okay, that's not how this works," he said.

"I don't think you need to step into this, Sheriff,"

Kara said. "I know a very good attorney who loves to sue the cops."

"Okay," Orson said. He planted his hands on the table and stood up. "Toby, if you would like to have a conversation, one on one, you know how to reach me. This dinner is over with. I am tired and I want to say goodnight."

"Are you serious? You coward! I can't believe you're going to run away from your responsibilities again," Kara shouted. The nasal quality of her voice only increased when she raised it. "Slime! You are nothing but a slimy, grimy man!"

Orson pushed his chair back and walked away from the table. He made it as far as the counter before he collapsed into a heap on the floor.

Brooks was the first one to Orson's side. He eased him onto his back and checked his airway. Myra was right behind him. She knelt beside him and burst into tears. Maggie looked up at Brett. He moved to the side of the room with his phone up to his ear. Wordlessly he handed his cell phone to Brooks.

Maggie watched helplessly as Brooks attended to Orson with the phone to his ear. Sirens wailed in the distance while Myra continued to cry by his side. Ruby stepped back and behind the counter. Maggie

noted her stare as she kept Toby and Kara in her line of sight.

Kara continued to eat the slice of pizza in her hand while the ambulance pulled into the parking lot. Lights reflected off of the stainless steel refrigerators behind the counter. Maggie would remember this moment for the rest of her life.

CHAPTER FOUR

Maggie stood up again and made her way to the water fountain. She glanced at the clock. It was just after midnight. Myra and Brooks had gone home around ten o'clock to see Lexi. Naomi texted her after she left the Macklin house. She planned to join Ruby to open the donut shop the following morning.

No one had come to see her since she arrived behind the ambulance just after eight. Brett had gone home for the night and Maggie had argued with him about leaving. She was determined not to leave the hospital until there was more word about Orson and his condition.

Around three in the morning, someone shook her by the shoulders. Maggie woke up, looking into the face of a nurse she had not seen before. He offered

Maggie a Styrofoam cup filled with piping hot black coffee and asked her to follow him.

"You're here with Mr. Hawley, is that correct?" he asked her when they moved to the hallway.

Maggie nodded her head. "Is Orson alright? What happened?" she said.

"Mr. Hawley has suffered a transient ischemic attack also known as a mini stroke," the nurse said. "We are still unclear how much damage he has suffered, but since he was brought in so quickly there is a very good chance of recovery. However, given his age we can't be sure just what level of recovery we are looking at."

There was a momentary pause. Maggie tried to calm her thoughts, unable to think of questions to pose.

After a few moments, the nurse spoke again. "He is currently under sedation, just so we can give his brain and his body a rest." Another long moment passed. "Can you tell me what happened last night? Was Mr. Hawley drinking or under any severe emotional stress?"

Maggie wiped away the tears from her face. "There was a young man who just showed up and started making claims that Orson was his father."

"Oh, wow," the nurse said. "That can be a very

stressful situation. Was there anything else that happened right before he collapsed?"

Maggie nodded. "We had arranged to have a meeting at my place of business with the man who claimed to be his son," she explained. "There was a woman with him that none of us had met before and she began tearing into Orson about being a bad father. Even the man claiming to be his son tried to get her to leave Orson alone, but she was relentless."

The nurse nodded. "It sounds to me like this was brought on by acute emotional distress in addition to age and high cholesterol, although the official call will have to come from the doctors," he said. "Was Mr. Hawley not aware that he had a son?"

Maggie shook her head. "The man claims his DNA matched another online profile which is linked to Orson," she said. "But Orson claims that he has never once submitted a DNA sample. I don't know what is going on."

"Wow," the nurse said. "That's some mystery to solve there."

"It's not the only mystery we have to figure out," Brett's voice called behind her. Maggie turned around to find him standing ten feet behind her, dressed in his work uniform.

"What's going on?" Maggie asked him. The nurse waited next to her.

Brett sighed and nodded his head at the nurse. "I suppose you're discussing Orson's condition," he said.

"A mini stroke possibly brought on by acute stress and high cholesterol," Maggie said.

"Well, if that was brought on by stress, we sure don't want him hearing about what we just found," Brett said.

"Okay, it has been a long night, and now you're scaring me," Maggie said. "What's going on?"

"We just got a call from a motel out on the highway halfway between here and the state line," Brett said. "Kara Donaldson, the woman who showed up with Toby, was found in the parking lot behind the motel, run over by a vehicle and left for dead."

"And Toby? Is he hurt? Even if he turns out not to be Orson's son, that will really upset him."

Brett shook his head. "Right now, Toby is sitting in a cell at the sheriff's department waiting for his lawyer to get back in touch with him," Brett said. "We have just picked him up for questioning in Kara Donaldson's murder."

CHAPTER FIVE

Maggie left her car at the hospital. She followed Brett through the hospital parking lot to his car just before four in the morning. Bradley had offered to pick her car up after work with his kitchen manager Zeke Soren and drive it back to her house later in the morning. For the time being, Maggie planned to go home and sleep for a few hours.

She was awakened at eight-thirty by a phone call. It was Myra. "The hospital just called," she said. Maggie wiped the sleep from her eyes. Her blood chilled.

"What did they say?" Maggie asked.

"Orson is awake, and he's talking," Myra said. "He's asking to see his family. I took Lexi to daycare

already and was going to head over to the hospital. Do you want me to come and pick you up?"

"Yes, please stop by here," Maggie said. "I just need a few minutes to get ready." Myra promised to be there within twenty minutes. Maggie rushed to take a fast shower and dress. She texted her son that she would pick her car up herself just before Myra pulled up in front of her house and beeped her horn.

"I don't know what we're going to find when we get there," she said when Maggie climbed into her car.

"What do you mean?" Maggie asked.

"I mean, I don't know if Orson will have any lasting effects from the stroke," Myra said.

Maggie understood what she was trying to say. "Whatever the case is, we won't let him see it in our faces," she promised. Myra turned slightly toward her. "As far as I know, he hasn't been told about Kara's death and Toby's arrest."

"I didn't think he had," Maggie said. "I have no plans of mentioning anything to him."

"But what if he asks us about Toby?" Myra said. "It's just natural that Orson is going to be curious about where the man claiming to be his long lost son is, and how he reacted after collapsing."

"I know." Maggie nodded. "I think we can tell him that he took off right after the ambulance left."

"Should we tell him that Kara ran back in and swiped a box of pizza?" Myra asked wryly.

Maggie shook her head. "That might force us to have to explain where she's at now. And if we tell him she is in the county coroner's office, the next logical question will be-"

"'Where is my son,'" Myra said. "Although, I just can't put my finger on it, but I don't think this guy is his son."

"He looks like him," Maggie admitted.

"Only slightly," Myra said.

"I can't get the DNA test out of my head." Maggie frowned. "How is it that the history site could link the two of them together, but Orson claims he never took the test?"

"Do you think he did take it, but just forgot?" Myra asked.

"Does that seem like something you would forget about?"

"No," Myra said. "It honestly doesn't sound like something I would forget about."

Maggie gazed out of the window. "But it also doesn't sound like anything Orson would ever have done."

Myra pulled into the hospital parking lot and parked close to Maggie's car. They walked in, gave their names to the receptionist, and were shown to Orson's room. Myra had to stop twice to compose herself before they entered the room.

Maggie kept to the edge of the room at first. An attendant was checking Orson's vitals when they stepped in the door. She could see his long form under the sheet and thin blanket.

"Orson," Myra said when the technician left at last. She picked up his hand and hovered over him. "Can you hear me? Orson? It's Myra."

Maggie stood at the foot of the bed. She had a full view of Orson, and watched as he opened one eyelid and peeked at Myra, then quickly shut it again. She watched him for another moment. When he looked again, Maggie was convinced that the old Orson was still in there somewhere.

"Myra," Maggie said. "Maybe you should run down to the nurses' station and tell them he needs more water. I think his pitcher is empty."

Myra looked up at her, questioning. Maggie held her finger to her lips, and then held it up in the air and pointed at Orson. Myra grinned and nodded. "Okay, sure," she said and even picked up the water pitcher from the table next to the bed.

"As a matter of fact, I think I'll go with you," Maggie said with a wink. "I could surely use some more coffee this morning." She marched in place for a moment. Myra followed suit. They stifled their giggles and silently watched Orson.

A moment later, his eyes popped open, and he sat up slightly. He was wide-eyed when he found Maggie and Myra staring back at him. "Welcome back, Orson."

"Thought you went for coffee," he whispered. His voice was weak, and he spoke slowly.

"Thought you had a stroke," Maggie said.

"Well, I sort of did," Orson said. He raised his right hand slowly. His fingers were drawn together, tucked in close to his palm. "It's hard to straighten my fingers out. And my foot isn't working so well, either."

Myra cleared her throat. "Can you walk?"

"I think so," Orson said. "I mean, they dragged me out of bed this morning by my hair and made me use one of those old folks' walkers to relieve myself. I made it to the bathroom okay."

"That's good news," Maggie said with an encouraging smile. "Have they mentioned anything about physical therapy?"

Orson shook his head. "Not yet, but they are

threatening me with it," he said. "In fact, they have said that I might need to spend a little time in a rehabilitation center, but I don't really want to do that."

"We should check into the possibility of having the physical therapy take place at home," Myra suggested. "That way you can get out of here and get back home to your own surroundings as soon as possible."

"Okay," Orson said. He seemed surprised by her statement. "But what about this guy, Toby? What if he tries to step in and take over things for me. Can he do that?"

Maggie shook her head. She hesitated before she spoke, The fear and apprehension were clear in Orson's eyes. "I don't think he can just claim to be your son and then swoop in and take over your life."

"Right. It isn't like you suddenly became a child again overnight and lost the ability to make decisions for yourself," Myra said.

"I don't see how this guy thinks he is my son," Orson said slowly. "No matter what that DNA test claims."

Myra and Maggie exchanged a look. "Speaking of that, are you sure you never, ever took a DNA test somewhere? Not even at the doctor's office?" Maggie asked.

"I have never taken a DNA test," Orson said. "Not even once. Not in my life."

"Then Toby must be lying about the test," Myra said.

"But you did know his mother, right?" Maggie confirmed.

"Sure. I knew her," Orson said quietly. "I think I even took her to dinner once or twice."

"But did you ever, you know?" Myra asked.

Orson began to chuckle. His laughter led to a coughing fit. Maggie watched with concern while he coughed and coughed.

"Not that I would ever kiss and tell," he whispered. "But I sure don't remember things going that far. I mean, we did go back to her place."

"Okay, we get the picture," Myra said with her hands up and her eyes shut.

"What happened to her?" Maggie asked. "This woman, whoever she was. Whatever happened to her?"

"As far as I know, she went on to be a nurse somewhere," Orson said. "She knew my brother better than she knew me. After our second date, I went into the army, and she stayed back home."

A nurse stepped into the room just then and announced that Orson needed to be moved for a test.

She waited patiently while Myra and Maggie said their goodbyes. As she was leaving, Orson gripped Maggie's hand with his good one. "Please don't let them get control of me and my life," he said. "Please stop them."

"Who, Orson? Are you talking about Toby and his girlfriend?" Before he could answer, the nurse stepped between them. Maggie nodded to Orson as she turned to leave his hospital room. She didn't know what had him so concerned, but no matter what, she'd go to the ends of the earth to protect Orson.

CHAPTER SIX

"What are you going to do now?" Myra asked when they walked out of the hospital's entrance together a short time later.

"What do you mean?" Maggie asked. She was still focused on Orson's request.

"I heard what he said to you," Myra said. "What are you going to do? How can we keep Toby from attempting to gain control of Orson's life? I'm sure that's why he's here. They seemed surprised when they found out that Orson's house wasn't much to look at and that he lived with us now."

Maggie was stalling a little with her answer because she was unsure herself what she could do. "That makes me think he knows where you live."

"He would have to know where we live if he sent

a letter to Orson," Myra stated.

"You're right," Maggie said. "I think the lack of sleep is getting to me. Listen, we're going to make sure nobody gets to Orson. There's no way anyone can change Orson's status without his permission, and a man with no proof that Orson is his father really ought to have zero legal standing."

"Maybe you better head back home," Myra said. "Are you sure you're okay to drive back to Dogwood Mountain?"

"I think I'll stop by the donut shop here first," Maggie said.

"Okay," Myra said. "I'm going to head back and help Ruby and Naomi out for a few hours. After that, I'm heading over to the Dogwood House to see Gretchen. I know she's having fits that she can't get away from the bed and breakfast right now. She said she's got a full house but hopes to be able to see him tomorrow."

"Poor Gretchen. I'm lucky I have the staff I do, otherwise, I don't know that I'd be able to see him either."

"I'll do whatever I can to help her and you," Myra said. "See you later."

"See you," Maggie said. "And thanks for bringing me along with you." She waved before getting into

her car and heading the short distance to the donut shop. Her son's truck was in the parking lot of the old filling station that had been remodeled into the donut shop. Maggie was pleased to see Zeke's motorcycle parked next to it.

"Mom? I didn't expect to see you," Bradley said from behind the counter. "I got your message about the car."

"Hey, Son. Any chance I can get a cup of strong coffee?"

"You bet." Bradley nodded. "Why don't you go in the back, and I'll bring it to you."

"Is Zeke back there?" Maggie asked.

"Yes. He's trying out that new scone recipe he got from Naomi. Or at least trying to figure out what she did to make them so good."

"Oh, so are we keeping recipes secrets from each other now?" Maggie chuckled.

"Not exactly," Bradley said. "Naomi shared the recipe, but he hasn't made them come out quite the same just yet."

"Ah, I see." Maggie headed back to the kitchen. Zeke stood over his table pressing the palm of his hand into a circle of scone dough. The table was a bit of an upgrade from the old baker's table he had used. "What seems to be the problem?"

Zeke looked up and jumped a little. He smiled slightly when he saw her. "You took me by surprise," he said. "I'm here working on my third attempt at the cherry vanilla cream scones."

"Is it the vanilla cream you have an issue with?" Maggie asked.

Zeke shook his head. "No, not the cream," he said. "I even stockpiled a bunch of that cherry jam you guys are serving with them. I'm having trouble with the scones themselves."

"What seems to be the problem?" she asked. She bit her lip to keep from laughing right out loud. "Is it coming out tough?"

Zeke's eyes widened. "Yes! That's exactly what is happening," he said.

"Show me how you're flattening out the dough before you cut the scones into shape," Maggie said.

Zeke nodded and moved the dough around in a half-circle, then began pressing his palms into it again. "See? I'm doing like I have always seen other bakers do," Zeke said. "I don't think I've ever had such a problem."

"I think I know what's wrong," Maggie said.

"Please tell me." Zeke stepped back from the table. "Enlighten me as best as you can because it's just gotten worse lately and I can hardly stand it."

"Worse since you have gotten this new table?" Maggie asked.

Zeke began nodding his head slowly. "As a matter of fact, yes," he said. "Wait, how did you know that?"

"Because the lower table gives you more power in your hands, Zeke," Maggie said with a laugh. "You are overworking the gluten. You're stronger than you realize and that makes the scones tough. I bet your homemade bread isn't great, either."

"Only the no-knead variety." Zeke laughed. "Okay. I see your point. I've noticed that I can pack more punch in everything with this new table."

"You'll have to let me know if the next batch turns out better," Maggie said.

"So, Mom," Bradley said. He entered the kitchen and set a large to-go cup of steaming coffee in front of her. "What brings you by? I figured you'd be at home trying to catch up on lost sleep."

"I thought I'd check in with you before I went back home," Maggie said. "I had a question for Zeke, too. I suppose you could answer this yourself, but he's the one with the career-long stint in the service."

"Those are a lot of words to say you came to ask Zeke because he's older and you figured he would know more than I would," Bradley teased.

"Pretty much." Zeke laughed. "So, what's

going on?"

Maggie sipped her coffee before she began. "Okay, here's my question," she said. "Is there any way that someone who served in the military fifty-plus years ago might have anything on file that could be used in a DNA test? Like a blood sample, maybe?"

"Why would the military do DNA testing?" Zeke asked.

"I don't know, but I'm just wondering if there is a way they could or would have," Maggie said.

"I'm not sure they would have had the foresight to do that fifty years ago."

"Where in the heck did this line of thinking come from?" Bradley asked. "Are you watching some sort of documentary series or something?"

Maggie chuckled and shook her head. "No, nothing like that. It's just... this man who claims to be Orson's long lost son said that he was matched with Orson through a DNA test online, but Orson swears he never took a DNA test like that."

"So, what brings the military into this?" Zeke asked.

"The army is the only place I could think of that Orson has been where someone would or could compel him to take that sort of a test," Maggie said. "He served long before there were DNA tests done, so

I suppose that question never made sense in the first place." She shook her head and tipped the coffee up and chugged it down.

"Someone definitely needs to get home and get some more sleep," Bradley said. He hugged his mother tightly and began guiding her toward the door.

"Hang on a sec," Zeke said. "The only alternative answer to that question is that someone took a DNA test and claimed they were Orson when they were doing it. As far as I know, those places don't check your identification when you send in the results."

"You're saying someone might have claimed to have been Orson and submitted their DNA in a test in his name? Why would someone do that?" Maggie sighed. "Whoever it was, turns out they were Toby's biological father."

"You have to remember something else," Zeke said. "Unless you see proof of it yourself, it's just this guy's word that he found out he was Orson's son online. They don't usually print certificates stating that sort of thing for people to carry around with them. I suppose he could share the results, but anything can be photoshopped nowadays."

Maggie nodded. "Good point," she said, taking in all the information. "Thanks, you guys. See you soon."

CHAPTER SEVEN

By the time she made it home, Maggie was yawning every couple of minutes. Despite her coffee intake, she was ready for a long nap. She unlocked the door and made her way inside the house, heading straight for her newly remodeled master bathroom. She changed into comfortable clothes, then drew the blinds and crawled back into bed, falling asleep right away.

Brett woke her a couple of hours later with a phone call. She answered groggily. "Hello?"

"Maggie? Are you at home?"

"Yeah," she said and threw the covers back. "What's going on?"

"Are you in bed? I'm sorry I woke you," he said. "I thought you were going in to see Orson."

"I did, and I stopped by the donut shop there, too," she said.

"You never called me," Brett said. "How is Orson?"

"He has had some weakness and his voice is a little off," she said. "His hand looks pretty twisted, too, but he has been on his feet."

"Is he, you know, himself?"

Maggie chuckled. "Oh, he is very much himself," she said. "I caught him pretending to be asleep when Myra was fawning over him a little bit."

"Sounds like Orson," Brett said.

"He asked me to do something for him when we were leaving, though," Maggie said.

"What did he ask you to do?"

"He asked me not to let them take control of his life," she said. "I'm assuming he meant Toby and Kara."

"So, he hasn't been told about Kara?" Brett said.

"I didn't tell him," Maggie said. "Neither did Myra. I don't think anyone else has said anything, either"

"I should stop by and visit with him on my break today," Brett said. "I'll shoot Myra and Brooks a call first, but he needs to be told before he hears it from someone else."

"I agree," Maggie said. "Especially if Toby has been charged with her murder."

"He hasn't been charged," Brett said. "Not yet anyway. We just don't have enough evidence. We do have the description of a vehicle, but Toby was not proven to have been involved. He might have been there, but we have no way to know right now if he was the one behind the wheel or not."

"Do you think he's going to try to go see Orson in the hospital? I don't think that would be good for him," Maggie said.

"I told him to stay away from Orson, but there is no law saying that he can't go into the hospital," Brett said.

Maggie sat on the edge of her bed. "Orson insists he never took a DNA test. Not once. How in the world would Toby Hawley presume that he is his son?

"First off, Hawley is not his legal name. It's Garrett," Brett said. "As for the rest of it, I have no idea. I know Orson knew the man's mother, but that certainly doesn't prove anything."

"Right, because it isn't like he carries anything around with him to prove that Orson is his biological father," Maggie said.

"I suppose Orson could demand that Toby take a new DNA test to establish whether or not he is the

father," Brett said. "Although I have to say, they do look a little bit alike."

"I noticed that, too." Maggie frowned.

Brett ended the phone call after insisting that she go back to sleep if she could. Maggie had promised that she'd try as she made her way down the hall to the kitchen to brew more coffee to help keep herself awake. She set her phone on the counter and started her coffee maker, then headed back down the hall for her laptop. She returned to the kitchen and yawned again as she sat down at the table.

While the coffee brewed, Maggie began searching for any information she could find about the man claiming to be Orson's son. She searched first for Toby Hawley. She found pages of social media profiles, but none that matched or even looked like him.

When she entered Toby Garrett's name, she found fewer profiles, but still no matches to the man she had just met. She stood up to fix herself a cup of coffee. Maggie walked to the back door and looked outside. Snow had begun to fall, typical for early February. She turned back to the kitchen and sat down in front of her computer again.

Maggie drummed her fingers on the keyboard for a moment, trying her best to think of another way to

find information about Toby. She thought back to the conversation with Brooks and Brett after Toby first came into the donut shop. Both seemed to think he had been incarcerated at some point, and now, both Brooks and Brett would know the truth.

She picked her phone up again and dialed Ruby. "How's work going?" she asked, glancing at the clock on her stove.

"We're out of cherry vanilla cream scones already," Ruby said. "I hate to say it, but I will be glad when the first of March rolls around and we aren't serving these scones any longer. They are so delicious, but everybody knows it!"

"Sounds like we have a good problem on our hands at this point," Maggie said. "Are you on your break?"

"Just sat down," Ruby said, and then giggled. "With the very last scone. Naomi is currently not speaking to me."

"That's hilarious," Maggie said.

"How was Orson?" Ruby asked, her tone growing more serious.

"Myra didn't say anything?"

"I haven't wanted to bother her with it," Ruby said. "She said a little bit when she got here but not much."

"When we got there, he was with a nurse taking his blood pressure and heart rate. Myra and I waited for her to go and then Myra got a little emotional," Maggie said. "He was totally playing possum, though."

"Oh, that is the best thing I have heard all day," Ruby said. "That actually makes me feel a whole lot better. I heard something about his hand being contracted and his voice being a little weak, but it sounds like we got off very lucky here."

"We did, and I think Orson is scared," Maggie said.

"Scared about his health?"

"More about the idea of this man coming into his life and trying to gain control of it," Maggie said. "Orson actually made a plea to me as we were leaving his hospital room not to let that happen."

"I have to go," Ruby said suddenly.

She could hear a few voices on the other end. The second Ruby hung up the phone, Maggie walked out the door and drove the short distance to the donut shop. She had to know what was going on.

CHAPTER EIGHT

"What are you doing here?" Ruby asked Maggie when she walked into the kitchen through the back door. "You're supposed to be at home resting."

"I'm rested," Maggie said. "At least as rested as I am going to get. I was worried that Toby showed up here and was causing some problems."

Ruby shook her head. "No sign of Toby Hawley today."

"It's not really Toby Hawley," Maggie said. "Brett told me his name is Toby Garrett."

Ruby sighed. "What are you doing after we close?"

"Probably going back home to try to find every-thing I can about this guy," Maggie said.

"Why don't you go by your house and grab your

laptop and head on out to my place?" Ruby suggested. "I have some steak and shrimp kebabs made up in the fridge and some wine chilling. You come over and we will work on things together."

"Sounds like a plan," she said. "I want to find out everything we can about this guy."

"And his recently deceased girlfriend," Ruby said.

Maggie nodded and got to work cleaning the display case out. While she worked, she had at least two people come up and request more cherry vanilla cream scones. She worked as quickly as she could to help close the donut shop down for the day. Naomi and Myra left a little early. Maggie was glad to see Myra head out before everyone else. She needed to rest a little before picking up Lexi from daycare.

Maggie arrived at Ruby's house a little bit after five. The snow had stopped falling and the temperature had warmed into the forties. Maggie hoped that meant some time around the bonfire, but for now, she headed inside the house and set her laptop down on the counter. Ruby was busy at the large stove turning over several kebabs she had over an open flame.

"Honey, I'm home," Maggie joked. She opened the fridge and helped herself to a glass of wine. Ruby sipped from her glass occasionally as she turned the kebabs.

"There's a quinoa salad in the white bowl on the top shelf of the fridge," Ruby announced. "If you want, take that out and give it a good toss." Maggie did as directed and wondered how Ruby found the time to create such beautiful meals when most of her time seemed to be eaten up by the donut shop, the city council, her farm, or writing another cookbook.

"Everything looks great." Maggie set the quinoa bowl on the table and waited while Ruby plucked the kebabs one by one off of the flame with a pair of tongs.

"Everything is great." Ruby smiled. "At least, I hope it is. I used a couple of recipes from the draft of the book I just sent over to my editor."

"Oh, let's hope so, then." Maggie chuckled. They sat together and ate without much conversation. When she was finished, Maggie sat back in her seat and sipped her wine.

"What are you thinking?" Ruby asked. She rose to clear their plates.

"I'm thinking Toby and his girlfriend must have been planning this for a while," Maggie said. "I wonder what that letter he wrote to Orson said."

"Kara was killed, and I don't want to speak ill of the dead, but if Toby did kill her, I wonder what led up to it."

"Are you thinking he might not have been the one who did it?" Maggie asked.

"That thought has crossed my mind," Ruby said. "Think about last night. Kara was the one with all of the vitriol toward Orson. Toby barely spoke a word."

"Except to try and shush her," Maggie said. "But that could mean she didn't let up when they were at the motel, and he lost it and snapped."

"And then walked around her, got into a car, and ran her over? That just doesn't seem very likely," Ruby said.

"Yeah," Maggie said. "That's true."

"The other part of this is the DNA test. If Orson swears that he never took one, how could his name be on the website?" Ruby asked.

"That's what I'd like to know," Maggie said. "There's something else, too. He all but said there was no physical way that he could be Toby's father."

"Meaning that they were never intimate?"

"Meaning he is not giving away much information, but that's what it sounds like," Maggie said. "I just wish we knew the name of Toby's mother."

"All we have to do is go on the genealogy websites and search until we find Toby's name," Ruby said. "There might be a family tree already there."

Maggie nodded and reached for her laptop. She opened it and began searching for the websites. "It looks like there are several sites to choose from."

Ruby stood up and walked around behind her chair. "These two are the main sites," she said. "I'll check one out and you do the other."

"Deal," Maggie said. She opened the site and looked over the top of her computer at Ruby, who had returned to her seat. "Do you think we should search for Toby Hawley or Toby Garrett?"

"I'd start with Garrett," Ruby suggested. "If you don't find anything, try the other name."

Maggie began typing the name into the search bar on the genealogy website. Within seconds, the search returned page after page of results. "Whoa," she said. "There are a lot of people named Toby Garrett."

"Just start with the top name and work your way through the list," Ruby said.

Maggie could already hear the click-clicking of her mouse. She worked her way through the first page and halfway through the second before she hit on something. "Got it," she said. "I found a Toby Jacob Garrett. His mother is listed as Gladys Jean Garrett."

"And his father is listed as Orson Hawley, confirmed by a DNA test," Ruby said. "I just found

the same profile on this site. It's interesting it's on both."

"Gladys Jean Garrett," Maggie read. "She died two months ago."

Ruby sighed. "So, we can't go and ask her any questions," she said.

"Were we going to ask her any questions?" Maggie asked.

"I think that is a logical conclusion," Ruby said. "But since we can't, there is just Toby's word against Orson's at this point."

"In other words, this was a dead end," Maggie said.

"Well, at least we have the mother's name."

Maggie shut the lid on her laptop. She pushed the computer away from her a bit and shook her head. She had no idea where to turn next, or how to help Orson.

CHAPTER NINE

Maggie stood at the baker's table next to Naomi and helped her with the scone dough for the morning's baking. She related the story of her interaction with Zeke at the Hunter Springs Donut Shop. The laughter carried on for twenty minutes as they each did an impression of how they pictured his manly muscles preparing the scones would look.

"Did we really promise that these scones would be on the menu for the entire month of February?" Naomi asked. She stopped mixing the vanilla cream sauce and rubbed her right shoulder. "I don't know how much more of this I can take!"

"The good news is that this is not a leap year, so there are only twenty-eight days in this month," Ruby offered.

"I suppose that should make me feel better," Naomi said. "But it isn't even Valentine's Day yet."

"It will make us all feel better on February twenty-seventh." Maggie chuckled. She pressed her hands onto another circle of scone dough.

"I'm sorry I picked this recipe," Naomi said.

"Don't be." Ruby smiled. "I was looking at the numbers last night after you left, Maggie, and we have been selling the dickens out of these scones. So, they are definitely a hit."

"They're just a very time-consuming hit," Myra added when she walked in the door.

"Good morning," Maggie said to her. "Any news about Orson?"

Myra nodded her head and yawned. "Gretchen is visiting him now, so he's not alone over there, which is good news. We're looking at rehab facilities for him for the first couple of weeks after they release him from the hospital. He'll need to stay just long enough for some intensive occupational therapy before he comes home."

"I thought they were going to try to work it out so he can do his therapy once he gets home," Naomi said.

"Physical therapy, yes," Myra said. "But occupational therapy will have to be done in the facility."

"I guess I don't understand the difference," Naomi said.

"Occupational therapy will help him relearn anything the stroke took away from him," Myra said. "It sounds like he doesn't need it, but his doctor told us that it is very important for him to go somewhere for a little while before they release him to go back home. He fared rather well and we're all very lucky, but any extra help he can get is going to be what's best for him, even if he doesn't want it."

"Okay, I get the difference, but can't they just have the therapist work with him at home?" Naomi asked.

Myra shook her head. "His doctor warned us that even though the stroke was light, one of the worst things that could happen to him at this point is a bad fall. If we don't realize that the stroke left him with a balance issue or a problem switching from one foot to the other when he tries to walk down the hall and turn the corner, he could fall."

"That makes a lot of sense to me, actually," Maggie said. "But the question is, how did Orson take the news?"

Myra shook her head. "Well enough that the doctor suggested we sedate him for the transfer to the facility," she said with a chuckle.

"They just might have to, just like when they move a stubborn animal in the zoo," Ruby said.

"Hey, do you hear that?" Naomi stopped what she was doing and put her finger up to silence their chatter. "I think someone is knocking on the door out front."

Maggie wiped her hands off on a towel and headed for the kitchen door. By the time she pushed through it, all she could see was a set of headlights shining across the parking lot. "Someone must have knocked and given up," she said.

"Probably because they wanted to get the cherry vanilla cream scones before we open," Myra said.

"Hang on," Ruby said. "I think someone just pulled into the alley."

By the time Maggie made it to the back door, someone was rapping hard on it. "Probably just Brett or Brooks playing around," she whispered as she opened it. She froze when she saw that the person on the other side of the door was Toby. He pushed his way inside the door and closed it behind him.

"Look, I don't want any trouble," he said. Maggie looked down at the knife in his hand and gasped.

"Now, it isn't like that! I just have this here so you will stop and listen to me. Nobody wants to listen to me and I'm tired of it."

"You're holding that knife in a pretty threatening way," Ruby said. "Maybe if you put it down, we will listen a little better." She moved slowly around the prep table and started toward them.

"Stop! Stay where you are," Toby commanded. Ruby stopped.

Maggie began to shake. "What do you want?" she asked.

"I want to know why you won't open the door for me," Toby said.

"You mean a second ago when you were up front?" Ruby asked. Maggie watched the knife out of the corner of her eye while Ruby spoke. "To be honest with you, we were back here working and chatting like we do every morning. We just didn't hear you until it was too late."

"Right," Maggie said. "By the time I heard you and I went up there to check it out, you were already leaving the parking lot."

"Yeah, well, so much for the bunch of you looking out for my father," Toby sneered. "You can't even hear the door when someone is knocking on it."

"Oh yeah? How about when he has a cold and I wake up in the middle of the night because I can hear him wheezing a little," Myra said. "Or what about when my daughter is sick, and I wake up in the

middle of the night to find Orson sitting in the nursery with her in his lap while they sit together in the rocking chair? You don't think we can hear things then?"

"That's a wonderful picture you painted, talking about your kid and all, but don't you think that's a little bit like rubbing salt in my wounds?"

"Okay, that's enough. The truth is that we do care for Orson," Ruby said. She spoke in her most rational and diplomatic voice. It was something Maggie had grown to appreciate. "But the truth is, Toby, the chances that Orson is your dad for real are not very good."

"I think the DNA test would disagree with you," Toby said.

Ruby shook her head. "Toby, we have spoken extensively with Orson, and he swears he never once submitted his DNA to any company for a test."

"What are you saying then? That someone else submitted the test in his name?" Toby asked. He waved the knife around a little as he spoke.

"That's a really good possibility," Ruby said.

"Okay, then who? Who would have done that?"

"I don't know the answer to that, but we did a little checking, and that test was only submitted a few years ago."

"Maybe the old man did it and forgot what he was doing," Toby said.

"I don't think so," Maggie said. "We have all known him for a while at this point, and my aunt knew him before that. I don't think Orson has had any issues with his memory."

"Fine, but that is a very loose theory," Toby said.

"There is something else," Maggie said. "Orson and your mother went on two dates. Just two. And from what he has been trying to say, there isn't any possible way you could be his biological child."

"I don't understand," Toby said.

"They're trying very carefully to say that Orson has indicated that he and your mother knew each other, but never in a biblical way," Naomi said.

"That's impossible," Toby snapped. "I told you that I wanted you all to hear me out and I meant it."

"Okay," Ruby said, attempting to calm him again. "What is it that you need for us to listen to?"

"First, I didn't kill Kara, no matter what the cops are trying to say about it," he said. "That car came out of nowhere and ran her down. She was still holding three slices of pizza when they got her. I was in the doorway trying to talk her into coming back inside after we fought."

"What were you fighting about?" Maggie asked.

"I don't know," Toby said. "Everything. Like the way she acted when we were here."

"She sure made it sound like you were here just to get all the money out of Orson that you can," Maggie said. She watched the blade of the knife as she spoke.

Toby dropped his head. "That's because I am trying to get money out of him," he said. "The man owes me for a lifetime of not being there."

"That's not very fair when he can't possibly be your father in the first place," Myra said.

"What do you know? You're going around acting like you're his daughter or granddaughter or something and you don't know anything!"

"I take care of him! I moved him into my house to take care of him the day I got married," Myra shouted.

"Hey, hey, let's all calm down," Ruby said. "Toby, you should know that we are all very protective of Orson. You should also know that he really doesn't have anything. Why do you think he came to work here? When we all first met him he was barely able to feed himself. He's definitely not rolling in the dough, like you seem to think."

"Before that, I lived with him in that old house of his just so there would be someone around to look

after things," Myra said. "And I paid him rent, more than I probably had to just to help him out."

"Why do you need money so badly?" Ruby asked.

"Because there are people who want money," he said. "It wasn't me who ran up the debts, it was Kara and I think they killed her for it. I thought if I found my dad he might be able to help us out before anything bad happened, but now it's too late."

"So, you came here and started demanding money from him and put him in the hospital," Myra said, choking back a sob.

"Look, I never meant the guy any harm," Toby said. "But unless you've owed money to the wrong types of people, you have no way to understand how much pressure it puts on you. That's why Kara sounded that way the other night. She was desperate because she knew they were going to kill her if she didn't pay up.'

"Why not go to the cops?" Naomi asked.

"Do you honestly think the cops are going to listen to a thing a couple of ex-cons have to say?"

"Have these people threatened you?" Maggie asked.

Toby shook his head. "I'm not sure how much they know about me. These were people Kara made mad when she was in the pen. They told her they

would find her when she got out and force her to pay them, but they haven't really said a word to me."

"Have they been back around since Kara was killed?"

"No, not yet," Toby said. "But you mark my words. Folks like them don't give up that easily."

Maggie's phone rang in her pocket. She jumped when she heard it. Toby jumped with the knife, too. "That's probably Brett," Maggie said. She cast a look in Ruby's direction.

"Don't answer it," Toby commanded her. "I don't need the sheriff coming around here right now."

"What do you think is going to happen if I don't?" Maggie asked. The phone was on the fourth ring.

"He probably will give up because he thinks you're in the middle of doing whatever you do back here," Toby said.

Maggie shook her head slowly from side to side, much like she did when she was teaching Wyatt that something was a no-no. "No, Toby," she said. "He will call right back and when I don't pick up, he will be on his way here. But not until after he tries first her phone, then hers, and finally, hers." She pointed to Ruby, Myra, and Naomi in order.

"Why would he come here?" Toby asked the

question just as her phone started ringing for a second time.

"Because he wants to look out for me," Maggie said. "I'm getting married to him in another couple of months and I think he's trying to make sure I don't get cold feet." She hoped the little bit of humor would diffuse his temper slightly. Her phone stopped ringing at last. Almost immediately, Ruby's began to ring.

"Okay, fine," Toby said. "I guess if I can't get any answers this way, I'll have to go looking in other places." He pulled the door open.

"Wait! Don't go to the hospital and try to get answers out of Orson," Myra said. "Please don't upset him or stress him out any more. They said the stroke he had was caused by emotional stress."

"They said that?"

Myra nodded once and looked away when her phone rang. It was a slight stretch of the truth, but Maggie knew her only purpose was to try and spare Orson the turmoil.

"Okay, I'll back off," Toby said. "I didn't want to have to do this, but there are other relatives, you know. There are other people I can force to give me the truth, and I may not be as nice to them." He ran out the door and sped away just as Naomi's phone started to ring.

CHAPTER TEN

As soon as Toby left, Maggie picked up her phone
and called Brett to fill him in on what had just
happened.

"Did he say anything about where he planned to
go next?" he asked her.

"No. Other than to say there were other family
members, but I have no idea what that means."

"I don't like it, one way or the other," Brett said.
"Despite his protests of innocence in Kara's murder,
he did just come in there brandishing a weapon and
threatening all of you."

"Which is enough to pick him up on some pretty
serious charges," Maggie said. "Is that what you're
saying?"

"That's what I am saying," Brett said. "I think you need to consider shutting down for the day."

"You want me to shut the donut shop down for the rest of the day?" Maggie was a little shocked at the suggestion.

"I think it might not be a bad idea," Brett said. "I know you won't do it, which is why I asked Brooks to send over a patrol car."

Maggie glanced over at Myra who herself was on a vigorous phone call with someone. She had a strong suspicion she was being told the same thing by Brooks.

"Why shut down when it's clear that Toby didn't get what he was looking for here? I doubt that he'll return."

"Alright, so, what about shutting down before lunchtime? That way if he doesn't find what he is looking for elsewhere or we don't pick him up by then, there isn't a chance he shows back up." Maggie covered the phone and repeated the request to the rest of her staff.

"I think that sounds reasonable," Ruby said. "I'll hit the social media channels and put the word out."

Myra nodded at Maggie and repeated the idea to Brooks. She looked up a second later with a smile and a thumbs up. Naomi gave her the same sign.

"Sounds like you win this time," Maggie said.

"Thank you, Maggie," Brett said. She could hear him breathe a sigh of relief. "I really do think this is for the best."

Maggie hung up the phone and turned back to the baker's table. "I suppose the good news is we're not likely to run out of these scones today."

The morning seemed to fly by. Despite her bravado on the phone to Brett, Maggie found herself watching out the front windows for any sign of Toby.

"Where are you going now?" Ruby asked when they walked out of the donut shop and to their cars.

"I think I'm going to take a little drive out to that motel," Maggie said. "The one out on the highway where Kara was run down. I want to see if there might have been a witness who saw what happened."

"I'll come with you," Ruby said. "I had another idea."

"What's your idea?"

"Well, I got to looking around on the genealogy website on my break a little while ago, and I found the name of a relative of Gladys Garrett's," Ruby explained. "This cousin of hers is living in an assisted living facility in Hunter Springs. I thought we could check in with her and see what she has to say."

"Alright, then," Maggie said. "First we visit the

motel and find out what we can there, then we'll head over to the assisted living place."

Ruby nodded and climbed into the passenger side of her car. They headed toward the highway motel. Maggie had driven past it from time to time, but when she slowed her car and turned into the parking lot, she was a little shocked that the place was able to remain open. She veered around five different potholes in the parking lot she figured were big enough to swallow her front tires whole.

"This place looks pleasant," Ruby said. "Look. There's the car Kara was driving the night they came to the donut shop."

"Then the police don't think that was the car she was struck with, otherwise they would have already impounded it," Maggie said.

"That's what I was thinking, too," Ruby said. She looked around the parking lot as they stepped out of the car. "Take a look at the way this parking lot is designed. There's only one way in and out of the alley behind the motel."

"That's where the police said she was hit," Maggie said. "Makes you wonder how the car would have gotten up enough speed to hit her." The parking lot narrowed to a single lane, barely wide enough for one car, and followed around the back of the building.

The way out on the other side of the motel was the same narrow lane. "Why was she even back there in the first place?" Maggie pulled the lobby door open and held it for Ruby.

"Oh, that's terrible," Ruby whispered. She covered her nose.

Maggie turned her head and forced herself not to gag from the overwhelming sulfur smell. "Is that the sewer?" she asked when she recovered herself enough to speak.

"I would almost bet on it," Ruby said. They walked toward the small front desk area. A man stood behind the counter with his back to them.

"Excuse us," Maggie said to gain his attention. The man cleared his throat and turned around.

"How long?" he asked.

"Pardon me?" Ruby replied.

"How long? You want a room, don't you?" He pushed a pair of thick, black glasses up his nose. Maggie noticed one side of the glasses was missing an ear piece. "You want it by the hour or by the day?"

"We don't want a room," Maggie said.

"Next!" the man shouted past them into the empty lobby and turned his back to them again.

"Look, we just want to ask you a couple of ques-

tions about the lady who got hit the other night," Maggie said.

"Already spoke to the cops," the man said, with his back to them. "Are you cops?"

"Nope," Ruby said. She reached into her back pocket and pulled out a small wad of cash. "But I have forty bucks that really wants your attention."

"Try again," the man said.

"Sixty bucks," Ruby said. "Final offer."

The man turned around and faced them. He reached for the cash in Ruby's hand. She jerked her hand back just in time, but peeled off a twenty and handed it to him. "Consider this the retainer," she said. "The rest is yours when you answer our questions."

"Fine," he said. "What do you want to know?"

"First off, where was the woman when she got hit?" Maggie asked.

"Out back," the man said. "That's where they found her body."

"Did you see her before she went back there?" Ruby asked.

The man nodded. "There's a back door down the hall and through the laundry room," he said. "I was up front here when it all happened."

"Do you have cameras on the alley?" Maggie asked.

The man laughed. "These cameras here haven't worked since I first started," he said. "Same thing I told the cops."

"Okay, then, do you know where the man who was with her was when she got hit?"

"Back there in the laundry room begging her not to go outside," he said.

"And you told the police this?" Ruby said.

"Yes, I told the police this," he said. "Anything else you want to know?"

"Yeah, there is, actually," Maggie said. "Was there anyone else here asking questions about the couple? Before or after the woman was killed."

The man smiled. "Now you're getting somewhere," he said. "There were a couple of guys here the day before asking about a Melissa, which is not the name she gave me, but they were definitely talking about the same woman. They didn't seem interested in the guy at all."

"What did you tell them? And no, we aren't cops," Ruby reminded him.

"I told them there wasn't anyone checked in under that name," he said. "Look, you two look like a couple of soccer moms trying to look out for a friend.

Trust me, these people are not your friends. That chick who got run down was hardcore. So were the guys that came looking for her."

"What about the guy with her?" Ruby asked. "The one the cops picked up for questioning."

"That guy? He definitely did time," he said with a laugh. "Anyone who has been in the joint will tell you that, but he was not at all what I consider hard. Desperate is more like it. He kept telling the woman that he was going to fix everything and that he was going to get the money together she needed to pay some people off."

"You heard all of that" Maggie asked.

"You'd be shocked how thin these walls are," he said. "I think she was the one with all of the ideas about what was going on. She spent most of her time telling him what a loser he was and how he was never going to deliver the money he promised her. And from the looks of the alley back there the other night, she was right."

CHAPTER ELEVEN

"I can't get the stench of that place out of my nose," Maggie said. She rode in the passenger seat on the way to the assisted living facility in Hunter Springs. Ruby was familiar with the place and took over driving from the motel.

"At least we know Toby isn't a murderer," Ruby said.

"I am slightly relieved, but I would really like for him to go back where he came from," Maggie admitted.

"That makes two of us." Ruby said nothing more until they arrived at the assisted living facility. Ruby parked the car close to the entrance. They walked into the front of the facility together and approached the first nurse they saw. "We're here to see Georgina

Barker," she said. "Can you point us in the right direction?"

"Are you relatives?"

"No," Ruby said. "Do we have to be?"

"If you're here asking questions about someone, you'd better be," the nurse said, then headed off down the hall alone.

"Okay," Maggie said. "What now?"

"Hey, you're looking for Georgina?" Maggie turned around to see an older woman standing in the hall directly behind them. She was about her height, wearing purple from head to toe.

"We are. Do you know her?" Ruby asked.

"I am her," the woman said. "Who are you?"

"I'm Ruby Cobb and this is Maggie Sharpe."

"Okay, and why are you here?"

"We're close friends of Orson Hawley," Maggie said. "Do you know who that is?"

"Yes I know who that is," Georgina said. "He's the man I wish had married my cousin Gladys instead of that jerk she wound up with."

"Do you know Toby Garrett?" Ruby asked.

"Of course, I do," Georgina said. "But he's been in prison for a really long time."

"He's out now, and he has come here looking for Orson," Maggie said.

"Let's go on over here," Georgina said. She ushered them to a small sitting area. She sat down on the small sofa and directed them to two wing chairs beside her. "Why would Toby come looking for Orson?"

"Well, he thinks Orson is his father," Ruby said. "There was a DNA test done online under Orson's name that revealed a direct parental connection to Toby."

"Well, that can't be right," Georgina said. "Anthony is his father."

"Who is Anthony?" Maggie asked, sharing a glance with Ruby.

Georgina stared at them for a long moment. "Anthony Hawley is Orson's brother," Georgina said. "He took up with Gladys after Orson enlisted. He was with her for two long years, right up until he found out she was pregnant."

Maggie's mouth fell open. "Are you sure about this? Orson is his uncle?"

"Of course, I'm sure about this," Georgina said. "I was there."

"And what about the DNA test?" Ruby asked. "I wonder how you would explain that?"

"If you want my opinion," Georgina said. "It was probably Anthony who took it before he died and

submitted it to the internet or however that works. I mean, why wouldn't that be the case? The same man took out credit cards in his own brother's name and ruined him financially for years."

"Orson's brother did that to him?"

Georgina nodded her head slowly. "You know him, so you have to know he is not a wealthy man," she said. "I hear he is still working at some donut shop over in Dogwood Mountain."

"That's our donut shop." Maggie smiled.

"Well, I'll be." The older woman smiled. "Anyway, you tell either of them to come on over here and see me if they have any questions. I'm in this place because I can't get around myself much anymore, but there isn't a thing wrong with my memory or my mind."

"Thank you," Ruby said to her.

"Yes, thank you very much," Maggie said.

Maggie practically skipped back to the parking lot. She smiled when she got back into the car and buckled her seat belt. "I can't believe what she told us," she said to Ruby.

"I know," Ruby said. "It makes sense now, though. Orson and Toby do favor each other. But he is his nephew rather than his son."

"Is that my phone?" Maggie rooted around in the console for the ringing culprit. "It's Brett."

"Maggie," Brett said as soon as she answered. "Where are you?"

"I'm with Ruby in Hunter Springs," Maggie said. "We just left the assisted living facility on the north side of town."

"What were you doing there?"

"We met with a cousin of Toby's mother, Gladys and we found out that Anthony, Orson's brother, is the father. He might also be the reason poor Orson has been so destitute all of these years. Sounds like he used his name for credit cards and that sort of thing."

"Well, that's really interesting, and it makes me more worried than ever," Brett said. "A little while ago, someone showed up at the hospital pretending to be a patient transporter. Whoever it was gave Orson something to make him sleepy and took him out of there, right under the hospital's nose."

CHAPTER TWELVE

"Myra went over to see how Orson was doing this afternoon and they told her that he was gone," Brett continued. "They reached out to every facility in the area and not one of them had heard from them. We don't know where Toby might have taken him."

"This is insane," Maggie said, putting him on speakerphone. She felt her heart beating in her throat. "Are you sure it was Toby, and do you think he is capable of hurting Orson? Is he going to do something to him?"

"We are sure it was him, but I honestly don't know what he's capable of," Brett replied. "The problem is, given Orson's condition, he might hurt him without even meaning to."

"What do you want us to do?" Ruby asked.

"Drive around," Brett instructed. "Look for his car. Do you remember what it looks like?"

"Well, Brett," Maggie said. "We saw his car earlier today at the motel over on the highway, the one where Kara was killed."

"What were you doing there?" Brett said. "You know what? Never mind. Don't even answer that question. Just tell me when you were there."

"About an hour ago," Ruby said.

"And you are sure it was his car?" Brett asked. Maggie could hear the roar of the motor in his pickup truck rev as he spoke.

"One hundred percent sure," Ruby answered. "There is a faded spot on the top of the hood that looks like green and yellow paint was splashed over it. You can't miss it against the brown paint."

"That's what I remember, too," Brett said. "You two stay back. We're headed over there now." He hung up the phone. For a moment, the two of them sat in stunned silence.

"Where are we going now?" Ruby asked when Maggie turned over the key in the ignition.

"Where do you think?" Maggie said. "We have to get to that motel."

Ruby nodded. "If he is planning to hurt Orson, what we just found out might change his mind."

Maggie headed out of the parking lot and followed Ruby's directions back to the motel. The parking lot was already full of law enforcement vehicles when they arrived, including police cars from the Dogwood Mountain and Hunter Springs Police Departments. She swallowed hard when she spotted two ambulances parked near the front.

"Get as close as you can and we'll just walk the rest of the way," Ruby said. Maggie parked her car and nearly fell when she got out. Ruby took her by the arm and led her up to the crowd gathered outside the motel lobby door. "I see Brooks."

"Let's get over there," Maggie said.

"I'm afraid the two of you are going to have to stay back a little bit," Brooks said. "He's got Orson over there in the laundry room."

"Is he holding him hostage?"

"He has a knife," Brooks said. A single tear streamed down his face as he spoke. "Brett is in there right now trying to talk to him."

"Brooks, we just spoke with a relative of Toby's late mother," Maggie said. "We have information about who his father really is. It was Orson's brother."

"Yeah, you should let us go back there and talk to him," Ruby said. "We might be able to end this more peacefully that way."

"Give me a sec," Brooks said. He muttered into his radio. "Okay, go on back."

"Thank you, Brooks," Maggie said. She squeezed his arm as she passed by him.

They wound their way through the other officers, stopping twice to explain that they were on their way back to speak with the sheriff. The man with the ponytail sat behind the counter and scowled at the officers. Maggie nodded in his direction as she passed through.

They found Brett at the end of the hall. He was just outside of the door. "Toby, you have got to let me see him," he spoke through the closed doors. "I can't do anything until I can make sure that Orson is alright."

"I just need him to acknowledge that he is my father," Toby said through the door. His voice was muffled.

"Brett," Maggie said softly. He looked up and spotted them, then pressed his fingers to his lips and pointed at the door. Ruby followed her to Brett's side.

"Toby? It's Maggie, from the donut shop," she said through the door. "Do you know who Georgina Barker is?"

"Why do you want to know?" Toby asked after a moment.

"If you looked on the genealogy site, you would have seen that she is a relative of your mother's,"

Maggie said. "Gladys and Georgina were first cousins."

"What about her?"

"Toby, she knew your mother and your father well," Maggie said. "She told us all about them. Orson is not your father."

"You're a liar," he shouted back.

"No, Toby," Maggie continued. "Listen to me. Anthony Hawley was your father. He is Orson's brother, and he was with your mother for two years."

"And before you ask about the DNA test, Anthony had a habit of doing things in his brother's name," Brett added. "Toby, Anthony is the reason your Uncle Orson wound up poor in his old age. Anthony stole money from him and ruined his credit."

"If you don't believe us, go on and ask Georgina yourself," Maggie said.

There was nothing but silence on the other side of the laundry room door. A moment later, the door opened, and Toby emerged with his hands in the air. His face was red, and his eyes were swollen. He looked at Maggie and shook his head. "I never meant to hurt him," he said. "I just wanted to hear him say he was my father."

"So, it was Kara who wanted his money?" Brooks asked from behind Maggie. She turned slightly to see him. Brooks shook with rage.

"I got him, buddy," Brett said calmly. "You go on in there and get Orson."

CHAPTER THIRTEEN

Orson tucked the blanket around his middle with his good hand. Maggie watched as he moved. He still favored his good side, although she had seen him walk across the living room in Brooks and Myra's home. She wondered if the weakness on one side of his body would cause him to fall more easily.

"I don't know why all of you are just standing there looking at me," Orson grumbled. "I only had a stroke. It's not like I just went and grew two heads."

"I think we have all earned the right to be a little worried about you, Pops," Brooks said to him. He laid his hand gently on Orson's shoulder. Orson said nothing, but reached his good hand up and covered it.

"You were taken from us," Myra added. "And whether you like it or not, that was horrifying."

"You can say that again," Brett chimed in. He was seated on the floor in front of Maggie. "You have no idea how worried I was when I walked into that hospital and found out someone had taken you."

"Yeah, well, I wasn't too happy about that myself," Orson said.

"That makes all of us," Maggie said. She rested her hand on Brett's shoulder. He reached up and took her hand in his.

"What's going to happen to Toby?" Naomi asked. "At least, what do you think will happen?"

Brett looked at Brooks. "Most likely, he spends another long stretch in prison," Brooks said. "Which at his age is not going to be fun for him, but his actions determined what his fate will look like, not any of us."

"That's code for 'it's not your fault, Orson,'" Orson said. "And I just want to go on the record to say that I know this for a fact, and I am not going to go insane blaming myself for my nephew's actions."

"That's good to hear," Naomi said.

"However," Orson continued. "I do plan to stay in touch with him. He is not an evil man, no matter what it looks like to the outside world. If I blame anyone, it is my brother for failing him while he was alive."

"Do you really believe your brother knew?" Maggie asked.

Orson nodded his head slowly. "That is the only reason I can think that he would submit his DNA online under my name like that," he said. "Anthony was as mean as a snake. He would whip anyone who looked at him the wrong way, man, woman, or child. Maybe he thought this kid would come looking for him one day and he decided to send him in my direction for kicks and giggles."

"Or maybe he sent him to you because he knew what sort of a scoundrel he was," Brooks said. "It could be that this was his one act of benevolence."

Orson snickered. "I don't think my brother had an ounce of benevolence in his entire body, but I appreciate the sentiment," he said. "You might be right, but my guess is Anthony did it as a sort of final joke on me. He always rubbed things in my face when we were kids, and tried to rub it in my face that Gladys sought him out when I enlisted."

"And you never knew she was pregnant?" Maggie said.

"Nope, not once," Orson said. "But let me just make this clear. I could not have been the father. We had one date where things got a little, how do you

people say this these days, hot and heavy? But it was never that hot and it never got that heavy."

"You're just old school, Orson," Myra said. "These days everyone kisses and tells."

"Or whatever and tells," Brooks said.

"Yeah, well, it may have been the middle of a war when I dated Gladys, but I was raised that a man doesn't do that," Orson said. "And I wasn't fifteen. I was a grown man, and she was a grown woman."

"I do have one question," Maggie said. "If you knew the whole time that Toby couldn't be your son, why did you meet with him in the first place?"

Orson shrugged his shoulders. "I did it because I had a feeling there was a family connection some-where," he said. "I had no idea how my DNA would have gotten submitted to those people online, but I noticed he looked a little bit like me and my father. I knew that his mother had gotten herself tangled up with my brother for a couple of years after I left. I guess I thought I could meet him, hear him out, and do my best by him."

"But his girlfriend didn't help that meeting go well," Brett said. "Her life was such a wreck."

"It's too bad all of that caught up with her," Brooks said. "I think we can assume Toby might have

been ready to turn over a new leaf and try to live a better life."

"Only if there was someone else around who could have encouraged him," Orson said. "I know it's harsh, but the one thing I learned about my nephew in the time I was with him is that he is about as malleable as Lexi's Play-doh."

"That's quite a comparison." Brett chuckled. "But I guess it works."

Myra stood up and headed into the kitchen. She returned with a tray filled with coffee mugs and a few cookies. "I thought we could spend a few minutes discussing other matters," she said.

"And what matters would those be?" Ruby asked. She picked up a cookie as Myra passed her seat.

"Well, in less than two months we have another huge event taking place," Myra said, with a sideways grin to Maggie. The change in conversation had been planned between them.

"That's right." Orson smiled. "These two love birds are going to get hitched, at last."

"Yeah, finally," Ruby muttered.

"You can say that again," Brooks whispered.

"Alright, alright, you all," Brett said. "What do we need to discuss?"

"Well, for one thing, how goes the wedding plan-

ning?" Myra asked. "I know we have our ring bearer and flower girl planned."

"Yes, we do," Brooks said proudly. "We have Wyatt and Lexi running the show."

"I was hoping we could change a few things around," Brett said. He took a mug of coffee from the tray and cast a knowing glance at Maggie.

"Oh no," Orson said, shaking his head. "Tell me you two aren't reconsidering."

"Well, I already asked you to be my best man," Brett said. "But I think I want to switch that up. What do you say, Maggie?"

Everyone stared at Orson as his face fell.

"I'd like for Bradley to stand up with me instead," Brett continued.

"And I'll have Ruby, Naomi and Myra." Maggie nodded.

"I thought this was supposed to be a small wedding," Orson grumbled. "I guess one way to make it smaller is to get rid of me. I get it. I'm old and feeble now. It's fine."

Brett cleared his throat. "Well, if Bradley is standing up there with me, who is going to walk you down the aisle, Maggie?"

Orson looked at her. "Are you just going to skip

that part since you're already a grandma and everything?"

Maggie wadded up her napkin and tossed it at him. "Very funny," she said. "Actually, Orson, that's one reason I wanted Myra to bring up the wedding this afternoon."

"Oh, boy," Orson muttered. "Here we go."

"I was wondering if you thought you could give that physical therapist a little less grief and make sure you're ready to walk down that aisle with me," Maggie said.

For a moment, a hush fell over the room. Orson stood up from his chair and slowly moved toward the window. His limp was a little more pronounced than Maggie had expected. He turned back and moved toward the couch where they were seated. He stood beside her and offered his good hand. Maggie took it in hers and smiled up at him.

"Darn it if you people don't keep an old man on his toes," he said.

"Does that mean you'll do it?" Brooks asked him.

"Yeah, yeah, of course I will," Orson said. He leaned over slowly and planted a kiss on Maggie's head. He looked down at Brett and nudged him slightly with his cane. "I suppose you and I need to go

in the other room and have ourselves one of those man-to-man talks."

Brett blushed instantly. "I already know what I need to know, Orson," he said.

Orson shuffled back to his chair. When he reached it, he looked back at Brett and slowly spun around and sat down. The move reminded Maggie of a jazz dancer's twist. Everyone gasped at his trick. "You know why they say you can't teach an old dog new tricks," Orson asked. "It's because us old dogs already know all of the tricks."

**

If you enjoyed Rolling in the Dough, check out the next book in the series, Do's and Donuts, today!

AUTHOR'S NOTE

I'd love to hear your thoughts on my books, the storylines, and anything else that you'd like to comment on—reader feedback is very important to me. My contact information, along with some other helpful links, is listed on the next page. If you'd like to be on my list of "folks to contact" with updates, release and sales notifications, etc.… just shoot me an email and let me know. Thanks for reading!

Also…

… if you're looking for more great reads, Summer Prescott Books publishes several popular series by outstanding Cozy Mystery authors.

CONTACT SUMMER PRESCOTT BOOKS PUBLISHING

Blog and Book Catalog: http://summerprescottbooks.com

Email: summer.prescott.cozies@gmail.com

And…be sure to check out the Summer Prescott Cozy Mysteries fan page and Summer Prescott Books Publishing Page on Facebook – let's be friends!

To sign up for our fun and exciting newsletter, which will give you opportunities to win prizes and swag, enter contests, and be the first to know about New Releases, click here: http://summerprescottbooks.com

33161278R00065

Printed in the United States
33637LVS00001B/15

9 781932 420371